P9-APJ-085

A Candlelight
Regency Special

hers alone with dreams in the air gazing into the
distance recalling his arrogant good looks, cool austere

CANDLELIGHT REGENCIES

A
Merry Chase

Rebecca Bennett

A CANDLELIGHT REGENCY SPECIAL

Published by
Dell Publishing Co., Inc.
1 Dag Hammarskjold Plaza
New York, New York 10017

Copyright © 1981 by Ruby Frankel

All rights reserved. No part of this book may be
reproduced or transmitted in any form or by any
means, electronic or mechanical, including photocopying,
recording or by any information storage
and retrieval system, without the written permission
of the Publisher, except where permitted by law.

Dell ® TM 681510, Dell Publishing Co., Inc.

ISBN:0–440–15596–7

Printed in the United States of America
First printing—December 1981

To Marsha, my daughter, for encouraging me
To Arthur, my friend, for hearing me

A Merry Chase

wit that is beyond compare. I cannot wait for you to meet

Chapter 1

The branches of the copper beech trembled and bent, and a whispered "Oh, blast it" could be heard. "Next time I'll wear Bertie's clothes . . . so much more sensible for climbing trees." As the leaves of the tree were parted by a somewhat disheveled lady, calls for "Betta" were heard coming from the garden beyond the villa.

"That parade of monkeys has found me again . . . must get back to my room before they see me. If I don't have quiet to think, I'll never finish the description of Rudolfo for the next chapter." The slender figure of Elizabeth St. John slipped from the tree, through the privet hedge to the broad terrace at the side of the gracious tawny stone building. The flirt of her pale-blue skirt caught the eye of the leader of the "parade of monkeys." A young man of eleven or twelve with shirttails flying ran a few feet ahead of three younger beings, all in a state of great anxiety. Trailing by several yards were a middle-aged man and a somewhat younger woman. In sharp contrast to the clamorous children, they were neither anxious nor upset. Rather they were in the throes of laughter and their once presentable garments were soaking wet.

"Betta, we see you . . . don't hide . . . come see what has happened. Wait till you hear . . . Betta stay a bit . . . Betta . . ." the chorus of high voices called urgently.

With an air of reluctant endurance, Miss St. John, known to her family as Betta, turned about and came forward. Taller than the accepted pattern of perfection, she was slim and graceful, with the movement of a dancer. Her beautifully shaped head graced a neck and shoulders that might have been the model for Botticelli's *Venus*. Eyes of unusual almond shape changed from gray to blue to violet, reflecting the colors around her or the mood of the moment. A delicately bridged nose above generous well-shaped lips and firm chin gave character and interest to a face that was both more and less than beautiful.

"What is it, Albert? What are you in a taking about this time?"

"Oh, Betta, if you could have seen . . . Mama and Papa . . ." Albert had arrived at the terrace with his followers, who could now to be seen to be three excited little girls. "Brindle was chasing a cat while Mama and Papa were feeding the goldfish, and the cat jumped on Mama and Brindle jumped on Papa and they all fell in the fish pond, and now Brindle has run to hide and Mama and Papa are very wet." The treble voices spilled information in a polyphonic counterpoint.

"Poor Brindle," sobbed Letty, the most sympathetic of canine fanciers. "What will he do for his dinner?"

"Yes, what will he do for his dinner?" echoed the twins, Pamela and Evianne.

"Poor Mama and Papa is more the thing." Betta's voice was sympathetic as she greeted her parents: "Oh, dear Ma'am, your lovely dress . . . you are wringing wet. Papa, how can you laugh like that? What a pickle!" Miss St. John had difficulty in keeping a straight face. "Evianne, Pamela, run and tell Thompson to have Miss Parker and Chub prepare baths for the parents—quickly, before they catch their death."

"Darling Betta, it's really too warm to take sick from a little dampness. Did you ever see anything so harum-scarum? At our age to fall in the goldfish pond! I declare, if word were to get out 'twould be more than life to hear the end of it." Mrs. St. John reached out to her eldest. "My sweet, the laughter alone was worth the wetting, was it not, dear George?"

"In this heat, Betta, the only disappointment was that the pond was big enough for the goldfish to swim but not for your father!" With this comment, Mr. St. John, a handsome well-built gentleman, drew his wife into the house. "Come, my dear one . . . your Parker will be at sixes and sevens over this, and Chub will never forgive me for taking my boots into the water with me. He is forever trying to refine my footwear, but this will surely put me beyond the pale with him."

Mrs. St. John, a quietly lovely woman, whose youthful figure was accented by her wet garments, quickly followed her husband, pausing only to give directions to her daughter. "Betta, my dear, see that the children are attended by Miss Aynsley. She must have Nan to help her bathe and dress them so that they will presentable for callers. We are expecting the vicar and his daughter. You will want to see them, I'm sure." The instructions were called out in a still laughing voice as the lady moved into the house.

As Betta turned to her brother and sister to accomplish her stepmother's directions, she thought of the warmth of the familial love she experienced. The daughter of Mr. St. John and his first wife, who had died in childbirth, she had become the beloved eldest daughter of his second marriage. Her stepmother, barely twelve years older than herself, was not only a beautiful woman, but was unusually well educated, with strong ideas of family life and the responsibility of family members to one another.

11

Betta's father, coming from the *haut ton* as he did, was unique in his close involvement with his family and in his belief in education for women. Although he himself was not titled, the members of his family, of impeccable origin, included a duke, a viscount, and two baronets, and were able to look down upon most of the world from their ultrafine perches in society. George St. John had eschewed this perch when he chose to follow his heart in marrying his second wife, Amelia, daughter of a scholarly pedant at Oxford, and to devote himself to his family and his avocation, the painting and study of nature. The family lived away from the fashionable haunts of the *ton* on a charming estate, about 100 miles from London, in Norfolkshire.

"Come along, young ones . . . time to become well-dressed young ladies and a gentleman again."

"But, Betta, we didn't find Brindle," a crying little voice reminded her.

"Don't worry, little Letty, Brindle's too wise to stay away when it's almost time for food. He knows that if he's not under your chair at mealtime (even though you and I know he's not s'posed to be there) he won't have his treats. Do please come before our visitors arrive and catch us all looking quite like ragpickers."

They entered the wide French doors, into a large, somewhat well worn room overflowing with comfortable furniture piled with books, drawings, various papers, and dried leaves, twigs, roots, and stalks of their father's studies. In the spacious hall beyond, they were greeted by Thompson, who was accompanied by Pamela and Evianne.

"What a rackety-looking group, to be sure, Miss Elizabeth. How could you young ones walk out of the breakfast room looking so well and return for luncheon looking so tattered?" Thompson addressed the children with the familiarity of one who cared deeply for them and was cared for in return. If the truth were told, the children regarded Thompson as a cross between a grandfather and the king, and probably were more concerned with winning his good opinion than that of either of those distant, shadowy figures.

"Thompson, please, will you watch for Brindle. He shall be so ashamed for pushing Papa into the pond. He might miss his food and starve." This plea was accompanied by several pats on the butler's arm, calling his attention to Letty.

"Of course, Miss Letty. Now you go along with your sisters and Mr. Albert and let your nurse and Nan fix you all for company. I'll see to that dog . . . he'll not miss a meal, you can be sure of that."

Satisfied with Thompson's promise, the children, accompanied by Betta, ran up the stairway, the youngsters to the nursery suite and Betta to her own room.

"Now I'll never get those lines down. . . . Oh, to see Mama and Papa laughing so . . . such absurdity." The violet eyes crinkled with amusement. "If only I shall have such a wonderful marriage, to have love and laughter. Why have none of the men I've met felt as dear Papa does about females? All they want are housekeepers and brood mares of good enough lineage to be presentable to their families. If any of them were to believe that I had two thoughts in my mind beyond what to wear tomorrow, I'm sure they would consider me to be a freak of nature. I wish I could write my own chapter . . . and bring on a hero drawn to my expectations . . . but only in my novel can I do that." The young woman's thoughts turned to her experience of the past six years.

She had made her come out late, at the advanced age of nineteen, having suffered the ignominy of measles the preceding year. Lady Godleham-Whyte, her godmother, had sponsored her in view of her stepmama's being in a delicate condition at the time. Neither her first nor her second season was successful in spite of her intelligence and wit. She was outside of the common mold and was too shy to make friends easily. She became tongue-tied when faced with the cruel humor and extreme formality of the *ton.* One of the popular macaronis had taken exception to her open remarks and informal ways and made her the butt of a cruel joke about country life and milkmaids of extra long dimensions. She had withdrawn to the safety of her family before the end of her second season and enjoyed moderate success in the social life of the country.

Her greatest disappointment was not to have met a man with whom she could share her thoughts and delightful sense of the ridiculous. But having been severely hurt by the cutting remarks she had overheard in London about her mind and person, she was very chary about offering friendship to anyone.

Two or three times in the ensuing years, she had joined her godmother or close family friends in visiting various English attractions and once spent some months in Italy but had not as yet met the man who engaged her emotions and entranced her mind. She was close to accepting spinsterhood as her portion in life. Once she had seen a man whom she might have admired, but the "on-dit" was that he was a rake of rakes. Now that she thought about it, he would make the perfect Rudolfo. . . . What was it about him? . . . His eyes, that's right; it was a long time ago, but she could never forget his eyes. They were of such a warm gentian-blue, but were colder than ice when he gave some encroaching mushroom a set-down. She would use a description of him for her villain, no one need know, and he was unlikely to read her book . . . if it ever was published.

Chapter 2

Sir Robin Petrie, Viscount Favesham, brother and heir to the sixth Earl of Halwick, was in a rare black temper. At twenty-three he was a personable, usually even-tempered young gentleman aspiring to become as much the Corinthian as his admired older brother. But today, having been banished to their Norfolk estate by the earl for gambling debts in excess of his allowance, he was beyond mere forbearance with himself, his brother, and the rest of the world. The trip from London had been wracked with unfortunate incidents. Against his groom's better judgment, he had decided to drive his curricle with his new team of horses. Three hours out of London an unlooked-for thunderstorm drenched the two men on a stretch of road offering no shelter. Later in the day, one of the horses cast a shoe, delaying the continuation of the journey until after noon the next day. Then, in an attempt to let out his animals, he took a sharp curve too wide, brushed the hedges, and loosened a wheel.

Fortunately the damage was minor, with none to the horses, his man, or himself, but the damage to self-esteem and temper was beyond reckoning. Instead of arriving at Possingworth the second evening, Robin found himself forced to spend the night at a small inn that offered the barest necessities and no distractions. Bored and in a mood of self-pity, he set out in the morning determined to arrive at the family home in time for the midday repast.

"Master Robin, you be taking the road too fast for the traffic . . . you'm a fair whip, but ye don't hev the judgment for this and ye don't know the horses yet."

"Dammit, Jackson, don't tell me how to handle the reins; I know what I'm doing." With an angry flick of the whip, Sir Robin touched the beasts. "This trip has been impossible, I've never known anything like. And Alec . . . he's been too damned unreasonable, not to advance my next quarter to pay my debts. Here I am of age and not of age. Why my father had to tie up my inheritance until I'm twenty-five is beyond me. I can't come or go without Alec's approval . . . might as well be thirteen as twenty-three. I can't even marry without his giving the nod because of the money."

"Be ye thinking of wedding, then, Mister Robin?"

"Of course not . . . I'm not ready to set up a nursery yet. . . . And aside from Judith Munsingham, who is bespoke to Peter Foulkes, there is no one worth looking at on the marriage mart. And there won't be anyone in Norfolk either, everyone's in London and there're just a lot of country loobies to be seen away from town. 'Tis beyond reason, Jackson. I suppose I may as well bury myself till I'm twenty-five for all the freedom I shall have. I tell you I'm fair hipped by it all." And sunk in misery and monumental self-pity, Sir Robin whipped his horses into ever more careless speed.

Suddenly, on the road ahead, as if from nowhere, there appeared a child.

"Master Robin, quickly . . . Robin, please . . . Oh, Lord . . . pull to the left or the brat's a goner . . . please, Robin . . ." Jackson's cries brought Robin to attention as he quickly reined his horses out of the center of the road.

"Hang on, Jackson, we're going to hit. Damnation, where'd the brat come from . . . ?" Robin had no time to finish his remark before the curricle swerved off the road and into the stone wall just off the verge.

The child stood trembling a moment looking at the overturned vehicle, one wheel spinning high above the ground, horses shaking and snorting with heads down and bodies lathered.

"Betta, Mama, Papa, help . . ." she began to scream as she turned and scrambled across the wall to the neatly edged drive that led to safety. "Betta . . . he's dead and the horses . . . come quick. . . . I didn't do it. . . . Please come."

It took only a few moments for the family to hear Letty's anguished cries and respond.

"Letty darling . . ."

"What happened, little one?"

"Where have you been?"

Mr. St. John's long legs brought him to Letty's side ahead of the others.

"Letty, what are you screaming about?" he asked as he caught her up in his arms. "Calm yourself and speak clearly so that we may help you."

Letty turned in his arms to point toward the road as she cried: "The horses and the man . . . I was calling Brindle 'cause he didn't come home, and suddenly the carriage was all overturned and it's my fa-ault." A torrent of tears spilled from her eyes.

"Amelia, get help, there's an overturned curricle. Someone may be hurt. Letty"—her father put her down—"run and tell Mrs. Simpson to prepare a bed and to send Jim for the doctor. Quickly now, that's my girl."

Groans could be heard coming from the scene of the accident, then a voice was heard: "Sir Robin, Sir Robin! Oh, Lord, don't let him be dead. . . . I told him to have a care. Oh, sir, thank God you've come." The battered groom saw Mr. St. John. "I'm just rare shook up, but my gentleman, I can't get to him . . . the wheel is on his leg."

Mr. St. John gestured to his daughter: "Betta, take care of this man while I look to the other. I wish to see just what the damage is." He looked at Robin's pale face but had difficulty determining whether the young man was still breathing. "First we must move the carriage." Turning to the two grooms who had arrived accompanying Mrs. St. John: "Joshua, you're the strongest, you hoist the bottom wheel. Bob, you give a lift at the back. Betta, take Bob's knife to cut the traces from this contraption." The young woman quickly began to saw at the leather straps. Mrs. St. John and the shaking Jackson went to work unbuckling the harnesses. In short order they were able to lead the trembling horses away from the equipage. Mr. St. John and his two helpers lifted the curricle onto its wheels and the injured young man could at last be examined.

"Oh, Mama, he's quite pale, but I think still breathing. Papa, does it seem to you that his leg is wrong somehow?" Betta was on her knees beside Sir Robin's head. "I do believe he is coming round."

"Oh, God . . . that child . . . Is the child safe?" Robin lifted his head slightly, looking around. "Oh, my leg . . . it's too much. Jackson . . . where's Jackson?" His concern gave a momentary strength to his voice, but as Mr. St. John examined the leg, the injured man weakened and fainted.

" 'Tis better if he's unconscious. That leg will need setting. Give me some cloths so I can splint it to the good leg. That will keep it steady while we move him. You did send Jim for the doctor, Amelia, my dear?" Receiving a nod from his wife, Mr. St. John directed his men to lift Robin to a carrier and proceed to the house.

"Jackson, is that your name?" he said, with a questioning look at Robin's groom. "Can you walk to the house, or shall we bring the cart?"

"Sir, I would look at the horses . . . and get them settled down. I'm just a mite shaky. Master . . . that is, Sir Robin, is that fond of them. . . . I tried to stop him, but he had to have his head, and when we saw the little one, there warn't no time to slow down. Will he be all right, sir? Oh, blast! Milord will have me whiskers for all I've been with him these many years."

"Come, come, Jackson . . . your master will be all right. Come along, I'll send one of the men to help with the horses. We keep a stable . . . you need not concern yourself with the animals. I want you to join the young man . . . he will feel more at ease if he sees a face he knows. A group of strangers won't comfort him as much as you will. Once we know exactly how he goes, we can send to his family. I am Mr. St. John, and once you've rested a bit you can tell me who you and your master are."

Chapter 3

In spite of the languid movements of the elegantly clothed gentleman as he lifted his quizzing glass, there was an air of suppressed vitality about him.

"My dear Philippe, that waistcoat should be shot at dawn"—he gazed through his glass—"an enemy, my friend, a veritable enemy."

Philippe Beaumont, French émigré and dear friend to Alexander Petrie, Earl of Halwick, Baron of Favesham and Frome, looked down at his striped garment, refusing to be baited by this remark.

"Be serious, Alex; sending Robin to Possingworth may keep him out of your way for a few days, but you may be sure he'll come galloping back to London *ventre à terre* as soon as he learns you are missing from your usual haunts."

"He won't learn anything he doesn't expect to hear. He thinks me off to Ireland to buy horses."

"And the mission to France will be finished within time?"

"If I am not returned at the end of the third week, you may intimate that I have found a new 'friend' in Ireland and that she proves too amiable for me to leave without fully enjoying such amity. . . . That will be reason enough for my not appearing sooner." The earl walked to his writing desk. "I've already written the letter giving this explanation should you feel the need to—ah—prove your intimations. No one will know it to have been written before I left. I am also leaving instructions with Parlow, my man of business, to book rooms in Brighton mid-June to July. That will keep Robin occupied; his thoughts will be more concerned with what to wear than where I am."

"And if the necessity arises, in the event of something serious happening, you will not be on a pleasure trip, *mon vieux.*"

"True. Parlow has my directions and the foreign minister assured me of giving Robin the whole story in the event of my too early demise." The earl handed M. Beaumont the letter he had taken from the desk. "And now, *mon ami,* let us make plans for this evening. I do not depart until tomorrow and we must look for gaiety tonight. The mesdemoiselles of the opera indicated a great need for our company." A wicked grin crossed the earl's face. "Shall we agree to meet here in two hours for dinner?" Again in the languid manner: "It will take me at least that long to create my *tailleur* . . . and then to the opera and perhaps Vauxhall."

M. Beaumont looked at his friend with a laugh. "You know, my friend, you never cease to astonish me. I don't see how people can look at you knowing you to be a sportsman—in fact, a top-of-the-trees Corinthian, as they say—and yet are willing to accept you as a veritable tulip with nothing between your ears but skin, bone, and hair."

"It's because I languish, my dear Philippe, absolutely languish, and am in a constant state of ennui with all the fatiguing matters of living. Although I must admit I am hard put sometimes to languish with a sword in my hand or sitting in my phaeton behind a fast pair . . . but then only a few have ever seen me with a sword, and even a languishing beau may be allowed to be a whip." He gave a laugh at the inconsistent foibles of the fashionable world.

"Ah, well, I hope your deceitful way speeds you along on your mission. You have a difficult journey ahead and a more difficult return. Your acting ability will serve you well this trip."

The two men continued to arrange their plans for the evening as they left the study. They parted in the large oval entry hall of the earl's townhouse, Philippe Beaumont to his home and the earl to inform his butler that there would be one guest for dinner and the carriage would be required for ten that evening.

Philippe's situation within the household of the Petrie family was that of a brother. His friendship with the earl had arisen when they met on the Continent during the traditional "grand tour" that young men of the upper classes were wont to make before attaining their majority. Both were gentlemen of means and young gentlemen of high spirits and became friends during a minor rebellion staged by Alexander in the throes of boredom at having to view his fortieth church campanile. Something to do with the Leaning Tower of Pisa, as Philippe remembered, something reprehensible that required a willing cohort to escape the attention of a watchful tutor.

The escapade had led to a discovery of mutual friends and interests and an open invitation to Philippe to visit with the Petries when in England. Owing to the circumstances in France, Philippe's visit was much sooner than expected. He had become persona non grata in France and had been forced to flee the country of his birth, leaving his sister and mother. Having inherited a fortune from his English uncle, he was not destitute, as were many émigrés, and was able to join Alec in his many pursuits without fear of need. As the two men matured, their respect and regard for each other deepened, so that each was privy to the other's most intimate hopes and plans. Philippe knew of the earl's secret work as an agent for the British government. The carefully conceived persona of a dandy and ineffectual tulip was the screen behind which the earl carried on his dangerous work. Philippe's contacts among the émigrés, some of whom were acknowledged agents of the French government, garnered bits and pieces of information that filled in the jigsaw puzzle of the spy network and occasionally actuated the earl's disappearance from the *ton* for a period.

Topping, the earl's valet, eased his master into his superbly tailored, black superfine evening coat and stood back to look at him. He saw a tall, well-built, albeit slender, man of four and thirty who carried himself with a certain air of assurance that gave notice to the world that here was a man of consequence. His black hair, worn in a Brutus, capped a broad brow, expressive eyes, a strong nose, and a wide, sensuous mouth. His countenance was of such attraction as to compel one to gaze at him, yet to cause one to be astonished at the attraction, since his features, except for the eyes, were not of a configuration accepted as a standard of masculine beauty. His eyes, though, were extraordinary. Fringed with dark lashes that might be envied by a woman, they were of almost a sapphire-blue, bright with intelligence and vitality. Upon occasion they could melt the most frigid matron or freeze the most insensitive mushroom.

"There, milord, the sapphires furnish the perfect touch." The valet admired the pin nestled in the pristine folds of the earl's neckcloth. "Did you want full evening attire packed for your trip?"

"This looks well, Topping. As usual you've turned me out very well. Yes, pack full rig—with proper clothes for town as well as country." Not even the earl's body servant was aware of his dual role. "I may need them on the return from Ireland if I stop at Bristol to see my aunt. You need not wait up for me tonight, but I will need your services in the morning. Inform Benson that I will want the traveling coach for nine in the morning and we shall be gone upwards of three weeks." There was a light knock at the door. "Come . . . ah, Stilson . . . has M. Beaumont arrived? Good. You are aware that I am leaving for Ireland in the morning?"

The butler nodded.

"I have arranged for Mr. Parlow to handle any emergencies that might arise. You have his address and may call upon him at need. You may look for my return in about three weeks."

Lord Halwick instructed his butler as he accompanied him down the stairs, "M. Beaumont and I will dine in ten minutes. Make my farewells to the staff. You may arrange for them each to have time off while I am away . . . discuss it with Mr. Parlow."

"Philippe," he greeted his friend, "shall we have something to drink before we dine? You are looking very fine this evening."

"Alec, please, you will put me to the blush. Shall I let myself be any less the rooster than my so fine *ami*? I also must be attractive to the ladies! But let me be serious for the moment. I am concerned for Robin . . . you know he was drawn into such deep play by Jeremy Wingate. Most charming man, but a total blackguard. I have it that he is trying to sell his daughter, only seventeen and a taking young chit. The man has not feeling. Supposedly she is still a virgin . . . fetch a higher price . . . and very innocent. He's kept her in the country until recently." Philippe saluted his host with the freshly poured wine. "Don't

24

believe he's approached Robin on that matter . . . I've heard he's offering her to a more discreet and older man. Knows Robin's too much the romantic to countenance such a havey-cavey scheme."

Lord Halwick looked at Philippe. "D'you know, I think it would be educational for Robin to learn of his dear mentor's plan for the girl. In all likelihood it will turn him off Wingate for good, and away from that whole group of jobsters. Don't think Robin would condone the thought of a man selling his daughter to the highest bidder for the blunt to pay his gambling debts. Not the thing. Yes, you must give Robin the word. Perhaps you would favor me with a trip to Possingworth before I return. He'll be well bored with country life and thankful for company in two weeks or so and will welcome you most heartily." The blue eyes danced. "He may even embroil you in whatever scrape he is into when you arrive."

"But naturally, Alec, he is as like you at that age as is possible to be. Perhaps not quite as wild, but then he has an older brother to hold him back." The Frenchman smiled. "I will be happy to disclose the news to Robin; it will also give me something to do now that the company in London is thinning out. The time between the town season and Brighton tends to be somewhat dull. I shall go on a repairing lease to Norfolkshire . . . possibly get in some fishing. Are the salmon running well this spring?"

Chapter 4

The pallid skin of Sir Robin Petrie's face had no more color than the crisp white bed linen on which he rested. The bulky mound beneath the coverlet indicated his splinted leg; the bottles of tonic and boxes of pills on the bedside table were reminders of the doctor's recent visit. In the quiet of the room, the crackle of the fire played a soft accompaniment to the sibilant scratch of the quill against the paper upon which Mrs. St. John was writing.

"Please believe, my lord, that we would have informed you sooner but were waiting Sir Robin's full revival so that he could himself assure you of his condition. However, this is the third day that he is still less than himself. Although the doctor feels this to be a response to his state of mind at the time of the upset as well as the shock of the injury and that he is to be considered in a recuperative process, I feel your presence would be beneficial to him."

Mrs. St. John ended her letter with an invitation to the earl to consider Watton Abbey his home for the duration of his brother's recuperation. She sanded the letter and as she folded it walked quietly to the door and opened it. There on a seat in the hall sat Jackson.

"How is he, mum? Has he waked up yet? Lord, it fair makes me wish 'twas me . . . if he were me own son, 'twould not hurt more to see him thus." The man's face was wrinkled with concern for the young viscount.

"Now, Jackson, I know your feelings, but he is strong and healthy and there is no fever. I'm sure we'll be hearing from him shortly, and then he'll be complaining about not being able to get about and the food and who knows whatall, and we will probably wish he were still asleep. I did hear him muttering just a little while ago . . . something about a high-flyer and then a reference to hitting the wall. You'll see, by the time you return with the earl, Sir Robin will in all likelihood be lively and impatient with being prisoner to the splints on his leg. I've written fully to Lord Halwick and asked him to return with you, so you must ride to him as quickly as you can. My husband will provide a mount and directions for the shortest route to town. You will want to say farewell to your master, I'm sure. Your voice does seem to bring him out of the depths of his sleep, so do you speak to him now, and see my husband. I'm going down to get his broth in case he comes to."

Jackson moved into the room and over to the bed. He looked down at the young man he had first seen as an infant.

"Oh, Robin lad, don't give up now . . . come along now, lad. Let's hear ye gibbling and gabbling about this and that again. I'd be that happy to hear ye cursing at me, Master Robin."

"Well, curse you for a gabster," came a thin whisper from the wan face on the pillow. "What are you in such a misery about?"

"Thank the Lord, ye've waked up. . . . I've been that worried. Don't yer remember, Robin lad . . . ye swerved the horses because of the child in the road and smashed into the wall. Ah, but never think of it now . . . you're too weak for this and it will wait on your feeling stronger."

"No, no . . . tell me all now. Where are we and how did I get here?" Robin looked around the strange room.

"Well, lad, we're in the home of Mr. St. John. 'Twas his youngest, Letty, who was in the road . . . looking for her dog, she was, and that upset when she saw you take a flyer . . . thought she'd kilt you, she did. And there're twin girls and Bertie, he's the only boy; and then there's Miss Betta, she's the eldest. They be a very friendly family and cared for you like you was one of their own."

"Yes, and since he is like one of our own, Jackson, he is to have some gruel and then rest. Mama will have to rewrite her letter to Lord Halwick now that the news is happier. Jackson, will you advise her that Sir Robin has awakened, and then you can be off to London." Betta sat down next to the bed. "How do you do, Sir Robin. It is too bad to have to be introduced in this manner. Not quite *comme il faut*, but I expect we shall get along for all of that."

"Very grateful to you all, shouldn't have been traveling so fast . . . was in a devil of a temper . . ." Robin tried to sit up. "My leg . . . what's wrong?"

Betta started to spoon up some broth for Robin as she explained the results of the accident to the ailing young man and assured him that with rest and care he would recover the full use of his leg, needing only the proper length of time to remain off the broken limb.

"And now Jackson must leave to inform your brother of the accident. He will be concerned when he fails to hear of your safe arrival at your home."

"He won't hear anything, because he's on a trip to Ireland. Left the day after I did. Gone to buy horses and won't be back for two or three weeks."

28

Betta continued to feed Robin while she digested this news. Cheerfully she told him that this was all to the good by reason of allowing the St. John family to give him the care called for as a result of Letty's unlooked-for appearance in front of his vehicle. Robin would be well enough by the time the earl should arrive at Watton Abbey to be able to receive him in the downstairs parlor rather than from his bed. And now Robin was to rest and not to worry about anything . . . just think about getting well.

Exhausted by the effort of staying awake, Robin quickly slipped into sleep.

Jackson's mind was greatly eased by the young viscount's return to consciousness. At worst now would be the length of time for the healing of the leg. It was a relief to know the earl was absent from town and not expected for so long a period. The dressing down he would get from milord would not be easy to face, and the more in health young Robin was when he and Jackson were confronted by the earl, the better. For now, the groom could make himself useful in the sickroom and give what help he could about the estate.

The next few days saw Robin's health improve rapidly. But for the incapacity caused by his leg, he would have been up and about and doubtless away. As captive to his bed, he found amusement in becoming acquainted with the members of the St. John family, his most frequent visitors being the younger ones, who applied themselves to the task of keeping the formerly active man from falling into the dismals during his enforced inactivity. Letty produced the originator of the series of events that had brought about the viscount's vegetation, the famed Brindle, to perform for the invalid. She adopted Robin as her very own, constantly keeping him advised as to events in the family, bringing him samples of flowers and precious things found in the gardens, and offering him bits of sweets that she'd garnered from the tea tray.

Pamela and Evianne, although older, were her loyal lieutenants, instantly obeying her every injunction, taking pleasure in doing their lessons at Robin's bedside, commanding his help when confounded by a particularly difficult geography lesson or a missing date in history. They were half in love, at nine, with this, their first town beau.

Albert at first resented the presence of one who so completely took his place in Letty's esteem, but when in the course of conversation he learned that this person was a frequent visitor to Gentleman Jackson's Parlor and an adept in the art of fisticuffs, his resentment quickly turned to an embarrassment of attention. He became Robin's confidant and told him of his desires to drive a high-perch phaeton and pair, be a lieutenant in the Light Bobs, ride to the hounds, and be a true top-of-the-trees goer.

It was well into June when the doctor gave permission for Robin to be carried to the lower floor, giving strict orders that at no time was he to put weight on his foot. "You will not want the healing to be crooked or the leg to be shorter than the other, Sir Robin . . . which will be the case if you should put a strain on the bone. It seems like a lengthy time, but once past, you will not miss it, and by the end of the month we may be able to put you on a crutch," were the doctor's cautionary words as he left the patient.

"Jackson, have a care there; Thompson, move the chair closer to the bed." Mr. St. John directed his two helpers to place the oddly shaped structure they carried. "You see what we've done, my boy; took the back and top off the old sedan chair m'mother used to be carried about in and added a support for your leg, and you can be carried with ease anywhere on the estate."

Jackson gently fitted Robin into a brilliantly embroidered scarlet robe and carefully moved him toward the edge of the bed. An audience of St. Johns, accompanied by Brindle, stood at the threshold of the room calling out advice to the master of the house and his helpers and encouragement to the sufferer as he was transferred from bed to sedan chair.

Game but pale, the houseguest made his bow to his vociferous fans and waved his willing carriers to take their places at either end of the conveyance.

"A most unusual way to travel about a house, I must say, but thank you for your goodness, sir, and brilliance of design. I thought I might be a prisoner to that bed for the rest of my stay here." He stifled a groan as the chair hit the doorpost and jarred his leg. "Here, Jackson, you're not supposed to kill me while you move me. I'm on my way to an improved condition, not a decline, which you shall put me into if you bang me around that way. When I told my friends I was going on a repairing lease into the country, I didn't realize I meant to repair my leg."

With much laughter, and admonitions from Letty and Betta, the group descended to the main level of the house and into the morning parlor, a room of comfortable size with a cheerful vista of the terrace and gardens and low hills in the distance. Along the long wall, opposite the entry to the room, were three pairs of French doors, now open in the late spring warmth, with small commodes of country design and family portraits above them, placed between the sets of doors. At one end of the area was a table and chairs used for informal family dining, all set in front of a high-manteled fireplace. Above the mantel were paintings and drawings executed by Mr. St. John of birds and flowers found on the estate. The other end of the room, also with fireplace, was furnished with a comfortable camp bed and several upholstered chairs and sofas. A round gaming table stood away from the bed with a beautifully carved chess set upon it, a game of spillikins and several decks of cards. Obviously a room greatly given to family use, there was an air of warmth and comfort in it . . . a feeling of love and safety.

"You will be able to join us for dining and tea here, Robin, and we will be a family for you until your brother arrives. It seems strange that we have not received word from him as yet." Betta fussed with the pillows on the bed while the men moved Robin onto it. "Of course, it may be that he is so relieved to be saved your scapegrace escapades that he pretends not to know of you."

Robin gave a laugh. "More like he is still in Ireland . . . or has met a 'lady fair' who keeps him occupied. My brother is the best, Betta. 'Tis just that he is eleven years older than I and had to take the responsibility of the estate and planning and care of me when he was but twenty-one. After a few years, it was as though he had to kick over the traces and enjoy some of the times he might have had at a younger age had our parents not died when they did. I am just as happy he does not come. I find being an intimate in your family circle a most diverting experience. Alec and I never shared such, our parents died when I was ten; and although he is the best of brothers, he has not been in such close rapport with me as you with your brother and sisters. Alec had been very close to our father, you see, and felt his loss in such a way that he could relieve it only by throwing himself into the work that had been my father's."

"I have always longed for a brother near my age," said Betta, "and you have become such a brother; the young ones already think you belong to them. Mama and Papa will have no objection to becoming your aunt and uncle

32

by adoption . . . although that will make the relationships a bit confusing!" Betta smiled and continued: "You must promise to listen to your sister when she advises you."

Robin groaned. "Why is it that women want to take over the reins . . . ? I'll promise if you'll promise to listen when I advise you; and no gammoning, now!"

"I could wish I'd had a friend like you, 'Brother,' when I made my come out. It would have been an easier time, to have been able to talk to someone near my own age. Country manners are not so formal as town, or so I found. I had been used to saying what I thought and answering with truth; but when I would do so in conversation with the gentlemen who spoke to me or even the ladies, they would profess to be confounded by my manner. I believe I came to be known as a bluestocking and an antidote."

"An antidote! How is that possible? You will forgive your 'brother' being so forward, but truly, Betta, you are a real looker. I'd be proud to name you 'sister' and show you off to the *ton*. It's too bad my brother wasn't on the scene . . . he would have seen you for what you are . . . he's not so high-flown that he can't tell a diamond of the first water when he comes across one."

"I'm sure your brother is a paragon; but even he, I'm convinced, would consider a lady novelist a bluestocking." Betta wrinkled her nose at the thought. "And you know, Robin, it is my ambition to finish my novel."

Robin pooh-poohed the idea and repeated his praises of Alexander Halwick.

Betta turned the conversation away from her disastrous season, remembering that the only man who had been the least bit attractive to her had been the Earl of Halwick, and that had been from a distance. The young woman's eyes were violet with dreams as she sat gazing into the distance recalling his arrogant good looks, cool manner, and sudden sweet smile when he spoke to his close friends. Though she had yearned to meet him, her precipitous flight from the unkindness she had met during that disastrous second season precluded any such happening. Besides, had she met him, the ordeal of standing up to his condescending examination would, in all likelihood, have tied her tongue in knots. No, better not to have been exposed to what would surely have been a severe setdown. And she would make sure not to be too much in his company when he came for Robin. Perhaps Robin would be wholly recovered even before the earl showed up at Watton Abbey. A feeling of regret for what had never been and most likely would never be stole over Miss St. John. Her Rudolfo—how delicious it might have been. Robin looked at her dreamstruck countenance and wondered at the blush on her cheeks.

Chapter 5

The smart black rig, drawn by a pair of smoothly paced chestnuts, was driven through the high wrought-iron gate that led into Possingworth, the Earl of Halwick's home. Wending its way up a driveway flanked with magnificent rhododendron bushes in the full bloom of mid-June, the chaise soon drew up in front of the sprawling seventeenth-century residence. A footman dropped the carriage step as Philippe Beaumont jumped lightly to the ground. He was greeted by Sedgely, the earl's butler and ruler of this awesome realm with its staff of more than one hundred, including maids, footmen, kitchen help, stablehands, yardmen, gardeners, and the upper hierarchy of housekeeper, chef, head groom, and head gardener.

"M'soo Beaumont, we are happy to see you again. You look to be in good health, sir," the very proper greeting went. "Are you expecting to meet the earl here? Or Sir Robin?" Sedgely led Philippe into the mansion.

"Do you mean to tell me that Sir Robin isn't here?" was Philippe's astonished response. "Has he left already?"

"He hasn't left, sir, because he hasn't been here in about three months. We are not expecting either of the gentlemen, although it has been the earl's habit to retire to Possingworth at this time of year prior to setting up in Brighton."

"The earl is in Ireland, but Robin departed London for Possingworth more than three weeks ago, just before the earl left. Sir Robin was directed to spend this month or more here . . . this is very unusual." M. Beaumont looked worried. "Perhaps you had better send one of the grooms to London with a message for him, should he have decided to return there rather than to continue on to Norfolk. In fact, I will write to both Sir Robin and the earl while you arrange with your people."

Sedgely left the hall as Philippe moved into the writing room to pen his messages. He had not expected to find the earl at Possingworth . . . the mission to France was sure to have taken longer than the original plan called for, with conditions there so unsettled and the need for complete secrecy necessary to its success. But certainly Robin should have been present. What mischief had the young scamp gotten into now, and what could or should he himself do about it?

Philippe finished the second note, sanded and sealed it, and rang for the elderly family factotum. While he waited, he considered the possible whereabouts of the younger Petrie, discarding the thought that he might have eloped . . . he had had no deep attachment for any of the young ladies on the London scene. Although of course with Robin one could never be absolutely sure . . . but in that case he would certainly have sent some notice of such action, knowing that there would have been no possibility of being discovered before he had accomplished his course of action, if that had been his aim. No, probably he was visiting a friend, knowing how empty of company Possing-worth was at this time of year. But again, for all his harum-scarum ways, Robin never disobeyed a direct order from his brother, and he had been ordered to retire to the country. All that was needed was to send to London and

36

await the answer. In the meantime he would start inquiries along the roads from London to Possingworth. Even with the lapse of time, a curricle and team such as Robin had been driving would be remembered by some of the innkeepers or tollgate men along the way.

Sedgely returned, followed by the head groom.

"M'soo Beaumont, Houseman here feels it would be best if he ride to London. He would rather not leave this to one of the other men. . . . We are all rather fond of Sir Robin and know his ways, and . . . Houseman . . . well, he knows some of the places he might be tempted to visit on the way, as it were."

"An excellent idea. The earl places much trust in your good sense, Houseman. I know you will know how to get about without creating a storm. Speak to Stilson and Topping when you get to Grosvenor Square. . . . They'll bring you up to date on the activities of the young rapscallion . . . that is, if they have knowledge . . . without creating a view-halloo among the *ton*. The earl would not want this to become one of the on-dits of the season." The earl's close friend worried at his fair hair. "Here are the letters and some money . . . should be enough for your lodging and tolls."

With directions not to set out until morning, Philippe wished the head groom a successful journey, silently reflecting on the problems that would arise should the younger brother not be found.

The six days' wait until Houseman returned seemed interminable. Philippe sent grooms out on various roads to question farmers and villagers while he himself took long rides to families known to the Petries to see if Robin was passing the time of his banishment with one of them. Houseman's return brought no word of either Robin or his brother, and Philippe made arrangements to return to

London to await Alec's arrival. Perhaps their two heads working together would be able to fathom the mystery of Robin's disappearance.

The house on Grosvenor Square loomed through the evening's mizzle, set off by the Italian poplars that cornered the forecourt plantings. The doorlamps shimmered through the fine mist reflecting softly from the back of the damp horse standing in the shallow court fronting the building.

The tall figure wrapped in a riding cape lifted the butt of his crop to the door. At that moment the door swung open and a look of surprise could be seen on the face of the footman.

"Why, my lord, welcome home. . . . Mr. Stilson," he called, "he's come home."

"James, lower your voice." A sharp command came from the earl's butler as he entered the hall, and with majestic wave of hand gestured the footman away. "I will see to the earl. If you will give me your cape, milord . . . We've been looking for you this past week, sir." He relieved his master of his hat and cloak. "M. Beaumont has just arrived seeking your return. He is in the library. May I say we are happy to see you."

"It's good to be back, Stilson. Please see if you can find something for me to eat; I've not had a bite since this morning and I'm famished, and bring in the makings for a hot punch. It's been a long wet ride and I'm feeling chilled. Are the mail and messages on my desk?"

"Yes, milord. I will bring them to you as soon as I inform Anatole of your needs."

The obviously weary man strolled into the library.

"Well, Philippe, what adventure brings you to Grosvenor Square on such a night and I not even at home?"

38

Philippe, already standing in response to the voices he had heard in the hall, walked to his friend and, in a movement characteristic of his French heritage, put his arms about Alec in greeting.

"Only you, *mon ami,* could return after so dangerous a trip with so casual a word. We have been worried beyond endurance, between you and Robin . . ."

"What do you mean, Robin?" the earl demanded.

"He's missing, Alec. Never arrived at Possingworth and no word there. We looked through your mail here but found nothing in his handwriting. Houseman made the trip from Possingworth but found no sign of him at the posting houses along the return. I am not enough acquainted with his many friends to set out the alarm, nor did I wish to, without consulting you beforehand." The worry in the eyes of the fair-haired gentleman was apparent.

"I'm sure you worry needlessly. He's probably rusticating with one of his friends. . . . I daresay he took off at me when I refused to make an advance to him. His letter must have gone astray and he will turn up full of his latest adventures, deeply enamoured of some country miss, to laugh at all your efforts at finding him."

"I hope you are right, my friend, but it is not like Robin to ignore his responsibility to you," was the rejoinder.

"Milord, I've ordered a supper for you and M. Beaumont. James will have it here in a trice. In the meantime, here is your mail." Stilson placed a large tray overflowing with envelopes of all shapes and sizes on the table next to the chair in which Petrie was lounging.

"Excuse me, Philippe, while I go through this pile. . . . Why don't you put together the punch? I would truly welcome the cheer such a drink would give me." He quickly shuffled through several envelopes. "This must be an invitation from Deighton for the rout . . . Chefley sends something. . . . I know this handwriting, 'tis that numb-skull cousin of mine, doubtless asking for another loan. . . . Here's a name that's new to me. St. John. Do you know a St. John? Of Watton Abbey in Norfolk. That's not too far from Possingworth. . . . 'My dear sir, regret to inform you . . . injured in an accident with his curricle . . . broken leg . . .' Good God, this letter is dated twenty-nine May . . . that's four or five days after Robin left for the country house. That's why you weren't able to track him down all this time. He's been a guest of the St. John family. This is signed by Mrs. St. John, who very nicely offers guest rights to us until Robin is able to be moved.

"I'll have to leave for Norfolk tomorrow. . . . No, that's impossible . . . perhaps the day after. You won't want to go with me, you'll have other things to take care of." The earl gave a quick glance at Philippe. "In fact, I have a feeling you'll be rather busy for the next few days escort-ing some . . . ah . . . friends to my estate."

"What nonsense are you talking, Alec? What can be more important than Robin's situation? Who shall I be escorting and why?"

"Just a moment and I'll tell you all. There is a letter from Robin . . . it must have come today. 'Dear Alec . . . hope you will be here soon. Still not walking, but doctor promised to put me up on a crutch by first of July in time for the birthday party. I have had the good fortune to have been taken in by a most wonderful family.' There must be a daughter. 'You will fall in love with them as I have. Their oldest daughter'—you see, what did I tell you!—'has become dearer to me than a sister. We share our deepest thoughts . . . never did I think to have such a friend. She has a clarity of thought and a sharpness of wit that is beyond compare. I cannot wait for you to meet

40

her. Please hurry your arrival, Alec. I know you will want to thank the St. Johns personally for their many kindnesses. Your affectionate brother, Robin Petrie.' That settles it . . . I definitely leave the day after tomorrow. I must meet this paragon for myself." The earl was distracted for a moment, then recalled to himself the news he had for Philippe.

"My very dear friend, part of my mission was to contact our agents in Rouen and Paris and to affirm our lines of information. But the other part, of which you were not aware, because I did not wish to raise your hopes, was to find your sister and her family, and I was successful! Even now they are but a short distance from here. I came on to prepare you for this reunion."

"My sister," the stunned Frenchman murmured. "But I had heard that she was dead and no family was left . . . that's why I never returned to France. Alec, this is a miracle . . . I can't believe . . . I shall have to rent a house, my quarters are not large enough. How many are in her family—Family . . . she was just a young girl when last I saw her."

"Well, she's grown up now, *mon ami*. You've told me she was the youngest in your family, but I never realized she was Robin's age. She certainly has three lively children; married at sixteen and gave her husband his heir the next year." His lordship stopped, caught by the look on his friend's face, "but what is it, Philippe? You have a look . . ."

"My sister would have been thirty this past May had she been alive. I heard she died five years ago." Philippe spoke in a barely audible voice. "I don't know who this woman is, but she's not Felicia. What does she look like?"

"Dark, slim, not an incomparable, but well enough . . . very taking eyes . . . ! Medium height, soft, pleasant

41

voice, and great patience . . . a pure wonder with those children. Taught them to call me Papa in a trice. . . . Well, I had to, you know. We were supposed to be a family." The king's agent began to speak in French: "You are speaking to the esteemed baker from Versailles, Pierre LaBrie, who until a few days ago had a wife, Jeanne, and three children, petit Charlot, Pierre, and Étienne, who were, in truth, supposed to be your sister and her children." He returned to English: "We will have to get to the bottom of this tomorrow. I beg forgiveness, Philippe, that I should give you such joy and then dash it to the ground in the same instant."

"But who could she be . . . to know of my sister, myself . . . enough to convince you? I cannot imagine."

The pain of remembering his loss when he had received word of his sister's death owing to an epidemic that wiped out most of the population of the country château in which she lived, stayed with Philippe through the night. By morning his pain had turned to anger against this unknown woman. Nothing she had to say would excuse the anguish she had caused. He would see that she was properly punished. Seething with anger and despair, he returned to Grosvenor Square to keep the appointment made with Alec to meet his supposed "sister" and her children.

The earl was found at breakfast in the silk-lined dining room. The glimmer of sunlight that filtered through the sheer curtains glowed on the rich colors of the Kirman rug that covered the floor, brought back by his lordship from one of his voyages. Mr. Sheraton's graceful dining chairs surrounded a table of his design, its polished surface reflecting the flower-filled epergne centered on it. A matching sideboard held warming platters of eggs, kidneys, steak, and hot breads; and pots of hot chocolate and hot milk sat next to the cups and saucers.

"Come join me, Philippe. I haven't seen a meal like this since I left England." The earl stood to pour the hot drink for his friend. "Sit down and calm yourself. You look positively hag-ridden. Bad night, my friend?"

"The effrontery of this woman . . . passing herself and her brats as my sister and her children. She's probably one of the maids from the village." The bitterness in Philippe's voice shocked Petrie.

"Not likely she's a maid, Philippe. She is cultured and educated. She spoke of you when you were a young man, so she obviously knew you or saw you then. In fact, she specifically mentioned your escapade with the so charming Yvonne and your escape through the window as her husband came in the door. You were a devil in your salad days! Still are . . . manage to stay ahead of me. . . . Sometimes I think my reputation for dalliance grew because of my association with you." The earl smiled warmly at his friend. "No, Philippe, this young woman is not a maid. . . . As to who and what she is, I am now as confounded as you. Drink up your chocolate and we'll be on our way. I left her with my Aunt Westrich. Couldn't bring her here without a chaperone, even with the children. She's too young (and beautiful) and I'm too talked about. Thought she was your sister; had to protect her. We planned a story that would cover her arrival without involving me . . . keep her from being gossip's meat. Did you ride or walk over this morning?"

"I walked . . . I felt I needed the exercise to work off some of the anger." Philippe's forehead was wrinkled in puzzlement. "Damned if I can think who she is. No one knew that story, not even Felicia. My God . . . there was one . . . but it couldn't be, she was such a child . . . to

remember . . . No, *c'est impossible. Pour une enfant
. . .*" In his agitation Philippe began to express himself in
French.

"Hold on, *mon ami,* you're not making sense. Who do
you think she is? And why is it impossible?"

"Oh, Alec, this child was too much. She followed me
everywhere. She was my mother's godchild and was staying with us when I was . . . I think . . . about nineteen,
so she was about eight years old. I think she had a passion
for me. I couldn't get away from her . . . not even in my
bath. . . . She would pop into my room to hand me a
sponge or towel . . . My word, when I remember . . . Very
quiet, with huge black eyes that would look at me
. . . she rarely spoke, just looked at me, until I would gladly
have sold her to the gypsies to get rid of those eyes. I think
it was the same year I met you. I had this little assignation
with Yvonne and the abominable child followed me."

The earl let out a yelp of laughter. "Followed you
. . . at night . . . ?"

"Oh, no, not at night. . . . How could one have the
affaire d'amour with a married woman at night . . . ? No,
it was in the afternoon. I find that to be the very best time
of day for such things. The husband is at work, the wife
at ease . . ." Philippe kissed the tips of his fingers and
flicked the kiss away with an insouciant grin. "But this
time the husband neglected to stay away and I tumbled
out the window, my boots in my hands, one arm not yet
in my jacket, and practically fell on this little . . . don't
know how to call her . . . admirer, for want of a better
word, and the two of us ran for my life."

The earl doubled over with laughter.

"My dear Philippe, the vision of you as a young buck
tumbling out of that window is too much." He wiped the

tears from his eyes. "But why didn't she tell me . . . I would still have brought her. . . ."

"Perhaps she felt so dashing a cavalier would be more solicitous in every way of her well-being if you thought her to have a brother to whom you would have to answer for your behavior." His laughter stopped. "But the children, can they be hers?"

Alec shrugged. "I know only what she told me, and that seems not to be true. Let's go, it's close enough to walk. I can't wait for you to meet this storyteller . . . to see if she's your admirer."

The two men donned their hats, accepted their canes from Stilson, and walked out to head toward Park Lane and Lady Westrich's abode.

Chapter 6

A rather harassed young lady of perhaps three and twenty was attempting to assist an even more harassed older woman of perhaps fifty to bathe three very active, slippery little boys.

"Étienne, Pierre, Charlot . . . *vous êtes comme des poissons . . . asseyez-vous, tout de suite!*" Water splashed over the sides of the tub and chortles of delight swept through the room.

"Mathilde, take Charlot from the water . . . he will drown . . . he is getting so . . . so . . . oh, this language. He slips from the hands . . . he . . . he . . . I couldn't be more with water if I should be in the bath."

The older woman lifted the three-year-old out of the tub and wrapped him in a large towel that had been warming in front of the fire, cooing to him in French as she tickled his toes and rubbed his hair dry.

"Ah, comtesse, *ce n'est pas gentil pour . . .*" Mathilde began to remonstrate.

"Mathilde, I am no longer la comtesse . . . and speak in the English. We are not in France and will not again be there . . . now we are to live in this England and must speak the new way . . . even though it sounds like bears growling in the zoo. Little ones, stop. . . . Oh, Pierrot, is the soap in your eyes? Let me wipe it out. Come, here is the towel, *allez*-oop." The woman, hardly more than a girl, addressed as comtesse by Mathilde, lifted Pierrot, a wriggling four-year-old, out of the water. "Now you, Étienne . . . you are going to meet your uncle today . . . Papa the earl, is bringing him here soon. So, quickly, let me dress you."

As the two women dried and clothed the youngsters they discussed their future. The maid with fear, the comtesse with a bravado that barely hid her own fears about the outcome of the waited-for visit from Étienne's uncle. Quickly putting the finishing touches to Étienne's apparel, she cautioned Mathilde to keep the children clean and quiet while she made herself presentable.

"Take the little ones down to the library. You can ask that so important-looking man . . . What is his name . . . ? Ah, yes, Umber, where it is, Mathilde. Here, take these toys with you. I ordered some food for the children and yourself; it will be brought to you there. I will be down as quickly as possible."

"Oh, madame, *ce n'est pas convenable.*"

"English, Mathilde."

"It is not correct for you to do this. There are servants in this house; they should be waiting on you. A granddaughter of a princess of the royal blood serving as a baby nurse . . . even for your own children. *C'est pour pleurer à chaudes larmes* . . . It is to cry the bitter tears. If your poor mother knew . . ."

"Well, she doesn't know, and times change. My royal blood will put no bread in our mouths. Now do as I say, and no more nonsense. *Mes petits chers* . . . *attendez* . . . you will go with Mathilde. Be as quiet as little mice. *Tante* Westrich is sleeping and we must not disturb."

When Mathilde had left the room carrying Charlot and sweeping the two other boys before her, Madame la Comtesse sank into a chair, exhausted. How life changed from one year, one week, one day, to the next, she thought. Here she was, Virginie Camille de St. Martin, Comtesse d'Ivrailles, being able to trace her ancestry further back than the time of Louis XIV, dependent on a stranger's kindness for the very food that passed between her lips. In fact, dependent for her living since she was six, when she had lost her parents in one of the many upheavals that had been plaguing France since the Revolution. If it hadn't been for her godmother, Antoinette Beaumont, Marquise de Genveille et de Coustignac, God alone knew what might have happened to her. The marquise had taken her godchild into her family, provided a calm, peaceful home, a good husband, and love. And now, bereft of husband, godmother, everything she had known, what would she do? And what of her two small sons? What would have happened if this mad Englishman, the Earl of Halwick, Papa the earl, hadn't come like a whirlwind and swept them up with him? What would she have done if he hadn't rescued them from the terror of the plague-ridden village in Provence, where the man who had been her husband had had his château? The earl thought she was Philippe's sister . . . but she couldn't tell him who she really was, he had too reckless a way with him. At least this way she had the protection of Philippe's name to stop him from possibly paying her unwelcome attention. But he had been only as an uncle might be, with no hint of such attention.

Virginie began to remove her bath-soaked clothes. Now she would have to answer to Philippe for her deceitfulness. Had he changed much from the days when she had been his worshiping follower? He would arrive expecting to see his sister Felicia. He would not know that Étienne was Felicia's son. Thank goodness that she had been able to rescue the certificates of birth and baptism and other family papers that would be necessary to Philippe.

Wearily the young woman finished dressing and walked to her mirror. The effort of maintaining a calm demeanor, supporting Mathilde and the children during the long, arduous escape from France, had drained her reserves. If only she had someone to help her; even to comb her hair required more energy than she had to give. But she must find the strength for a little longer. Then, when Philippe had taken Étienne, perhaps Lady Westrich would be good enough to house them for a few more days and Virginie would be able to rest. For now, she had done all she could. She was not in her best looks, *mais quant à ça,* she could do no more.

Downstairs, in the beautiful ivory and gold hall with its geometric black-and-white marble floor, a punctilious butler was greeting Lord Halwick and M. Beaumont. Graciously he accepted their hats and canes, remarking to himself on the extremely fine jacket Lady Westrich's nephew wore (undoubtedly from Weston) and the similarly clad M. Beaumont. Two top-of-the-mark men, a privilege to be connected to such of the *haut ton.*

"My lord, M. Beaumont, I believe you are awaited in the library. Will you take coffee?"

"No, nothing, thank you, Umber. We'll go right in." The earl took Philippe's elbow. "Courage, *mon ami,* you are not going to your untimely end after all."

The two started to the door on the right, from beyond which came sounds of childish voices. The earl reached for the door handle but was stopped by Philippe's hand on his shoulder.

He turned to see his mysterious lady on the stairs, motionless, face pale, and eyes enormous. The young woman's hand went out. "You, you are Philippe. I did not truly think I would ever see you again." The emotion of the moment overcame her, her voice faded, and tears glistened in her lovely eyes.

"But . . . who are you?" Philippe moved to the staircase. He extended his arm taking her hand in his. "I thought you to be Virginie, but she was such a scrawny, funny-looking little one. But how could you know such stories if you were not she?"

The young woman smiled through her tears, looking at the handsome man before her. He had not changed, her adored Philippe. His fair hair had a different style, his years had taken away the gawky, unfinished look; but the gentle curve of a mouth on the verge of smiling was the same and the mischievous laughter was still in his eyes. Suddenly, overwrought at seeing the most cherished memory of her childhood alive and well, standing before her, Virginie began to sob and speak at the same time. "I'm so sorry, I . . . I . . . I . . ." she wailed as Philippe put his arms around her and drew her down the stairs.

"Hush, hush, little one, you are safe now. Philippe is here. Little Virginie, it is you. Calm yourself, sweet one." Just as he had petted and cosseted the eight-year-old orphan so many years ago, Philippe soothed the distraught girl. As he held her, he glanced at Alec. "Thank you, my friend . . . you've brought me my youth. I had not thought ever to feel so moved again. Come, my pigeon, let me dry your tears so you can give me a proper hello." Gently he kissed her cheek and mopped her eyes with his handkerchief. "You are the finest gift my friend could have brought me. Ah, that is more like it."

A tiny smile, a mere twitch of the lip, began on Virginie's face. Tremulously she took a deep, shuddering breath, like a child once the storm of tears is over.

"Ah, Philippe, to see you again is to be a child again.

It is very hard to have such feelings after all that has passed. So unexpected, but so very welcome."

Philippe kept his arms around her, looking down at the appealing heart-shaped face with its huge brown eyes.

"I cannot believe that this is happening. You are like my home coming to me. Almost I can smell the almond blossoms of that last spring . . . But you must tell me, how came you to meet with Halwick? And why did you tell him you were Felicia?"

"There is someone you must meet first," said Virginie as she moved out of Philippe's arms. She opened the library door, leading Philippe and the earl into the book-lined, comfortably furnished room. The three children, who were sitting on the floor in front of the fireplace, jumped up on seeing Petrie and ran to him with cries of "Papa the earl, *le grand M'sieu.*"

"What a set-down to think they recognize the baker in the London beau. Is it that my valet was unable to effect my usual standard of perfection, or was the baker more of an aspirant to the fashionable world than I gave him credit for?" The earl addressed the world at large as he gave each of the boys a robust hug. "No, no . . . keep your hands off the coat, little ones. You are very fine in your new clothes, but I don't know how fine your hands may be."

The tumble of excited voices communicating to him all the events of the past twenty-four hours slowly came to a halt as Philippe's presence was recognized. The harrowing experiences before and during the escape from France had made the children wary of strangers; the two younger boys moved behind the earl, each grasping one of his legs as though holding on to a life preserver. Étienne sturdily stood his ground, looking up at the tall stranger from dark eyes remarkably like Philippe's own. He studied the man silently and then, making up his mind that this person was acceptable, he brought his heels together and bowed his fair head in greeting.

Philippe drew in his breath sharply. "My God . . . it is as though I see myself. But who is he?"

Virginie walked to the child. "Étienne, I wish to make you acquainted with your uncle, Philippe Beaumont, Marquis de Genveille. Philippe, may I present Felicia's son, Étienne Tironds, Duc de Blaiseau."

"But Virginie . . . I am in shock . . . this is unbelievable. I was told that Felicia's son had died at birth, with his mother."

"It was felt that it would be better, safer, for the *petit duc* to die. Étienne's father had been opposed to the regime in a way that aroused great hatred for his line among the officials. Once they rid themselves of the threat he represented to them, they were not satisfied; they kept hounding the family until all were gone . . . except Felicia, and once she died"—the young woman shrugged her shoulders—"we felt it was best to say that he was Mathilde's grandson, my son. I had just been married. . . ."

"Married?" Philippe's voice expressed shock.

"Yes, Jean de St. Martin, Comte d'Ivrailles. We were so lonely and frightened and very young. We needed each other to . . . hide our losses from each other. We were married a few months before Étienne was born . . . Jean was cousin to Felicia's husband . . . we lived close to them. In fact, after Felicia's husband was . . . killed . . . we moved into the château to be with Felicia. Then when Étienne was born and Felicia died, we left with him and became plain citizens, daughter and son-in-law to Mathilde. Farmers, my dear, on your estate. . . . We were cared for by your mother's people, who taught us to be true farmers. I am a very good milkmaid and can make cheese and sausages and kill a chicken and pluck it. And then, after a time, Jean and I had our own two." Gently Virginie put her arms around the two little boys who had gradually relaxed their life grip on Petrie's legs and moved to her. "This young man is Pierre and this little one is Charlot . . . Charles, and they are pleased to make your acquaintance. We no longer use the titles, they are so meaningless now. Except Mathilde, who insists." She turned toward the woman. "My dear Mathilde, who has been with us through the whole. She has been my nurse since I was born and my mother and friend. . . . I do not know how I would have survived after Jean died if my Mathilde hadn't been there to support me and bully me and direct me. So you see, my dear Philippe, so much has happened . . . and I am so glad to be able finally to give you your gift from Felicia. It has been such a long trip and a longer time, and I am so very tired." Virginie sank into a chair . . . tears streaming down her face, unable to support herself any longer.

"My dear Virginie, you are undoubtedly the bravest woman I have ever met. I cannot even begin to tell you how I feel, how grateful to you, to have my nephew and you. . . . I said you are like my home coming to me. To know that I am not the only member of my family . . . Étienne, son of my very dear sister. *Mon Dieu*, Alec, I am overcome with joy. I wish to leap and shout and . . . and . . . and run with happiness. How can I thank you! Forever I am in your debt."

The earl brushed a speck of dust from his sleeve. "I do hope, my friend, you will restrain yourself," he drawled. "The sight of you leaping and shouting would undoubtedly shock the fashionable world to such a degree that it would never recover."

Virginie's teary little chuckle accompanied Philippe's laughing protestations that not for the world would he wish to shock the *ton.* Mathilde clucked at them and scolded the earl for his lack of sensibility to ascribe such an action to M. Beaumont.

"I do not believe myself," Virginie said as she dried her eyes. "I have turned into a veritable watering pot since I arrived. It must be the English climate . . . although this time of year is supposed to be very dry. *Eh bien,* we have much talking and planning to do. Mathilde, will you take the boys into the garden. Étienne, you may run upstairs to get a ball, but very quietly. It is warm enough outside so that you will not need your jackets. Go please, Mathilde." Quickly she arranged for time to make plans for the future.

"Now, my dear friends, we will have a space to talk and plan." The exhausted girl smiled tremulously at the two men, the one so darkly urbane, the other fair and amiable, both so important to her. "I have decided to become a housekeeper, for some elderly gentleman who needs to be well cared for, perhaps with young children of his own, preferably girls, so that I can teach them sewing and cooking and deportment. Not of the *ton,* perhaps on the edge of it, living in the country."

She looked at them brightly. "Don't you think that's a good plan? I would take a position only where I might have my sons with me. That way I won't have to sell my jewels until it is time to send them to school. You see, I have thought it all out. It is the answer to everything."

As Philippe began to make sounds, Alec slowly took his snuffbox from his pocket and with an elegant gesture offered it to him.

"Please, dear boy, do stop gobbling. You sound for all the world like a turkey."

"Gobbling!" Philippe waved away the snuffbox. "I swear I shall call you out. Did you hear this girl?

54

Housekeeper! How do you remain calm? I know when she was a child she was impossible to control, but to arrive at the age of three and twenty and still to think in such a way. Housekeeper!"

"Philippe, please, display a more temperate aspect or you will totally disillusion me. I have been of the opinion that you have a degree of understanding . . . of *savoir-faire,* but you have become totally chicken-witted."

Lord Halwick looked at Madame la Comtesse with the flicker of a smile.

"Virginie and her children and Mathilde and you and I shall repair to Possingworth, accompanied of course by my Aunt Westrich to certify that we are above reproach. Above all, Virginie needs rest and peace to pull herself together." He looked at her, stopping her protestations with a raised hand: "You both need time to catch up on the years, and while we are there we can come to whatever decisions are necessary. At the same stroke, I shall be able to visit Watton Abbey and ascertain Robin's progress and meet the wonderful St. John family, since it is but a two-hour ride at most from the estate." Alec surveyed the two. "Don't you agree? It will be best for all, and I shall not accept 'no' for an answer."

A murmer of protest started again from Virginie's lips but was overcome by vociferous concurrence from M. Beaumont.

"Well, then, we are agreed, and if all goes well, we leave tomorrow. My aunt is aware of the plan and has already begun to prepare. We will use my traveling coach . . . much different, Virginie, from our other conveyances. My aunt will want hers, a baggage wagon, and . . ."

The earl continued to enumerate the vehicles and horses they must have to include valets, lady's maids, and the various appurtenances necessary to a comfortable trip. He planned a leisurely journey, taking three nights rather than the usual one-night stop. "It will be less of an effort for the children and my aunt this way. The pressure of early starts and late stops is not for them. We should arrive at Possingworth by the twenty-ninth, and I shall see Robin the next day. I've already sent word to Sedgely to prepare for guests, so all is in order."

Chapter 7

At Watton Abbey, preparations were under way to celebrate Albert's birthday. Cook was at sixes and sevens, what with decorating the cake and shooing the interested children out of the kitchen. Mrs. St. John was instructing a new parlor maid, hired for the occasion, in her duties. Betta was helping Mrs. Simpson count tablecloths, and the three little girls, when not in the kitchen, were helping the gardener arrange pots of plants around the terrace.

Mr. St. John and Robin, who was not yet on crutches, were involved in a chess game designed to keep them separate from the frantic activities about the house.

As part of her duties, the new maid was instructed to fill a nuncheon tray for the two men in the morning parlor. Fearfully, the young girl, dressed in her gray stuff gown with the long white apron tied in a bow at the back, entered the bustling kitchen.

"Excuse me, please, excuse me . . . can you . . . I need . . . oh, dear." Her voice was so quiet and her manner so unassuming that no one took notice of her. Seeing that the only person in the hubbub staying in one place was the commanding-looking dame in cook's habit, she approached her and pulled at her arm just as that worthy was placing a sugared rose in the border decoration of Albert's cake. Rose squashed and icing splashed.

"There, now, look what you've made me do. . . . Don't go pulling my arm when I'm doing such a del-li-cut placement." Cook turned to see who would be so idiotic as to do such a thing. "And who are you?" she asked the frightened girl in a voice approaching the sound of thunder.

"I beg your pardon . . . I didn't mean to interrupt . . . to cause an upset. . . . It's just that I . . . I . . ." The tears trembled on the edge of the very young parlor maid's dark lashes.

"Now, then, don't be a-crying, nothing's done that can't be undone." Cook took mercy on the girl. "Tell me what you want and where you came from . . . we haven't seen you around here before . . . and no tears . . . they'll salt the icing and then what shall we do?"

A tiny giggle could be heard from the downturned head. "I'm Lucy, the new parlor maid, hired for the party, and ma'am directed me to take a nuncheon to the gentlemen in the . . . um . . . oh, yes, the morning parlor, and I'm afraid I don't know what to take or who to ask." The girl looked at Cook with worried eyes.

"Here, now, you're a bit of a thing . . . no wonder no one saw you. I have a tray all ready for the master and Sir Robin. Just let me put the meat pies on it and you can take it up." Deftly the woman moved about. "And how did you come to be hired here? Your face is new to the area."

"I'm staying in the village with Thompson's family . . . and he thought it would be good for me to see how the household is run because I'm thinking of going into service." A breathless voice told the story: "I think I'd like to be a cook . . . is it very difficult? I cooked for my father and sometimes his friends when we had no money for the caterer . . . but sometimes the results weren't so very fine."

Cook listened to this disclosure, not knowing whether to laugh or cry over such blithe ignorance. She recognized the very young woman, certainly not above seventeen, as being of the class not usually called into domestic service. Yet here she was, and brought in by Mr. Thompson. Sounded like a gammon to her, and she'd get to the bottom of it sooner or later. Meanwhile, best send the pretty young thing on her way with the nuncheon tray so the cake could be finished and the job of cooking for the party started. Company would begin to arrive tomorrow, and the great day would start the day after.

Robin and his host had just finished their chess game and were discussing the fine points of training racehorses when the door opened and a small female figure carrying a large, heavily laden tray with great difficulty, sidled into the room. Mr. St. John, observing her, jumped up to relieve her of the tray.

"Oh, sir . . . that is not your . . . oh . . . I'm supposed to . . . oh, dear," were the confused words from her lips.

"We'll do very well if you will make a place for the tray on the table next to Sir Robin, my dear. You've done extraordinarily fine to have brought the tray this far, but to make sure it reaches the table I will undertake the delivery." Mr. St. John chuckled. "For a moment I thought 'twould be more suitable for the tray to deliver you . . . you are quite a little dab of a girl, aren't you? I haven't seen your face before, have I?"

Lucy blushed in confusion at such an unlooked-for response to her difficulties in her new position. She moved to the table, placing herself under Robin's scrutiny.

"I say, don't I know you? Yes, of course I do. You're Wingate's young'un. What are you doing here in that getup?" In astonishment, Robin reached for her hand. "What kind of Maygame are you playing, my girl?"

"I'm not your girl, and I'm not playing . . . I'm in service as parlor maid here, helping out for the party.

Please, Robin, do let go of me. I shall be in trouble, and I need the place." Lucy tried to pull away from Robin.

"Robin, my boy, what is this . . . ? How is a new parlor maid known to you? Who is Wingate? What kind of a riddle is this . . . that guest and maid know the answer and master is in the dark? I must hear the story."

In great good humor Mr. St. John seated the girl and settled himself to hear what promised to be a convoluted history.

"Oh, sir, please . . ."

"This is too much . . ."

The younger man and the girl began to speak together, stopped, and then started again.

"Silence," commanded the master of the house. "Peace. Lucy, you speak first."

"I have run away from my father," Lucy blurted out, "and I will not go back. He is a wicked man and behaves like a villain, not a father."

"How is this, Lucy?" Robin asked. "All was well when I saw you last; your father is a gamester, but surely he cares for you. He has great pleasure in taking you around and presenting you to his friends. True, I do not think it proper that you meet some of them at your tender age, but he must . . ." Robin stopped in memory of a hint that had reached him that he could not or would not credit. "But he cannot do else, since he has no way of bringing you out and wants to make a good marriage for you."

"He doesn't want to make a marriage for me. . . ." Lucy hesitated, and tears began to fall from her large gray woe-begone eyes. "He sells me to the highest bidder. He is deeply in debt and has no other way to raise money. My grandfather disowned him years ago and will not even speak my name, he is so angry with my father."

Mr. St. John was silent in shock. Himself the father of

four daughters whom he dearly loved, he could not conceive of a man so debasing himself as to sell his own flesh and blood. Rather, he would perform the most degrading drudgery available to prevent any harm from affecting his loved ones.

"Gammon," was Robin's response. "Your father is a good fellow . . . look how he introduced me to his friends when I was just come up to town. He took me to the gaming houses when my brother wouldn't, and he . . ." The viscount's voice slowed. He began to examine Wingate's motives in befriending a fledgling with pockets a-jingle and began not to like his conclusions. "How know you for sure, Lucy?" He spoke more warmly to the now mute girl. "Tell us what happened."

"You must know I have been living in Kent," she began, "with my dear nurse; she was my mother's nurse before me and has a cottage near Chatham. I turned seventeen four months ago and my father sent to Pennit (my nurse) to have me taken to London, saying it was time for me to get some town polish so I would be able to make a fine marriage." After the first rush of words the story slowed as though reluctant to be released from her lips. "I was thrilled to go; I hadn't seen much of my father as I grew up . . . my mother died when I was very young . . . and he always seemed so exciting and dashing and . . ."

"Bang-up to the nines," inserted Robin.

"Yes, exactly. . . . I was flattered that he wanted me with him. When I arrived in London I had Pennit's daughter with me, but she had to go back to Kent, and I thought it odd that my father didn't find an abigail for me. He told me that he would be with me whenever I had need to go about and that our landlady had offered her services as dresser if I should need her. Then he began to take me about . . . to gaming parlors and other places I'm sure I shouldn't have been.

"I met you, Robin, but you were the only young man I was introduced to. He kept making me acquainted with old men . . . and not nice like you, sir." She turned her innocent face to Mr. St. John. "But nasty, cold . . . who looked at me as though I were a roast chicken on a platter ready to be eaten. And then he told me, when I questioned going about to such places, that I was his property and I was up for sale and shouldn't cry about it for he wouldn't change his mind. He had received a bid from the Duc de Selles and I would meet him the next night. If the duc liked me, he would take me with him then and would set me up in a nice little house with my own carriage and horses (as if those would make me happy), and he would cover all my father's debts with something extra for him to leave England.

"I couldn't believe what was happening. . . . I think I fainted, because I had seen that horrible old man, and the thought of being touched by him filled me with such disgust that I became very ill. I knew the only solution was to kill myself or run away, for there was no one that I might turn to for help. If I went to Pennit, I would be found immediately.

"Then I remembered Pennit's sister had married and moved to near here, so I decided that I didn't like the idea of dying at such a young age and I would try to make the trip to Mrs. Thompson."

"Mrs. Thompson . . . ?"

"Yes, she is married to your butler, sir."

"Go on, child, go on," urged Mr. St. John.

"My only friend was the lady who sold us eggs and sometimes greens and she came from Hereford. The next morning, when she came to the door, I asked her if she and her husband could take me in their wagon and told her why and she did. Then she gave me over to a friend in Hereford who was traveling to Suffolk, and she made arrangements for me to travel in a cart to Thetford, and I walked the rest of the way."

"You walked . . . it's over twelve miles."

"I know, but my friend gave me a pair of sturdy boots that no longer fit her daughter; and the last person, Mr. Higgety, gave me a parcel of food, and I slept under the hedges off the verge so no one would see me in the night." Exhausted with her storytelling, accompanied as it was with many tears and sighs, the poor child finished in a rush. "So I'm here and have to work because there's nothing else to do."

The meat pies had become cold; the nuncheon tray stood forgotten on the table.

The gentle demeanor of Lucy Wingate, the reluctant manner in which she spoke, and the depth of feeling exposed by her words indicated the truth of her tale. Robin was aghast that he had befriended such a man as her father; that he had not been able to discern the monstrous treatment of the girl. He reached for her hand, and as he grasped it he declared himself her friend.

"The Petries shall stand by you, child. There must be some way out of the coil you find yourself in. Your father must be exposed for the monster he is."

Mr. St. John excused himself. "I must get my wife, Lucy. You shall stay with us . . . as our guest, not our maid."

He left the room, calling for his wife and Betta, urgent to relay this tale of horror to them.

"Lucy, if ever I had guessed what was happening"— Robin looked at the piquant face, eyes still teary—"but what of your grandfather . . . surely he would help you;

he cannot be as dissolute, your pardon for being so direct, as your father? Do you have his direction?"

"I only know my papa hasn't spoken to him for fifteen years, and I have seen him only once. It was when I was very tiny, and I have no memory of it. I believe he lives in Dorset or Cornwall and is quite retired from society." Lucy looked up from pleating her apron. "As long as I can stay here, Robin, I'm very happy to be parlormaid. 'Tis such a pretty, happy house to be in. I've never lived in a house like this," she confided, "only in Pennit's cottage or let rooms."

The sympathetic young man became enraged at the scoundrel whose selfish, profligate ways had thrown his only child into this fix. As she sat on the chair beside him, Robin felt an unfamiliar response within himself. A need to care for this lost, naive waif arose, and he vowed to himself to do all in his power to put her on a happier course.

Lucy jumped up as the St. Johns bustled into the room.

"Dear child, what a shocking situation to have found yourself in!" Mrs. St. John went to the girl and, taking her in her arms, said, "You have a home now and a family to love you. You are so brave to have traveled as you did. Were you not frightened to walk all that distance alone?" She turned to her husband: "There will be so many coming for Albert's party that her presence will never be noted. And if anyone asks, we can say she's a . . . a . . . cousin."

Betta embraced Lucy. "Welcome to the family, Lucy. It will be lovely to have a friend living here. I need someone to take my side against that stubborn man, Robin. He's become a veritable sultan with his autocratic ways. Too shockingly spoilt, being waited on hand and foot as he is."

"Well, if my second foot were fit, I should only be waited on hand," said the young man, laughing.

The easy camaraderie of the family soon diminished Lucy's feeling of awkwardness. It was decided that Mr. St. John and Betta would accompany her to Mrs. Thompson's cottage to gather her belongings. She would return to share Betta's room until the expected houseguests left after the party.

The amazed young miss was speechless at the rapid change in her circumstances; the warmhearted acceptance by the St. Johns, the comfort she felt in their company, and above all the sincere regard of the handsome viscount soothed the terrible ache left by her father's actions.

Within minutes, Thompson was apprised of the surprising turn of events and went off to order the carriage and team.

"Betta, my love, Lucy will need a dress for the party; what do you recommend? Is she not a pretty thing? Her face has the look of a kitten." Mrs. St. John beamed at Lucy. "In truth, she is so tiny, she could almost be a kitten."

"Oh, ma'am, I do have a very pretty dress in my box. You shall see it directly when I bring it here." Lucy blushed. "I think I look quite well in it"—and with a little giggle—"in fact, I was told by a renowned Tulip that I was quite a taking little thing when last I wore it."

Robin looked her up and down as though peering through a quizzing glass. "Quite a taking little thing, to be sure," he declared. "Too small to be an incomparable, but she'll do until she grows up."

"Robin"—Betta pretended to look shocked—"mind your manners. You're not with your fly-by-night friends now. There are ladies present . . . not the . . . other kind."

There was a gasp of laughter from the St. Johns, followed by Robin's protestation that she was doing it too brown with her intimation that his manners needed minding when all along hers needed mending.

The assurances of the family's concern for her and offerings of protection produced a remarkable effect on Lucy. In the role of parlormaid, she had appeared meek, almost unnoticeable in her dun-colored apparel, but as she responded to the warm friendliness of her newly found friends, her personality unfolded like the petals on a flower opening to the sun. Gray eyes sparkled, pale cheeks flushed delicately, a rosebud mouth smiled easily; the very curls on her head seemed to bounce in saucy black profusion as the tightly reined fear for her future dissipated.

"Really, my dears," exclaimed Mrs. St. John, "we must contain ourselves and let Lucy leave to get her belongings. If we keep carrying on like this, we'll be very behindhand in our preparations for the party."

It seemed no time at all before the merry group had made its trip to the startled Mrs. Thompson's cottage to take possession of her guest's belongings. In less time than that Lucy and Betta were setting things straight in Betta's bedroom. Shyly Lucy thanked Betta. "I never imagined such friendship . . . to take in a stranger . . . and Sir Robin . . . so handsome, so kind."

"He is a dear person, and has become my beloved brother in every way," agreed Betta. "I have never had so amicable a friend before. To be able to confide in someone so close to my own age but with a different understanding is quite a novel experience. I wonder what his brother is like. Robin calls him top of the trees and has great respect for him."

"Oh, I've seen him in London driving his phaeton and once at Vauxhall Gardens when my father took me there. The earl was accompanying a real beauty, but not one he would introduce to his family." Lucy's artless disclosure brought a momentary quiver to Betta's heart. "My father has said that he is well liked by the high-flyers. He is generosity itself and cares nothing for the more sedate life. There is much talk about him. . . . I think my father hoped for an offer from him . . . for me. But sometimes he has a very coldness about him that frightens me just to see him. He is well-enough-looking, but so high in the instep I would quake if he were to notice me. I do not think I could like him."

Lucy's chatter suddenly caused a flare of intense anger in Betta.

"How despicable of the man . . . to send Robin down for gambling when he is guilty of much worse . . . what a hypocrite. I hope I need never meet him. It would be difficult for me not to give him the cut direct, knowing what you've told me about him." Betta's magnificent eyes sparkled. She was shocked by the intensity of her feeling, not all of it anger. There had been jealousy and betrayal involved in her response. She thought about the earl's possible involvement in Lucy's problems, trying to let her better nature and good sense speak to her. Surely Lucy must be mistaken; this doesn't sound like Robin's *non pareil*. And yet . . . and yet . . . What does a loving brother really know about his own kin? Robin sees that side of his brother that the earl permits him to see. He probably does many things unbeknownst to Robin. The unwelcome debate continued in Betta's head until it ached with the effort. Finally she achieved a semblance of quiet when she wept a few tears into her pillow and wished that it were she, not Lucy, who had caught the earl's roving eye.

Chapter 8

The next day dawned gloriously fair, promising a kindly greeting to the few houseguests whose arrival was anticipated by the St. Johns. Betta, not quite in her best looks, was already breakfasting in the morning parlor, listening to Robin animadverting upon Lucy's hardhearted parent. His tirade was interrupted by the appearance of his heroine, accompanied by a veritable army (although, in truth, only four) of enthusiastic children with their beloved comrade Brindle. Visibly wincing at the spirited voices, Betta directed the newcomers to their respective seats and signaled the footman to pass their plates.

"For you must know that my brother has described him as a shabster and . . ." Robin's voice came to an abrupt halt at Betta's irritated "enough."

"What do you mean, enough? Enough what?"

"Enough of your superior brother and what he says and thinks. I have other things to be concerned with today, or had you forgotten that we are expecting aunts and uncles and cousins? Why, your brother hasn't had the thought even to inquire about you or to visit you, and certainly he could have bought half the horses in Ireland by now. He could have paid for all the lightskirts there also."

"What's gotten into your head, making such remarks?

Too unladylike, my girl," Robin said in disapproval. "That's not talk for little ears to hear."

"I beg your pardon, I don't know what . . . I have a headache . . ." Betta tossed her head. "How lowering to realize that even one so fine as I must have a moment's fall from grace." She smiled and repeated softly: "Please, Robin, do forgive my haggishness. I would not cause you pain for anything."

"Of course Robin will forgive you. You have had too many things to think of, and now having me in your room . . . I know your sleep was disturbed, for I heard you tossing and turning during the night." Lucy stoutly supported Betta. "The best thing for you would be a nice gallop . . . I have heard that the air rushing past one's face when riding at a rapid pace is very beneficial for blowing away the vapors."

Robin let out a bark of laughter at this unusual remedy, then seconded the suggestion.

"Come with me, Betta," Albert petitioned. "You haven't been riding with me all week, and there won't be time again until after the party. Please, Betta, you know the horses need the exercise."

Lovingly urged by the gathering, the out-of-sorts young woman went to change into her riding habit. Since it would be but herself and her young brother, she would ride astride as her father so often encouraged her to do. She dressed herself in the old riding breeches of her father's that she had altered and the elegant boots her father's bootmaker had cobbled for her. "No guests have arrived, so as long as we stay on our land," she thought to herself, "no one will see me and I can be comfortable."

Looking like a tall young boy with her slim figure and long legs, Betta strolled down to the stables, swinging her crop, already feeling on the up. Her lovely eyes sparkled with mischief when she saw the look of disapproval on Jackson's face. With a nonchalant move of her hand, she flipped the end of her neckcloth at him and jauntily mounted the sleek gray mare he was holding.

"Why so gloomy, Jackson? Do you not think I make a dashing young beau?"

" 'Tain't right for a genteel young lady to go jauntering about dressed like that. No knowing what kind of trouble you'll get yourself into," Robin's dour groom grumbled.

"Oh . . . piffle! We shall be riding on our land and no one is around to see me but those who know me. And I shall be back within the hour, which is well before anyone is expected to arrive. So stop your nattering and let go the bridle. Come on, Bertie. I'll race you to the oak in the pasture."

With a shout, young Albert wheeled his horse and started down the path closely followed by his sister. A short while later the two reined down to a trot as they passed the oak neck and neck. Betta's normally good spirits were restored; as Lucy had said, her vapors were blown away. Her face was pensive as she thought about the earl. Having more sense than sensibility, Betta realized that her feelings about this man, whom she had never met, only seen, were unduly strong. After all, his behavior was in keeping with the society in which he moved. That society which, when faced, caused her to retreat into a tongue-tied little miss with no speech or polish. And perhaps there was a perfectly good reason for his not having arrived in a pelter wanting to know his brother's circumstance; although upon reflection, she could not see that toplofty swell arriving in anything resembling a pelter, more likely a leisurely stroll.

Feeling much better now that she had soothed herself by finding so much fault with the undefended nobleman,

Betta chatted amiably with Albert, remarking that his rapid growth brought him to a point where he was as tall as she and would be needing a larger horse. The boy flushed with pleasure and commented on their looking more like brothers than sister and brother, both wearing similar clothes. Their direction took them along the outer boundary of the St. John acres and to the lane that led into the property from the northern edge of the land.

Albert confided that he was both excited and fearful of his coming experience at Eton. He said that he had spoken to Robin about it, but Robin's experience had been with tutors at home because of the circumstance of losing his parents and being subject to severe nightmares when he was Albert's age.

So involved were the two in their conversation that they were taken unaware when their horses, by now slowed to a walk, stepped into the lane to make the crossing. Suddenly a phaeton drawn by a matched pair of bays was bowling down upon them. Had it not been for the superb handling by the driver, riding horses, pair, vehicle, and company would have been in a lamentable tangle that might easily have resulted in severe injuries to the parties involved.

"Since when do chuckleheads like you go riding out into a country road without the merest caution," the driver raged. "My horses could have been seriously injured . . . to think nothing of myself."

"Your horses?" Betta's eyes flashed ice-blue fire. "What about our persons? And our horses? And what right have you here? You trespass upon our property, and not only trespass, but drive at such an excessive speed as to endanger any beasts or men that find themselves in your path. You are fortunate that you were able to stop them in time."

Atop her nervous mount Betta was almost on a level with the driver of the phaeton. She looked him over, taking note of his dashing driving coat with its many capes, the gleaming boots, the flat-topped beaver hat. Her lip curled disdainfully. He was to her eyes the epitome of the London beau . . . a dandy, careless of anything except his own immediate pleasures . . . everything she remembered, even to his eyes.

As the driver's temper cooled, he examined the riders. The younger one he dismissed after a cursory glance. The older one, sitting straight-backed, controlling the restive beast with knees and hands, was a superb rider. Rather slightly built for a man, although something about him . . . It dawned on the driver that the rider was a young and very attractive woman, improperly clothed, but a veritable young Diana: hair tousled by the wind, cheeks flushed, and eyes afire.

With a cool look at Betta, the man in the vehicle addressed his tiger, who was perched at the back of the rig: "Announce me to this . . . lady, Mathis."

"This 'ere is Milord Alexander Petrie, Earl of Halwick . . . and 'e dun't need fortune to 'elp 'im with 'is 'orses, 'e's got knowhow." The cockney voice with its missing aitches was full of pride.

Betta's rage was suddenly tempered with awareness of her appearance. She blushed at the pause before the word "lady."

"I am Elizabeth St. John." She offered her name in an icy voice, unable to be forgiving. "This is my brother, Albert. He will conduct you to the house."

Before Albert could protest, she instructed him to show the earl the route to the stableyard and then to accompany him to Robin. Her final words were given over her shoulder as she wheeled her mare around and took off through the hedge and across the fields at a gallop, looking for all the world as though she were fleeing for her life.

Albert watched his sister, startled by her unusual behavior.

"I beg pardon, sir. I don't know what's gotten into my sister . . . she's usually very quiet and good-tempered . . . and . . ." He paused, perplexed. "Maybe she wanted to get back to tell my parents and Robin. We've been wondering . . . that is, Robin said you probably found a new high-flyer and we shouldn't worry. . . ." Suddenly the boy began to blush, aware of what he had said. "I beg pardon, sir, but I think he was beginning to be concerned. It's almost five weeks since he smashed into the wall and he was, well . . ." Albert let his words dwindle away. Never one to be at a loss, he quickly changed the subject. "If you like, I could get up into the rig and tie my horse on behind. I'd like that. I don't have much opportunity to ride a phaeton."

The boy's artless prattle was of interest to Petrie, and cordially he invited the lad to tie his mount on and climb up beside him. It was not quite the thing to question the son of one's host so closely about the host's family, but Alec knew nothing of the St. Johns, other than the enthusiasms in Robin's letter, and wished to determine for himself Robin's feelings about this country goddess. If he knew Robin, the boy was completely in love and might even have made an offer. The elder Petrie was aware of the overwhelming attraction that could exist between a beautiful nurse and a weak, grateful patient. And there was no doubt that she was breathtakingly beautiful. A fiery nature, too, he'd be bound.

The earl set about putting Albert at ease by complimenting his riding ability.

"Oh, thank you, sir. I'm sure I don't hold a candle to

Betta. She's a marvel. Why, she can ride any horse in the stable including my father's new stallion. And even my father has trouble with that one. She says it's much easier to control when you ride astride . . . that's why she wears riding breeches . . . but only on our acres and only when it's just family riding. She'll most likely feel the same when Robin can ride, 'cause he's like family . . . he's a splendid fellow, sir, plays a tight game of jackstraws, and always has time to listen to one . . . and doesn't brush one off . . . takes time to answer. He's top of the trees with us. But I expect you know that, seeing that he's your brother."

The earl's eyebrow rose at this encomium. "Yes, he is truly a great gun, Albert, and I am happy to hear he's . . . ah . . . like family."

"He really is, you know. He and Betta have been planning a musical entertainment for my birthday celebration, and he and Letty, she's my youngest sister, have been teaching Brindle, that's our dog—only really he's Letty's, because he only listens to her—special tricks, and no one has seen them yet; it's to be a surprise for tomorrow. And he helped the twins, that's Pam and Evy, with their studies, and he's promised to teach me to drive a pair when he's all well, although we don't have any as fine as yours." Albert ran out of breath, but his beaming face supported his declaration of appreciation.

I had no idea my brother enjoyed family life to such a degree. Can it be he has found his place? mused the earl as Albert rattled on. But she looks to be older than he . . . I don't know whether I like the idea of such a match. What a stroke of good luck for this family . . . to win a title and a fortune in exchange for caring for the victim of an accident . . . a very attractive exchange . . . but not for my brother. We'll see how anxious they are when they learn that he is pockets-to-let until he's twenty-five.

Petrie didn't express his cynicism to the young son of his host; the boy would play no part in any kind of machinations that might be taking place.

The two continued to chat . . . or rather, Albert chattered and the earl listened and inserted occasional comments until the briskly paced horses brought them to their destination. Standing ready to greet them, obviously bursting to speak, was Jackson. The earl courteously greeted him, then commented on Robin's situation: "You've watched over him for many years, Jackson, but he's still almost too much for you."

"Oh, sir, ye know how headstrong he is betimes—well, not headstrong, he is a good lad, but he was that angry . . . partly at himself because he knew he'd been wrong, mostly because the trip up was fair beset with bumble-stumbles." He continued to recount the woes of the trip from London, explaining exactly how the accident occurred and why he and Robin were still bound to the St. Johns' hospitality.

"You've done your best, Jackson; not to worry any further. I shall deal with Sir Robin and will discover his condition from the doctor as soon as I have paid my respects to Mr. and Mrs. St. John. Please see to my horses. I'll speak with you later."

The earl turned to Albert. "If you would take me to my brother now, Albert, I should be quite grateful to you." A singularly sweet smile lightened the austerity of his face. "I have enjoyed your company and look forward to taking you up with me again; perhaps you may even take the reins. Your ability as a horseman gives you good recommendation and you look to make a good driver."

Albert flushed at praise from such a Corinthian and immediately began to dream of the day when he would be tooling down the avenue behind not a pair, but a team of matched grays . . . or bays—no, blacks—with a black phaeton and . . . His delightful visions of the future carried him along to the morning parlor, the earl following close behind.

The scene that greeted the earl's eyes was one of laughter and harmonious sound. Robin was seated in his unusual converted sedan chair surrounded by three very pretty, very young ladies, who were attempting to harmonize to the tune of "Greensleeves." At the large dining table a woman of about eight and thirty worked with a much younger, pertly pretty, tiny young lady moving what looked like small calling cards around, as though playing whist with them. At the central open door, calling directions to someone on the terrace, stood a man in his early fifties, obviously a country gentleman who had kept his looks and physique.

In a stentorian voice, he was admonishing his listeners to set the awning carefully so it wouldn't collapse as had Squire Douglas's in the middle of the country dance, fairly suffocating the dancers and causing untold embarrassment to all concerned. As he finished cautioning and instructing his cohorts, he turned to the lady at the table and started to make a comment. He spied the earl standing at the entry to the room.

"You must be Robin's brother. You have the look of him."

On hearing this address, the members of the group turned to the newcomer, pausing for a moment to take in his elegant appearance, his ruggedly handsome good looks lightened by his startling eyes, and his total assurance of manner. The pause was broken by Robin's shout of greeting and the middle-aged gentleman's movement forward.

"My lord, we are very happy to at last welcome you to our home." He extended his hand to the earl, examining his face for an indication of the humor that could have kept him away from his injured brother for so long a time. "Come, make your hellos to Robin and then be introduced to my family." He gestured toward Robin, who was entrapped in his chair, not yet having been allowed to try his crutches by the doctor.

"Well, hello, brother. I've been expecting you these two weeks past. Where have you been? I warrant you've bought out Ireland's horse farms and then some. I only hope there's a good nag for me amongst the cattle." Robin smiled in welcome. "I am glad you're here . . . I was beginning to worry . . . thought you might have eloped with one of your fancy pieces. Damn . . . pardon my mouth, ma'am. I feel so easy, I forget my manners with you. Alec, let me make you known to a most wonderful, generous family."

The young man presented each of the St. Johns, heaping praise on their heads, expressing his overwhelming gratitude. At last he came to Lucy and paused to call her to his side.

"May I make you acquainted with Lucy Wingate, Alec. Her story is very special; I will tell you all about her later, with her permission. We have adopted her . . . or rather, the St. Johns have adopted both of us, but I choose to make her my special care." The girl blushed, her eyes downcast, as Robin took her hand. "She has not one to care for her, and I told her the Petries would see to her well-being. She is but a little thing and could easily be lost . . . and we would not want that to happen."

Lord Halwick could only respond to the appeal in his brother's face, and agreed that if Robin felt honor-bound to take care of the young lady, then the Petries were united in that stand. His thoughts as he examined this turn of events were less than orderly. His brother had really thrown him for a fall; he would have to redefine the whole plot as he saw it. Who was this chit, so shy and demure, and what of the magnificent Betta . . . where was her place in Robin's heart? Could he have been wrong? But the letter from Robin was of nothing but Betta. And all these children, and parents; a something less than tranquil environment, but nonetheless a warmth of feeling among the members. This must be discussed with Robin in private.

As he looked at the newly presented family, Alec laughed. "It will take me a while to sort everyone out"— he turned to the three youngest—"especially three such lovely young ladies." The three little ones bridled and blushed. "Your son, Albert, was of great help in conducting me here, but I do not see Miss St. John. I met her when she was out riding with Albert.

"I must confess that I was coming down the back lane of your property at a most thoughtlessly rapid pace." The earl turned on his full charm. "I am ashamed to say that I lost my temper and was rude to her. I would like to beg her pardon."

Mrs. St. John gave him a look of understanding. "My lord, Betta told us of the incident. She was startled herself by the occurrence and explained that she was not the most polite . . ."

"Ah, she was very polite," Petrie replied, laughing. "She was so polite, she was ice and I was left frostbitten."

"Well, you will have to smooth it out between yourselves. She shall be with us for luncheon. We are planning to have it alfresco on the terrace. The weather is lovely at this time of year. Letty, help Pammy and Evianne with the music . . . you shall practice later with Robin. Lucy, my dear, will you help me with these place cards. Let us put them away for now. My lord, I am sure you are longing for a private reunion with your brother. He is still unable to walk, but we shall be out of the room in short order. You will have half an hour with him before luncheon is announced; until then we will all try to stay out of your way. Oh, I had forgotten—Albert will show you to your room when you are ready to freshen up . . . if you will give me your driving coat, I'll see that it's put in your room. We are quite in a horrendous mix-up with the preparations for tomorrow. No, no, do not disturb yourself further. . . ."

"Madam, you are too kind. But please, since the circumstance is informal, and you have already reached such familiar terms with my brother, how can you continue to address me with such formality. Am I any less than my brother?" The fascinating face broke into a winning smile. "Please, call me Alec, or Petrie, or Halwick, whichever makes you comfortable, but no more 'my lords' between us. I appreciate your thoughtfulness at providing us with a few moments alone; Robin and I have much to catch up with."

Mrs. St. John returned his smile and then stood a moment caught by the intense blue of his eyes. With those eyes and that smile, she thought to herself, he must be a danger to every woman between eight and eighty. She beckoned to the hovering Albert, who was so obviously reluctant to leave the vicinity of his new hero, and left the room to the two brothers.

Chapter 9

"Well, Robin, for all you've a broken leg, you look well."

"Well, Alexander," mimicked Robin, "for all you've been carousing in Ireland, you look well also."

"You certainly fell . . . or rather, overturned . . . into a very unusual family."

"Didn't I just. Never knew young'uns were so interesting, and Mr. St. John; his knowledge is immense. No nonsense about him. He'll talk to you about horses, enclosure laws, breeding sheep, agrarian reform, a Weston coat versus one by Schultz, or the number of petals on a rose. He's tops, Alec, as is his wife."

"And his oldest daughter?" The earl pulled a chair over to Robin's settee. "What of her?"

"We-e-ll, Betta is a very special person, kind and good and knows how to listen and when not to give advice, and is very beautiful. She doesn't know just how beautiful. But she's a bit shy . . . fearful of meeting people who are too high in the instep. She had a difficult time of it when she was in town to make her come-out, wasn't really ready, couldn't handle the scene. You know how false it is. If you can't play the game or if you're too honest, you can get cut to pieces . . . and that's what happened to her. Instead of getting a town bronze, she was town burnt. Came running back to the country and refuses to go up to London anymore. Won't even go the Bath in Season. Freezes up, she says, just thinking of it. But she's witty, and bright, and most enjoyable to be with. I couldn't wait for you to meet her." Robin looked meaningfully at his brother. "I know you'll love her just as I do."

The earl listened to Robin's words, sure that his brother was asking him to accept Betta as the future Lady Favesham. Obviously Robin had never seen her for the shrew she was, as she had shown herself to be at the meeting this morning. And the boy was definitely, tenderly in love. It would take tact and planning to remove his attention from the St. Johns. It was the family as much as the girl that appealed to him. Perhaps Virginie and the three little ones would prove more attractive; Philippe might object to that, but it would be a start. Important to get Robin away from here as soon as possible. Who thought a gaggle of children could be so seductive to a young man. The earl evaluated and planned as he listened to Robin singing praises about the St. Johns.

"And that Letty—I'm almost inclined to wait for her to grow up. Wait until you see her at work. I swear she could twist the whole of Parliament around her little finger. So . . . enough of me. What happened to you? Not like you to stay away when you must have received our letters. Why are you so late in arriving?"

Knowing that he would no longer be executing any more government missions to France, Alec felt free to describe his rescue of Virginie, Mathilde, and the children. The lines of his face softened as he spoke of the difficulties of the baker LaBrie and his family, and the courage of the children and the young woman. Robin watched his brother's face light with laughter as he recounted the trials and tribulations of the escapade, brushing away the dangers. To the younger man's mind, his brother was displaying the habit of a man in love, possibly unaware of it himself. Philippe would have to be consulted about the situation as soon as possible, especially since Betta was his own choice for Countess Halwick and his sister-in-law.

"It's so good to have you back, Alec. Your Virginie sounds quite the heroine. I can't wait to meet her and hear her opinion of the baker. Will you send Jackson to escort her and Philippe here for tomorrow? I know the St. Johns would like to include them in the festivities. It's young Albert's birthday and there's to be a grand celebration. Evidently this is the highlight of the local social festivities each year. With the whole world invited including tenants and gypsies. The doctor is to bring my crutches this afternoon so I shall be able to get about a bit. 'Twill be a rare opportunity for your French family to begin to enjoy a social life. Not to mention that I shall be directing part of the entertainment."

"Not my family, Philippe's," interrupted the earl.

"All right, to introduce Philippe's family to our neighbors and to see an English fête. They'll be here from all over the county."

"If the St. Johns give me leave." Alec leaned back in the chair, long legs stretched out, and casually asked, "And what of this Lucy? I take it she is Jeremy Wingate's daughter."

"That blackguard." Robin almost spat the words out. "I once thought him the best of fellows. A top-of-the-trees goer. Gad, I've heard of men doing low things to pay debts, but his is the lowest. Can you believe, he has been trying to sell his daughter on the open market . . . turning that innocent child into a barque of frailty . . . his own daughter. I can't think of anything so wicked, so . . . so . . . ." The viscount was unable to find a word expressive of the iniquitous action of his former friend.

"I told her we would help her, but I don't know what we can do if he comes looking for her. I wish you could have heard her tell her story. Wingate had arranged a sale . . . Gad, to think of it sets me aboil . . . to the Duc de Selles, and you know what a dirty piece of linen he is, and dangerous, too. Didn't you have a business with him at one time, over a . . . a . . . What was it about, Alec? I can't remember, if ever I knew."

"Um, yes . . . for all his high birth, he's scum, the dregs of the earth." Alec looked thoughtful. "Does her father know where she is? Unbelievable how you can get into a fix. One would think you settled, having a broken leg; but here you are, ready to do battle with two of the worst around. Does she have any grandparents who might help her?"

"Wingate's father is still about in Dorset, or Kent, but he disowned Wingate and according to Lucy has no wish to see her. She didn't say anything about the mother's people. If only I could get about, I'd look up the old man and see if he'd take her. His authority as head of the family would stop that devil."

"Let it go for now, Robin." The earl paused in concentration. "We can invite her to Possingworth to keep Virginie company. She must return with us after the celebrations. Even if her father traces her this far, if all keep mum about the Petries' being involved, the St. Johns can hint that she left with guests from the Welsh border or Cornwall who needed someone to help with their children. That should keep him out of our way for a few days. I'll talk to the St. Johns about it.

"It's almost time to dine, and Albert is waiting to escort me to my room. I believe I have found myself a squire, should I need one when I go slaying dragons. Can I do anything for you before I go up?" A trill of giggling

83

preceded three little girls into the room. "Here come your handmaidens. I can see you won't need my help."

He turned to leave the room, making a most polite bow to Letty, Pamela, and Evianne, who bobbed in return and scampered to Robin for protection from this too elegant stranger.

"Jackson's coming with Jem to take you outside," Pamela and Evianne, ever a duet, chimed.

"And you're to sit next to me, because that will be at the end of the table, so your leg will have room," decreed Letty.

With orders, directions, and instructions, Robin was moved to the terrace to await the gathering of family and guests for the midday repast while the earl was conducted to his chamber by his new squire.

The huge terrace, paved in the Italian manner, ran along the length of the house and had a low colonnaded balustrade edging two sides. Set atop this wall at intervals were urns filled with colorful blooming plants that added color to the summer landscape. Beautiful plantings directed the eye to an avenue of stately elms that shaded travelers approaching the manor.

Mrs. St. John had caused a comfortably large table to be set upon the terrace under the spreading branches of a particularly fine chestnut tree. The party was gathered around, prior to seating themselves, awaiting Miss St. John's presence.

"Pamela, run up to Betta and tell her we are waiting," requested Mrs. St. John.

The little girl turned to comply with her mother's request but stopped when she heard Betta's voice signaling her approach from the garden.

"Here I am. Dear Mama, I hope you will excuse my tardy arrival. It is so lovely, I couldn't resist a stroll while

84

I waited for you to assemble. I was too early, and now I'm too late."

The young woman tried to look penitent, but her endeavor was spoiled by the little chuckle that came from her throat. Her eyes were alight with enjoyment and her whole being crackled with vivacity. The earl, so engaged by this joie de vivre, moved to her side.

"Miss St. John, I am at a loss to explain my infelicitous conduct this morning. To have behaved in such an unmannerly fashion . . . the remembrance quite puts me to shame. I beg you will forgive me. I should not like to be in your bad graces else my brother may try to call me out in revenge." Petrie smiled, his eyes admiring Betta's loveliness. "Can we start afresh and pretend that that earlier ill-tempered fiend was someone neither of us has ever met? I should like to be counted a friend of my brother's dear friend."

Betta stood still a moment, studying the fascinating face, the sweet smile. "My lord, I am pleased to meet you and more than pleased to forget the most unpleasant encounter this morning with a very uncouth person. Shall we join the others at the table. They won't start until we are seated."

Coolly the young woman moved away from him, still sustained by the anger the earl had initially aroused in her. She had been polite for Robin's sake and accepted his apology for the morning's fracas, but she could not forget Lucy's words concerning the business between her scoundrel father and Petrie. She couldn't understand why her knees had such a tendency to tremble when she gazed into those remarkable eyes or why her stomach felt as though it were sliding downhill. Surely it was just her extreme hunger . . . or was she coming down with a megrim? She reached the table and responded to the loving greetings of her family. She sat down in the empty chair next to Robin, commenting on his approaching session with the doctor.

Before Mrs. St. John had a chance to appoint him to another place, the earl sat himself at Betta's left. He was somewhat puzzled by her less than cordial response to his apology, but being a determined man, continued to address himself to winning her friendship.

"Now this is what I call a pleasant occasion," pronounced Mr. St. John from his place at the head of the table, "to have such an honored guest and our loving family, which now includes Robin and Lucy, all together under this fine chestnut tree, on such a perfect day. I must make a toast to the salutary circumstance."

Lifting his glass of wine, Mr. St. John stood up and made a little bow to his audience: "My dear wife; my loving, beautiful, and mischievous children; my honored guests, may this be but one of many such gatherings where we meet to celebrate happy circumstances." He quickly drank his wine to loud huzzah from Albert, "Hear! Hears!"'s from the earl and Robin, and enthusiastic applause from the female members of the party.

"Papa, that was very fine, but I am hungry." Letty's voice rose above the applause. "Please may we eat now?"

"Your sister goes directly to the heart of the matter," murmered the earl to Betta. "I agree with your father's wish, but quite happily second Letty's desire to eat. These strawberries look particularly fine. Are they from the estate garden?" Halwick was determined to establish an amicable relationship with Miss St. John.

"Yes, my lord," Betta gave short answer and turned to Robin: "Robin, when will you want to hear the girls sing again?"

Robin had been watching the earl's unsuccessful attempts to establish a harmonious association with Betta.

In a low voice he queried her about her lack of cordiality. "I had thought you would welcome my brother with the same feelings you extend to me."

"Ah, but you are my dear friend, and he is my friend's brother, not mine."

"Betta, there can be no difference. You are very cold towards him. Did he not apologize for the mishap this morning?"

"Oh, yes. He expressed sincere regrets for the incident, which I no longer remark upon. It is just that I do not know him as yet . . . and even though he is well loved by you, Robin dear, there is the possibility that he may never be loved by me. But do not repine; one never knows how the play will unfold, and there is always hope that the villain will be reclaimed."

"Villain?" Robin's eyebrows went up. "How came Alec to be the villain?"

A deep blush stained Betta's face upon her realizing the careless way she had exposed her inner thoughts about Robin's brother. In confusion she stammered an answer, excusing her words. "Really, Robin, it's just a way of speaking. I meant nothing more than to compare life with seeing a play enacted on the boards. You make too much of it."

Turning toward her father and mother, Betta addressed them with a question about the arrival of the other guests, leaving Robin to stare thoughtfully at the back of her head.

Albert meanwhile had triumphantly engaged the earl in further discussion about the merits of Gentleman Jackson over those of Black Humphrey, to the accompaniment of lamentations from the twins and Letty that he was monopolizing their guests' attention and not permitting the younger females a chance to work their wiles.

"Children, please," cautioned Mrs. St. John, "you will have your chance after luncheon." She laughed as she bespoke the earl to visit the rose garden with the three girls. "You have an experience ahead of you, Alec, that every man should go through to gain a greater understanding of womanhood. I will anxiously await your opinion. I would ask Betta to accompany you, but that would . . . um . . . dilute—yes, that's the word—would dilute the ineffable entertainment you will enjoy in the company of my young daughters."

Pamela and Evianne looked confused at this high-flown language, and Letty exclaimed: "Mama, you are turning dear . . . dear . . . Oh, I do not know what to call you"—she turned to Alec in surprise—"Robin is Robin, but we've know him forever, and it's my fault about his leg, so it's all right for me to call him Robin, but what shall I call you?"

Although surprised by the unfettered naturalness of the St. John children, Alec was not displeased at the honesty of their responses.

"Well, I've never given too much thought to a situation like this, Miss Letty. Perhaps we could start with Lord Alec, and then if you feel that you can accept my friendship"—he glanced at Betta as though to address himself to her—"we can come to friendlier terms. Now, will that suit you?"

"Oh, splendid. Have you had enough to eat yet? I'm ready to show you the garden. Aren't you ready, Pam . . . Evy?" Letty pushed away from the table in a hurry to develop her new friendship. "We can take Brindle. Come along, Brindle dear." She pulled the shaggy, mop-like dog from under the table. "Lord Alec, this is Brindle . . . isn't he lovely? He's the best dog in the world, and if

88

it hadn't been for him, you and Robin wouldn't be here now."

A shout of laughter arose from the older members of the circle around the table.

"Dear, dear Letty, you mustn't give away all our secrets," wheezed Mr. St. John as he chortled at his youngest child's open appreciation of the villain of Robin's accident. "Lord Alec and Robin may become fearful of our designs upon them, eh what? Take the earl to the gardens before he changes his mind. Go along now."

The earl turned to Betta and gently took her hand in his. "May I hope that you will join us, Miss St. John? I am thinking I will need a chaperone to protect my honor, especially after what your mother said. I can see these three are very determined ladies."

Betta pulled her hand from the earl's, wishing the tremor in her throat would go away. "I . . . I . . . we are expecting my aunt to arrive at any moment . . . I must be here to greet her."

"Betta, do go with Alec. You know how persuasive Letty can be. Lord knows what mischief she'll tie him in if someone isn't there to protect him," Robin urged with a twinkle. "Who knows . . . she may even return from the garden betrothed to my brother . . . and that I can't allow. I wish to save her for myself."

Cajoled and encouraged by the laughter and beseeching of the children, and a secret wish within herself, Betta agreed to join the troop, missing Robin's unexpectedly calculating look as she let herself be drawn down the steps to the garden.

Just let them enjoy each other's company, Robin planned, and the interest each felt for the other would be nourished. Even with all the young'uns, a walk in the garden should be helpful.

The two adults, almost herded by the three little girls, proceeded to the garden. Betta had continuous difficulty with her breathing when Alec took her elbow to support her along the flagstone path. The shrill comments of the little girls were enough of a distraction so that Betta felt no call to conduct a conversation (had she the breath to do so). Alec was too busy responding to the comments of Letty and her sisters to converse with Betta, but by his attentive manner and helpful support made her know that he was completely aware of her presence. Finally deciding that the youngsters had had enough of his attention, he gave them leave to go.

"Young ladies, your tour of the garden has been most edifying and delightful, for which I thank you." The earl bowed politely to each of his three guides. "But now I . . . that is to say, your sister and I, are worn to the bone, being so much older than you. Of course, Miss St. John, I am not casting aspersions upon your advanced age." The earl grinned at Betta, looking much like Robin when wickedness was upon him. "We would like to sit for a while in this delightful folly to recuperate from our exertions. You may go and play." With a brushing motion, the earl shooed away the children, who ran off in high good humor.

"I trust I was not too forward, Miss St. John." Alec took Betta's hand and tucked it in the crook of his arm. "But I'm truly exhausted. Not being accustomed to such youthful enthusiasm, I find I must rest my weary bones."

Suddenly the sun seemed to shine more brightly, the sky seemed bluer, and the day more beautiful than ever a day had been. I can't be letting this happen, Betta thought. He's unscrupulous, a rake, and all I abhor . . . but his eyes are . . . I mustn't stay here.

"My lord . . . I . . ."

"Yes, Miss St. John." Petrie walked up the steps to the miniature Greek temple. "Here is a bench where we can sit for a while. The shade is more comfortable after the heat of the sun, don't you agree? Now, you were saying?"

"I . . . I . . ." Betta felt as though her mind were filled with cotton batting in which nestled pictures of herself in fantastic situations being rescued by Sir Alexander Petrie, this man she was determined to snub. For the first time since her coming-out season, she was again experiencing that incoherence of thought. This time there was a difference; she had an almost overpowering desire to throw herself into Alec's arms so that he would protect her from herself. From herself! *Elisabeth Honoria Anne St. John, what are you doing?* a voice in her head screamed. *Get away from here immediately . . . you great booby, run . . .*

The earl had been studying Betta's face, waiting for her to pick up her conversation. He was entranced by the play of expressions as her brows lifted, then drew together, and again arched in surprise, accompanied by a startled look in her violet eyes. His face reflected his astonishment as she suddenly jumped up, said something that sounded like "I can't lo . . . oh, no . . . I mustn't" and ran away from the folly as though devils were pursuing her.

"What did I do or say that caused that? I can understand why the girl had a difficult season; first she's a virago, then an iceberg, then as she starts to melt, she goes off like a thirty-pound cannon. That look in her eyes was very appealing, if one could but understand what was going on in her head . . . evidently she didn't behave in that shattered way with Robin. Must try to approach her again.

"Come, come, Petrie . . . as experienced a man of the world as yourself . . ." Alec's soliloquy continued, "should

91

certainly be able to charm an inexperienced country miss
. . . if she'd only stay in one place long enough. Well
. . . if I'm not near her, I can't charm her, so . . . have at
it, Alexander." Petrie concluded his ruminations and
strolled toward the house.

Chapter 10

The day of Albert's birthday celebration dawned bright and clear. The dew had hardly begun to evaporate before Letty was running from room to room to remind her family that this very important day had arrived.

"Why are you still sleeping, Betta? It's morning. Everybody must get dressed."

The sound of Alec's husky voice whispering words of love while he nibbled her ear became Letty's shrill, excited soprano.

"Oh, Letty, how can you be so cruel! It can't be time to rise . . . I've hardly slept."

"Ooooh, is it light yet?" Lucy pulled the coverlet over her head.

"No, no, you mustn't do that." Letty stripped the covers from the recumbent girl. "Truly, it's time to get up. Mama and Papa are dressing. The breakfast will be ready instantly and all the company will be arriving before we're ready if you don't hurry. Hurry, hurry, hurry."

Letty began to dance around the room to the accompaniment of her chanting: "Time to get up . . . time to get up . . . Ouch!" The pillow thrown by Betta silenced the youngster.

"Out . . . out . . ." Betta jumped from her bed, swooped Letty up, and deposited her outside the room. "Go waken

93

Brindle or Robin or anyone else. We're awake. We'll be down posthaste . . . so GO!"

Letty ran along the corridor as Betta turned back into the room, closing the door behind her.

"Ohh, I can't believe it's time to dress. Come along, sleepyhead . . . Lucy, get up. This is the very important day. Albert must be so excited. Lucy, if you don't come out from under those covers, I shall dump this pitcher of cold, cold water on you."

"I'm up, I'm up. . . . How can you be so cruel." The tousled head emerged from under the blanket. "I know you're right, Betta . . . this is a most exciting day, but I wish it wouldn't start until tomorrow. No, I don't, not really. Now that I'm more awake, I'm glad it's Albert's birthday, and it's also Robin's walking-on-crutches day, and it's a bright and shiny day and a day for me to celebrate my whole new life." By now Lucy was imitating Letty's dance around the room, chanting: "A new life, a new life." She threw her arms about Betta in her joy. "You're my new sister and I have new friends and it's all wonderful."

The two girls collapsed into laughter, Betta caught up in Lucy's infectious excitement.

"Calm down, Lucy . . . contain yourself for a moment. We must get dressed. There'll be no breakfast for us if we don't hurry. Parker herself has pressed your dress. It's hanging in the clothes press and your shoes and bonnet are on the shelf."

"Oh, Betta . . . I feel so fine." Lucy peered in the mirror as she brushed her tangle of dark curls. "I don't think I've ever had such a good feeling. Here, let me do up your buttons. Oh, these sleeves are elegant." The excited girl finished fastening the dress and stood back to examine her friend. Betta was in unusually good looks. Attired in a pink-and-white-striped percale half-dress with a flounced embroidered border and mameluke sleeves, she was the picture of a country beauty. Her eyes reflected the deep-blue bows adorning the neckline and sleeves of her gown and sparkled in anticipation of the day's happenings.

Lucy's dress, a white muslin, was caught under the breast with a band of delicate pink that was the same pink that colored her cheeks. As the young women played lady's maid to each other, Betta placed a thin gold chain with a cloisonné pendant about Lucy's neck.

"Papa asked me to give you this as a welcoming gift from him and Mama. And this shawl is from the rest of us." She quickly draped a handsome shawl of sheerest beeswing cashmere over Lucy's shoulders. "Now, no tears . . . your eyes will be all red and . . . oh, come along before you start me off."

The two friends walked down the stairway arm in arm. Each exceptional in her own way, harmonizing but complementing the other's good looks. They were the last to enter the breakfast room, where the rest of the family sat laughing and chatting around the table with the Petrie brothers.

Robin stood at the sideboard making a choice from among platters heaped with meats, fish, breads, and cheeses. As the two women called out their good mornings, he turned to greet them and stopped in amazement.

"Oh, I say, Betta . . . you do look fine . . . and who is this ravishingly beautiful lady with you? Pray, make me known to her."

For a moment Lucy stopped in confusion and then realized that Robin's reaction was too pronounced. She stuck her nose in the air and came back with "I don't know whether I want to be introduced to you . . . you're rather too forward for me."

Dramatically Robin clutched at his heart, almost losing his crutches. "Ah, you strike me to the quick to turn upon me so. I prithee, sweet maiden." Lucy covered her mouth to hold back her giggle. "Oh, I can't go on with this. You do look fine, Lucy . . . and you, too, Betta." This quickly added afterthought elicited shouts of laughter from the group around the table. The two young women went to Albert to salute him on his birthday. Betta's sisterly kiss was received calmly, but Lucy's kiss, chaste though it was, was received with a bright-red blush and mumbles of embarrassment.

Betta listened to the laughter and the easy repartee, surreptitiously glancing around to find Alexander. Suddenly her eyes were held by the sapphire-blue of his gaze. She felt as though her heart would suffocate her, it seemed to swell so. She could feel a blush start at her toes and creep up her body until her cheeks were stained crimson. Ohh, she wailed within her mind, what is happening? Why do I do this? Her eyes finally broke the contact, but not before she saw a welcoming smile start with a crinkle at the edges of his eyes.

He's a villain, a villain . . . but oh, lord, he's so attractive . . . I wish . . . her thoughts rambled . . . I wish we were alone and . . .

"Betta love, do sit down and have something to eat." Her stepmother's gentle voice broke in on her turbulent thoughts. "We really must hurry. The tenants will be coming along anytime now, and your father must be in the middle of the goings-on, else he won't be happy. Will you, my dear?"

Mr. St. John beamed at his wife. "She's the only one in the world who understands me and puts up with my fribbly ways. What a mother you have, Albert. A priceless treasure, that's what she is."

"Of course," murmured Mrs. St. John in agreement, "your father is a very intelligent man, Albert, and I always find myself in total agreement with him. Particularly when he is telling everyone how wonderful I am." The delightful woman paused a moment, chuckling. "To be sure, I never tell him about the less-than-wondrous moments I have. I couldn't bear to disillusion him! However, we are not gathered here today to pay compliments to me, but rather to help our son celebrate his birthday."

Rousing cries of "Hear! hear!" were heard from the family.

"George, my dear, as host of the day's festivities, it is your honor to be master of ceremonies. Now, do your duty, sir. As only you know how!"

Mr. St. John rose from his chair, smoothed his hand over his hair, pulled down the points of his waistcoat, and caressed the folds of his neckcloth.

"My dear friends and family, there comes a time in the life of every young man (and I use the term advisedly) when his heart yearns that he be acknowledged a man. One of the symbols of manhood is to become a property owner. Today, my beloved son and heir, Albert George Fitzwilliam Clyde Edward St. John, is about to acquire his first property . . . and you are invited to share the joy of the moment. If you will all follow me to the side terrace . . ."

Mr. St. John put his arm around Albert's shoulder, gestured to the rest of the group, and led the way to the terrace. Once arrived there, Albert and his father again became the center of attention. Mr. St. John emitted a piercing whistle and a whinny was heard coming from the thicket of shrubs down the walk. Again Mr. St. John whistled. This time he was answered by the appearance of a beautiful gray colt, already saddled, prancing daintily down the drive, saddle leather lustrous and metalwork gleaming in the sun. Albert's face was no less bright with delight as he realized that his birthday gift was walking toward him.

"Oh Papa, Mama . . . Oh, my . . . What's his name? May I mount him now? Oh, thank you." He threw his arms about his father and gave him a huge bear hug. "How did you keep him a secret? Where did he come from?" The boy stroked the velvety nose of the colt. "Oh, you are first-rate . . . a real top-of-the-mark winner. May I try him now, Papa? I shan't get myself mucked up . . . just a little canter down the path and back."

"Go, go . . ." Mr. St. John advised with a broad smile, then turning to his family and guests: "You see how easy it is to make a twelve-year-old boy happy? What concerns me now is, Will it be as easy when he is eighteen or twenty-one? Well, we have a few years to prepare for that."

"Papa, Papa . . ." Letty's voice piped up, "what shall you do to make a six-year-old girl happy?"

The laughter of several adults sounded in the clear morning air.

"I shall take her with me to see that the workmen are setting up the booths properly," responded her father. He swung the little girl to his shoulder, bid his guests entertain themselves while he attended the final preparations for the festivities, and quickly moved away, bouncing his youngest up and down as he went.

Mrs. St. John excused herself to attend to the final bits of business for the evening's entertainment, leaving the two brothers and the young women to their own devices.

"Lucy, I want to watch the men raise the banners. Mr. St. John devised a way to have them mounted so they would form a partial cover over the booths, and I've never seen anything like it. Help me along . . . I'm not quite steady yet with the crutches, so you can run for help if I fall." Robin made his request sound like a command, which Lucy smartly "Aye, aye"d as she jumped to attention. The two then moved off to watch the proceedings with Robin yearning to give his opinions to everything.

Betta and Alec strolled to the balustrade of the terrace, Betta still ill at ease in Alec's presence. In the distance they could see Mr. St. John bustling about checking on the final touches to the game booths and fortune-teller's tent. His words of encouragement and advice carried through the crystal-clear air. The sounds of agreement from workers and attendants were a soft accompaniment to the rich tones of the master's voice. The morning sun shone on the brightly colored bunting that decorated the tables and formed the banners flying above them.

A parade of tenants and villagers arriving for the festival was strung out across the lawn, the children laughing and running among the sedately strolling adults.

"Shall we take a closer look at the activities, Miss St. John?" Alec grasped Betta's elbow, determined not to let the provokingly elusive damsel escape him. "This reminds me of the Public Days we used to have at Possingworth when I was a boy. I think I shall have to revive that custom. . . . Robin should enjoy arranging it, from what I see of his actions here." As he talked, he guided Betta down the steps to the lawn. "Some of the booths are of very original designs . . . I judge it will be easier to examine them now than later when all the company are arrived. Tell me, does your father do this every year for Albert's birthday?"

"Why, yes. He was so thrilled at Albert's birth that he ordered a huge celebration and enjoyed it so much he's repeated it every year." Betta looked at Alec with a shy smile. "I am fully convinced that if Albert's birthday were at a less salubrious time of the year, he would still find reason to celebrate something now!" For the first time the young woman seemed at ease with Petrie and appeared to bloom as a result. As they walked she picked a stalk of iris and held it to her cheek as she continued speaking. The violet of the flower enhanced the color of the satin texture of her skin, the thick lashes that brushed her cheeks, and the sensuous curve of her delicate lips. I wonder what it would be like to kiss her, he thought; her lips look so soft. I'd like to be the one to teach her . . . Good God, what am I thinking of! He stopped walking for a moment and stood looking at her. Betta, startled by the abrupt cessation of their stroll, looked up at the earl. The intensity of his gaze disrupted her placid mood and set the drums beating in her body. Suddenly, she was aware of herself as a woman, a desirable woman. In that timeless moment there were only the two of them questioning, answering with their eyes, their breath, their being.

"I . . . yes, of course . . ." Petrie dispelled the mood with a rather incoherent utterance. . . . I've fallen in love, he thought . . . Lord, without even being aware of it, I've fallen in love. She won't be easy to capture . . . so, easy it goes, Alec, don't frighten your quarry. "That is, I find it interesting that people who do such humdrum work everyday can rise to such heights of creative endeavor as we see here today. The banners are quite unusual." Alec chatted on about the appearance of the grounds and guests in the most ordinary way possible. He had decided not to remark on his change of perception; he was not sure that Betta had felt the same reaction.

The thoughts were scurrying around in Betta's head. Did I imagine? Is this what being in love is . . . ? I could drown in his eyes . . . I'm just being fanciful. . . . Gradually

100

the calm tones of Alec's voice brought her to a semblance of poise. Outwardly, she had just paused and then strolled along with the earl. Inwardly, a volcano had erupted and the edges of her being were feeling somewhat scorched. She came to herself as Alexander was speaking of his friends.

"Philippe and Virginie have never been to an English fête. I imagine they will find it a very pleasant experience. I hope you and Virginie become friends. She will find it difficult trying to build a life in a new country with no female acquaintances. I have observed that women need other women for companionship."

"Just as men need other men," Betta answered. "I suppose it is easier to become friends with someone of one's own gender. There doesn't seem to be the confusion . . ." Betta's words trailed off.

"Oh, do you find us confusing, Miss St. John? It seems to me that you ladies are not in the least confused, you take such delight in setting us straight." Alec's smile took the sharpness from his words.

"Well, I . . . I . . . How old did you say the comtesse was?" Betta refused to rise to the bait.

"I didn't exactly say, but you shall judge for yourself. I think that commotion on the terrace is their arrival. Come, let me introduce you to my friends."

Betta looked at the newcomers as she and Alec moved to the terrace, trying to gauge Alec's relationship to Virginie. Her heart dropped as she took in the visitor's appearance. The Frenchwoman wore a simply cut ivory-colored muslin walking dress. As she adjusted the silk shawl around her shoulders, she greeted Alec with a ravishing smile and a flutter of lashes, chiding him for having deserted them for greener pastures.

"You must instantly introduce me to the so beautiful Miss St. John who has kept you by her side."

"Oh, no, madame, you misunderstand." Betta, though older than Virginie, felt like a schoolgirl in the face of the comtesse's sophistication. "Lord Halwick remained to be with his brother. I am happy to welcome you to Watton Abbey. Did you have a comfortable journey from Possingworth?"

"Oh, yes, of the most enjoyable. The countryside is particularly verdant, *n'est-ce pas?* Did I say that with correctness? The language offers some difficulty to me. You look just as Robin described in his letter . . . does she not, Philippe? I know we will become friends. Already I feel for your parents and this so lovely place. Alec, you have done me much happiness to have made me known here."

Prattling artlessly, Virginie linked arms with Betta. "Do you like my Alec? Is he not bang-up-to-the-mark?"

She was interrupted by Betta's muffled giggle and varying degrees of laughter from the men.

"But what is it I have done? Why do you laugh? Immediately, tell me!"

Philippe continued to chuckle as he instructed Virginie on the niceties of English cant expressions and the do's and don'ts of English usage.

"Ah, bah . . . is he not of the most high elegance? So . . . what difference. I will not speak again of it. Betta . . . I will call you Betta because you are going to be my good friend and you shall call me Virginie. . . . What do you think of my so wonderful Alec? Was he not of the bravest to have rescued me?"

"Here, here, what's this?" Mr. St. John had joined the conversation. "What's this about a rescue?"

Alec quickly introduced Philippe and Virginie to Mr.

St. John. Virginie turned to her host: "You do not know about the brave baker La Brie? Alec, you must tell the story; his glory must not be kept hidden."

"It would be too boring, my dear, and do not flirt those wicked eyes at me." Alec refused to take the line. "I did a service for someone and at the same time was able to help Virginie and her children."

"And Mathilde."

"And Mathilde."

"And Étienne."

"And Étienne."

"Such an air of mystery, my lord . . . it becomes a challenge to hear the whole of it." Betta's eyes dared Alec.

"No, not today, Miss St. John. It's old hat today . . . perhaps we shall save it for a cold winter's night." Alec's glance held a promise. "Today we shall forget La Brie and all he stands for. Virginie, no more of the past . . . only the future is of interest."

"Oh, la la . . . you make me to feel I have committed the *grand faux pas*. But I will not beg pardon, because, *enfin*, it is your fault."

Alec looked stunned. "My fault? What . . . what?"

"Aha, my friend . . . you are gobbling." Philippe joined in triumphantly.

"Gobbling . . . Philippe, name your seconds. . . ."

"I have waited to be revenged upon you. Now you have the same experience of this low set-down since you so described me to myself one day. Aha, I am at last vindicated!"

Soft sounds of appreciation from the ladies joined the laughter of Mr. St. John and the Frenchman as they enjoyed the exaggerated gestures of the earl.

"You have struck a mean blow, my erstwhile friend, a blow to the heart. What can I do to redeem myself? I fear

I must withdraw to calm my torn emotions. Ladies, Mr. St. John." Gracefully Alec doffed his shallow-crowned beaver and sketched a bow to the young women. "Philippe, I will deal with you alone. Now. By your leave, ladies, sir."

The two men walked off, Alec pantomiming his overwrought nerves, Philippe with a broad grin on his face.

Betta turned to Virginie in amazement. "I had no idea my lord had such a sense of humor. He always seems so stiff and proper. . . ."

"Ah, bah! That Alec, he is of the best . . . but does not always wish to reveal himself. Me, I think Philippe and I will always owe him our happiness. For many days my children and I were in his company and he was only of the greatest kindness and . . . and, how you say, concern for us, can I tell you. He played with *les enfants* when they were out of sorts, he took care of my so dear nurse Mathilde when she was overcome with fear for all of us, and he was like *mon oncle* to me. He is a very special man . . . and me, I love Philippe, but I say this."

"I believe what you say, and yet the stories we have heard seem to be about a different sort of man." Betta was stunned by Virginie's disclosure. Hesitantly, she told the young woman Lucy's story, explaining the arrival of the girl at Watton Abbey, then describing the plan of her blackguard father to sell his daughter. Somewhat shamefacedly, she made known to Virginie Lucy's supposition that Alec was the potential buyer of Lucy's favors.

"Oh, no, we will be enemies if you tell me such lies, Miss St. John. My Alec is not such a man. He is so good you cannot know. See how he has brought me to my beloved Philippe and now he gives to me and my little ones a home. Never, never did he behave *comme un bête*, he is *un gentilhomme. Vraiment, il est comme un*—oh, this English . . . I have not the word—he is like one who wears the iron suit."

"Iron suit . . . oh, you mean a knight in shining armor."

"Ah, *oui. C'est ça.* He is truly such a one."

Virginie took note of the confused expression on Betta's face. "Me, I think you have a little feeling for Alec, no?"

Betta looked startled. Could her feelings show? "How did you know . . . ? I never . . ."

"You become too angry, dear Betta, and it to me tells the story. And he I think has feelings for you." Virginie looked gleeful. "Ah, never did I hope to see Alexander, M'sieu La Brie, throw his heart over the moon! I wonder if he knows. Have you lost your heart altogether?"

"I don't know . . . I never gave it any thought. No, no, it's impossible . . . it's just that he is so devilish handsome. When I first made my come-out, I was used to seeing him dancing with other ladies and I remember thinking them quite fortunate, but that was because I had no one to pay me court. I didn't take, you see. When you have no one," confided Betta, "you build dreams about the unattainable."

Betta stopped speaking, realizing that she was sharing her most secret thoughts with a stranger. "Oh, please don't think anything of it. I don't know what's come over me that I should speak so. I am really the most levelheaded of our family. It must be the excitement of the day . . . or the sun . . . or something."

"Do not concern yourself. We women sometimes think foolish thoughts." Virginie laughed gently. "Sometimes our foolish thoughts are all we have to keep us from falling into the what-do-you-say . . . dismals, *hein?*"

As she spoke, the comtesse began to evolve a plan of action designed to bring Betta into a more harmonious relationship with the earl. She recognized Betta's inexperience in matters of love, and though younger in years than Betta, she felt infinitely older in her experience of the human condition. Not wanting to awaken the older girl to her emotions too quickly, she began to speak of less disturbing things.

"I will tell you about Philippe. I have loved him since I have seven years . . . always to me he was the strength and the protection and"—she giggled—"the sillinesses that sometimes we need. But he was older and a young man when I was eleven, twelve. I think he had feelings for me even though he didn't know how they would be when I grew up. When Alec brought me to England, I knew I would see him and I knew I would love him. But Philippe was surprised to see me, and he is more surprised to find he loves me. But it is of the most wonderful to be in love and to be loved."

Virginie stopped speaking, caught by the expression on Betta's face. Don't worry, my friend, she thought, I will see that you get your wish. Already I am sure Alexander has turned to you in his thoughts. We will contrive.

"What?" Betta looked fuzzy. "Oh, yes, to be sure. . . ."

Chapter 11

"Betta, wait for me." Lucy's voice broke into the day-dreams Betta was weaving as she listened to Virginie. "I haven't met Virginie yet and I want to tell her how brave I think she is." Lucy ran up, slightly out of breath. "Please introduce us."

Virginie turned questioning eyes to Betta. "And who is this pretty one, so breathless and eager to meet such a one as I?"

Betta put an arm around Lucy, drawing her closer. "This is Lucy Wingate; she is another heroine. Like yourself, she has escaped a wicked villain . . . but he is her father."

"Her papa. Oh, yes, you have told me. How could such a pretty *jeune fille* have a wicked papa?"

"Oh, her father is shocking bad form."

"Bad form?"

"Why, he took me to market just as though I were a calf for sale," was Lucy's indignant comment. "I suppose he saw that I had grown up and I was sort of pretty and . . . and . . . he knew some men might pay him for me."

"Ah, pauvre petite, mais c'est incroyable! This is a bad man. You will excuse my speaking so, Lucy, but are you sure he really is your true father?" Virginie's active mind

107

was at work. "Perhaps he stole you from your real papa and mama and . . ."

"No, no." Lucy laughed. "He is truly my father . . . although at times I wish he weren't. When I was tiny he was good to me and very loving, but I think he began to love gambling more than he loved me, and so he just forgot about me for a while . . . and forgot he loved me, too, I s'pose." Tears formed in Lucy's eyes.

The two older girls were quick to comfort her and fuss over her as Betta took up the story.

"You should know, Virginie, that Lucy is quite resourceful. She managed to escape and foil her father's plan." Betta recounted the tale of Lucy's flight from London, her connection with the St. Johns' butler, and her arrival and discovery at Watton Abbey.

"But you are a refugee like myself . . ." Virginie marveled, "without the baker La Brie to help you."

Which remark led to the story of Virginie's escape aided by the earl in the person of La Brie.

"The two of you make me feel that my life is very humdrum . . . I haven't escaped from anyone." Betta's complaint elicited bursts of laughter from her two companions.

"Now I wish to know what plans we make for the future to keep Lucy from the so wicked papa," la comtesse commanded.

"It's not only from her papa," Betta explained, "but there is a truly bad villain, the Duc de Selles. He is infamous for his deeds and he is the man who has offered (not marriage, you understand) for Lucy."

"Ah, I have heard his name. Philippe and Alexander spoke of him, but I did not pay attention at the time. Now we must make a plan in case he discovers your hiding place, Lucy. Your father would have the power to force you to leave here, so if he comes, he must not find his daughter."

As the three young women spoke they moved toward the house. It was still early enough in the day so that the grounds had not become crowded with new arrivals. Mr. and Mrs. St. John could be seen on the main terrace greeting arriving friends and family. Off in the distance, where contests of physical endeavor were being held, a group of young men were seen encouraging two contestants in a weight-lifting match. Robin's hobble-and-bob way of moving on his crutches made him visible to onlookers as he walked around followed by the younger St. Johns. The sounds of the village musicians tuning up for a songfest could be heard, not always harmonious; the occasional sour note causing the listeners to wince.

Betta's brow was wrinkled in thought as she listened to Virginie's pronouncement.

"Of course he must not find her . . . we know that. In fact, the earl suggested that she accompany you to Possingworth. If her father shows up we would tell him she left as nursemaid or companion to a family heading south."

"But that is of marvelousness. . . . Lucy, you will be nursemaid to my boys."

Lucy's eyes lit up. "I should like that," she said in a soft voice, "and I would work very well, and take very good care of the boys."

"*Stupide,* it is not for working I say you will be a nursemaid, it is for a . . . a . . . *un masque.* . . . What do you call it?"

"A disguise. That's wonderful, Virginie." Betta applauded Virginie's idea. "Oh, come, let's go find Lucy an outfit . . . we shan't be missed, there is so much going on. Do you know, you two, I haven't had such fun in . . . well . . . ever. I hesitate to tell you, but I feel as though

109

you are both like sisters to me. I shall use this very adventure in my novel. You won't mind, will you, Lucy?"

"Oh, no. How thrilling to be a real heroine. . . . Shall I be the heroine, Betta?"

"Well, not really. Actually I shall have to change the story somewhat; I've just found out my villain isn't really a villain." Betta looked meaningfully at Virginie, who began to laugh.

"Oh, well, *ma chère* Betta, there is time enough after all is over to write. . . . Perhaps this will make your novel more exciting . . . and there is a true villain in the Duc de Selles. Which way shall we go now?"

The three had reached the foot of the stairway. Betta beckoned the comtesse and Lucy to follow her as she took the lead and guided them to her room.

"Lucy, what did you do with the parlormaid's dress you were wearing the other day?" she queried.

"What kind of dress is a parlormaid's dress?" asked Virginie.

"It's very plain, gray in color. Lucy will wear it with a long white apron and a white mobcap to cover all her hair. The very costume will hide her in the crowd, because people don't look closely at a servant. If you will walk a little differently, Lucy, kind of drag yourself instead of bounce around as you do . . ." Betta started to laugh as she spoke.

"Bounce around," the indignant Lucy cried out, "bounce around . . . whatever do you think I am, Betta, to say I bounce around?"

"It's just that you have a certain zest and eagerness . . . well, maybe not bounce, but . . . well, just walk more slowly." Betta gave in.

"Is it not truly amazing we should be such friends so quickly? Never have I been able to have friends since I was a little child. . . ." Virginie's comment caused the other girls to stop their hunt for Lucy's costume. "To feel so at home with you, not for a moment did I feel as *une étrangère,* a stranger. It is a lovely feeling." The svelte, sophisticated countess threw her arms about Lucy and then Betta, who responded to her warmth. "Almost I could cry with my happiness to feel so good."

"There's no time, Virginie, we've got to dress your nursemaid first. Then later we can cry about being friends." Betta rolled her eyes in an exaggerated way. "Fancy crying over a nursemaid and me . . . Whoi, oi'ld 'ave a lake of tears in 'ere, mum, if ye'd do such a dafty thing."

Betta's clowning dispelled the intensity of the moment even as she and Lucy shared Virginie's tears.

"Oh, here's the dress, I've found it." Lucy pulled the plain dun-colored dress from the wardrobe. "It's rather a colorless color, isn't it?"

"That's the whole point, child, to make you without color. You are so small you could almost be a child yourself. . . . We might even be able to dress you as . . . no, no, that would never do, this is better. . . . Although, if there were no extra females at all . . ." Virginie snapped her fingers. "I have the better idea . . . she shall be another Albert, not a nursemaid. When we leave we will take with us cousin Lucien. He has twelve years, like Albert."

"Virginie, that's outrageous," Betta exclaimed, "but you know, I do think you are right. She's even smaller than Albert, and in his clothes with a cap covering that mop of curls, no one would guess."

Lucy clapped her hands with excitement. "Now, why didn't I think of that?"

"For now, be the nursemaid," Betta instructed. "I'll fetch an outfit of Bertie's for you to try, but don't wear it until it's time for Virginie and Philippe to leave for Poss-ingworth. That way no one will see a small girl, and you know no one will notice another harum-scarum boy. Just a moment while I fetch some of Bertie's clothes."

Betta returned shortly with a bundle of garments. Soon Lucy was attired in pantaloons, shirt, jacket, and scruffy shoes. A peaked cap covered all her curls.

"She really looks like a little boy . . . and a real mischief" was Betta's comment upon examining her handiwork.

"*Vraiment* . . . this is much better disguise. . . . I think she should wear this from now on. Forget the nursemaid. We will tell no one, not even Robin or Alexander." Virginie began to instruct Lucy: "You must not talk to them, but run past them to the booths where the other children are. They'll not even notice you. Now, let's go down and see what happens."

As the three, now two girls with a boy, descended to the garden, they were joined by Mrs. St. John and an elderly neighbor who had just arrived for the celebration. Lucy, keeping her head down, ducked around the two ladies, mumbling something about "lookin' for Albert, very im-portant."

"Who was that boy, Betta? I don't think I've seen him before," Mrs. St. John asked.

"Younger generation is going to go to rack and ruin the way they're brought up. No manners, no manners at all." The visitor thumped her cane to accent her pronounce-ments. "Never mind that one. Who is this gel? Introduce me, please," the outspoken old woman demanded.

Betta made the introduction, explaining that the Com-tesse d'Ivraille had recently arrived from France and was visiting at Possingworth.

"Humph, know that top-lofty fellow Halwick, do you?

Well, well, you'd better watch yourself; he's said to be too appealing to the ladies."

"No, no, madame, you need have no worry. I have the understanding with another. All is *comme il faut.*" Virginie laughed as she assured the inquisitive neighbor. Then, turning to Mrs. St. John, she asked, "Do you make the visit to the earl's estate at this season? It is so beautiful, the gardens and the lakes, very soothing to the spirit, *n'est-ce pas?*"

"Well, perhaps . . . a visit hasn't been mentioned," Betta's stepmama answered, "unless Alec has spoken to Mr. St. John about it."

Before she could continue on the subject, her elderly guest addressed the two girls, advising them to be off to see to the party. "If you don't protect your interests," she cautioned Virginie, "the other pretty young things may take over!"

Protesting her Philippe's fidelity, Virginie took her leave, glancing significantly at Betta as the laughter bubbled in her throat. The girls ran off, muffling their giggles as they went.

"That's a beautiful gel you have there, Amelia. She should be married and busy with her own children, not with her sisters and brother." The old woman and Mrs. St. John made their way to the terrace. "George really did himself proud this year. The booths and decorations are beautiful."

Mrs. St. John began to thank her guest. Then, spotting her husband, said, "There's George, you can tell him yourself. Just let me get him. It will soon be time for the family to gather with Albert so he can receive the presentations from the tenants. So absurd, really, quite like *petit* royalty . . . but very sweet of them to go to the trouble. George . . . George . . ." she called out to her husband,

"Come and receive some compliments. Now, don't turn his head too much, ma'am, or we shall never hear the end of it."

114

Chapter 12

"This is insanity, *m'amie.* One can't turn a girl into a boy and expect to get away with it," Philippe adjured Virginie. "Alec, my very dear friend, tell this jewel of my heart what she is all about in the head!"

Alec shrugged his shoulders and pretended to turn away from his friends. "I would hesitate to come between two people who are having problems, particularly when one is male and t'other is female. I don't want to end up with my head separated from my shoulders."

"Philippe, truly if you would only believe me . . . I know . . . if you can pick Lucy out of the crowd of children, then I will say you are right." Virginie challenged the upset Frenchman. "When you think about the situation, you will see that it is more the better for there to be no Lucy and perhaps a Lucien instead; anyone looking for her will not think of looking for a boy. Is that not true, Alexander?" She appealed to the earl.

"I just said that I wouldn't interfere, Virginie, but I do think there is something to be said for the disguise. What will you do with her? She can't stay here."

"Oh, I told her we would take her to Possingworth with us."

"You what?" Alec erupted. "How could you do such a thing . . . what will we do with her dressed as a boy?" He shuddered. "I no sooner finish with one rescue than I have to be involved in another. Is there no rest for the weary?" He appealed to the world in general.

"Who's weary?" asked Robin as he and Betta joined the three. "What's the problem? I say, did you see Lucy? She looks unbelievable. A real little horror as a boy!"

"A horror—Robin, that's too much." Betta pushed his shoulder. "Really, you know you said she could be Virginie's younger brother with her coloring as it is. Big black eyes, dark curly hair, and rosy cheeks . . . certainly better than a nursemaid. Virginie, I thi k you are a genius."

"It is not of my genius," modestly replied Virginie. "I have learned all I know of the disguise from the baker La Brie."

"Oh, are we back to that scoundrel again?" moaned the earl. "I vow I shall be so jealous of this person, I shall almost certainly challenge him to a duel! That is, if I could. We really must put him away for the remainder of our acquaintance, my dear Virginie, otherwise we will have a very short relationship!"

"Be serious, my lord." Betta took up the cudgels. "We must find some safe way to get Lucy away from here in case her father does find her trail, and what better than to show him that he has made a mistake? She will no longer be here, there will be no one here other than one of the undermaids who resembles her in coloring, and no one who looks like her will have left the estate. He will think that he was given the wrong information because the undermaid has just recently come to work here and, and . . ."

"Ladies and gentlemen." Mr. St. John's stentorian voice could be heard trying to get the attention of the visitors: "If you will all gather at the pavilion, please

. . ." His request was repeated by various servants walking through the crowd.

"It's time for the entertainment. . . . Robin, you'd better find the girls so you can do your part. This is one year that I am going to enjoy myself and be part of the audience instead of being a performer."

"As long as you are going to enjoy yourself, let me enjoy with you." Alec took Betta's hand to lead her to the pavilion. "This looks to be a very unusual experience for my brother. You may have to instruct me on the niceties of the program."

Before Betta could pull back, Virginie agreed with Alec and gave her friend a not too gentle shove in the direction that Alec was taking. "That is a wonderful idea. We will come in a moment. I wish to make sure that Lucy is hidden among the children."

"But, but . . . oh, all right." Betta started laughing. "I feel as though I have been plotted against, but I shall go along with the plot." She smiled at Alec. "If you would not pull my arm with so much effort, my lord, I should find it more comfortable to walk with you."

"Oh, lord, I didn't realize . . . I'm glad you are no longer on the outs with me, Miss St. John. I was almost ready to give up the ghost! Ruinous to one's self-esteem to find oneself at loggerheads with a brother's dearest friend . . . and through no fault of my own."

Betta's cheeks turned rosy. "I can only beg your pardon, my lord, for a misinterpretation of certain information that had been relayed to me." She stopped walking and turned to him with a sweet sidelong glance. "Shall we agree to try to keep the peace between us? That is, I will agree to that if you will not tease me about it."

"I find I can not refuse so reasonable a request. We shall be friends . . . while we get to know each other better."

"Better? . . . Oh . . . yes . . . well . . ." Betta decided that she could make no better response to Alec's warm regard and quickly resumed their walk.

By the time the two arrived at the pavilion, the crowd of tenants, family, and friends had gathered to witness the presentation of a gift to Albert from the tenants of the Abbey's farms. With many fine speeches and much huzzahing and clapping of hands, Albert received a beautiful fob watch and chain that he would be able to enjoy for many years.

"Lookee here, Master Albert, if ye push this little thingy, the hours chime, and if ye push this little one, the lid opens and . . ." The directions for the use of the watch were given by the enthusiastic leader of the group. Albert's speech of thanks brought great satisfaction and a few tears to the many witnesses, and he must needs display all the wondrous capabilities of his grand new timepiece to his friends and relatives.

"Well, now." Mr. St. John broke into the emotional moment. "Is anyone hungry? If we have no takers, I shall have to throw away a fine roasted sheep and a side of beef. . . . Just step over there and take your seats and we'll soon see if there's aught to give away!"

He turned with a gesture to wave the company to the serving tables and seats, almost knocking Thompson down in the process.

"Thompson, I didn't see you. What is it, man?"

"Sir, there is a Mr. Wingate waiting to see you."

"Wingate, but . . . Alexander, Betta, I think we have a problem on our hands. Lucy's father is here." He turned to Alec. "What do you recommend, my lord? Shall I see him or shall I have him shown the gate?"

"Oh, that's a leveler; let me think a moment," Alec answered. "I'll tell you what; I think you should see him purely as a politeness, but not immediately. Have Thompson convey to him the message that you have guests and cannot take time to interview him now. After all, if Lucy had not come here, you would have no reason to meet with him, so you must behave as though you had never heard of her. Do you agree?"

"Yes, I think you have the right of it. We will carry on in as normal a way as possible. I certainly would not see any strangers on a day like this unless they had previously informed me of their proposed visit and had received my permission to call. Thompson, inform the . . . gentleman . . . that I am busy with my guests and cannot possibly see him today."

"Immediately, sir." Thompson nodded in agreement and left with his message.

"Where is Lucy? I haven't seen her since breakfast." Mr. St. John addressed Betta.

"Lucy? Who is Lucy? We have no one here named Lucy," Betta answered.

"Sir, I think it would be better if you were to believe that there is no Lucy here," Alec advised Mr. St. John. "No one other than the family has seen her up until now, and no one will see her after this moment . . . that is, until time for her to come forward."

"Yes, Papa, this way you can lie with a clear conscience!" seconded Betta.

"Either you have the makings of a scoundrel, Betta, or a very good tactician," her father said. "I don't know what kind of April's fool game the two of you are playing, but we have never seen Lucy, I agree. I think I can handle that blackguard with no trouble. Better tell your mother where I have gone . . . she will be looking for me."

"It would be more in keeping if you were to wait until

Thompson calls you a second time, sir," Alec suggested. "It shouldn't be too long."

"Yes, you're right. Well, I shall sit here under this tree and wait for Thompson to summon me. Betta, you will have to look to the entertainment."

"Robin has it well in hand. He is leading the songfest as soon as the musicians finish tuning up." Betta gave a little giggle. "Did you think Letty would let him get away without conducting her performance today? She is in the limelight with her hero!"

"You go along, then, and enjoy the music while I enjoy pulling the wool over this rapscallion's eyes" were Mr. St. John's parting words.

Chapter 13

Mr. St. John stood in the doorway examining his unwanted guest. He saw before him a slender man of medium height, dressed in London fashion of a sort. His jacket was a trifle too narrow in the waist and a bit too wide in the shoulders. His waistcoat was of the finest material, but the stripes were the merest hint too pronounced, and the several fobs at his waistline were just beyond good taste. It was the points of his collar (so high, he had to turn his body in order to see to either side) and the intricacies of the folds of his neckcloth that truly acclaimed Mr. Wingate for the dandy he was. His face, which was handsome, had a weakness to it about the mouth, and the mark of dissipation was visible about his eyes.

Mr. St. John had decided that his best course of action was not only to pretend ignorance of the existence of Lucy Wingate, but to be cordial and welcoming to the intruder. With this in mind, he extended his hand and jovially greeted Jeremy Wingate.

"I beg your pardon for not coming sooner, Mr. Wingate. I don't believe we've met. I am George St. John. It is my son's birthday and we are entertaining quite a large number of people. Do sit down and tell me what has brought you to Watton Abbey, my dear sir."

Wingate was rather surprised at Mr. St. John's bluff

joviality. He began his attack by refusing to take a seat. He then gave out a story about the disappearance of his daughter at the same time one Robin Petrie had fled the London scene. As he strode about the room he began declaiming: "Sir, I have been told that my dear motherless daughter was brought here by that rascal Robin Petrie. I do not make so bold as to accuse you of complicity. . . . In fact, knowing what I do of the young wastrel, I would hold you innocent of his scheme to offer my dearest Lucy carte blanche. He is the lowest sort of rascal . . . inveigling her to join him in flight. I know how high in the instep his brother is, and I know he will never offer her marriage. And, my dear sir, she has had an unexceptionable offer from another that would be to her great advantage to accept. I wish to see the two miscreants instantly!"

"My dear Wingate, you must be foxed. Your daughter isn't here, and if you think that Robin Petrie brought her, you're badly mistaken. He's here by virtue of having had an accident in front of my gates several weeks ago. In fact, he broke his leg at the time and is only now able to get around on crutches."

"I hesitate to doubt your word, St. John, but I have it on the best authority that Petrie eloped with my little Lucy." Wingate made as if to wipe a tear from his eye. "And for that I will have his hide. I shall challenge him—No, I shall horsewhip him; that is what he deserves for such a dastardly deed."

"My dear sir, I will forgive you the slur because of your obviously distraught state," Mr. St. John said dryly, "but I do assure you that for Robin to have run off with your daughter would have been impossible. When did you say she disappeared?"

"Two weeks ago, she was taken from my bosom two

122

long weeks ago, and I have spent all this time in trying to find her. She has an understanding with a very fine nobleman, you see, and he is suffering from a broken heart this very moment because of her loss."

"Why did you think that she would be here?"

"I thought she might have gone back to her nurse, but realized that she would know that I would look for her there and I then recalled that her nurse had a sister in this area. When I confronted the nurse's sister, she claimed she knew nothing of my daughter, but one of her neighbors told me that she had seen a young woman leave Mrs. Thompson's house in your carriage. So now you see I have proof positive that she is at present in this house." Wingate looked triumphantly at Mr. St. John as though expecting him to fall on his knees begging forgiveness.

"Mrs. Thompson, you say? Of course, Thompson's wife; that is to say, my butler. Naturally you saw a young woman leave their home in my carriage. I have hired Thompson's niece to be a parlormaid here during the celebrations of my son's birthday. Would you like to see her?" Mr. St. John walked to the bell pull and hauled away at the embroidered cloth hanging with the greatest nonchalance in the world. "I can quite understand your anxiety. I have a few daughters and would certainly not want them to run away from home with a scoundrel. . . . Thompson, please bring your niece in here, the one who just started working."

"Certainly, sir. She's just here in the hall." Thompson answered this unusual request graciously. "Betty, you may come in to the master now."

Wingate's mouth dropped open when he saw the pretty girl walk in. In truth, superficially she did look like Lucy and could easily have been mistaken for her. Her dark curly hair was short and her dark eyes were large and she was short, as was Lucy. Without a pictured likeness to portray the real features, a spoken description would not differentiate between Lucy and Betty.

"Is this your daughter, Wingate?" Mr. St. John asked politely.

"Of course not, but I could not have been mistaken. There is some trick here. . . . That Petrie creature has played a hoax on all of us. Of this I am sure." Wingate was sputtering, he was so angry.

"But I had thought you to be one of Robin's best friends, Wingate. He himself told me what a good fellow you are. Surely he wouldn't, even had he been able to, take advantage of you in such a way. After all, friendship does count for something in our circle, does it not?"

"You . . . ah . . . yes . . . well . . . you will have to forgive a father, St. John. . . . You can understand, especially since she was to have made such a splendid connection." Weakly Wingate excused his actions.

Perhaps you had better repair to wherever it is that you are staying and rethink your ideas. Since your daughter is not here, she must be somewhere else. Correct? Now you will have to look further afield for her."

"Yes, I can see that I will have to do a great deal of rethinking about this. I am staying at the Inn of the Two Doves tonight. A friend is with me. He will have some ideas about all this. I'll go now, but with your permission will return in the morning." Abruptly Wingate departed, convinced only that something was not quite as it should be and that he would understand better once he discussed the matter with his friend de Selles.

Mr. St. John took himself back to the party, concerned that all was not as it should be, certain that they would have trouble with this rascal unless he could be put onto another scent.

While the two fathers were having their talk, Robin, Betta, and Alec were making plans to send Lucy (as Lucien) to Possingworth with Virginie and Philippe.

"Damn, what bad luck that he should find her here so soon." Robin railed about Wingate's arrival. "What are we going to do now?"

"Philippe, were you able to pick Lucy out in the crowd?" Virginie reminded him of her challenge.

Before he could answer, the earl took it upon himself to comment: "I couldn't pick her out and I'm fairly familiar with the way one changes one's walk and stance to disguise oneself. What did you do with her, Miss St. John? I'll warrant she isn't even out here among the guests." Alexander was peering at the various groups, trying to spot Lucy. "If it weren't for the fact that her father has arrived in the vicinity, I would say that she should remain disguised as she is. You are to be commended, Miss St. John, for your competence in the art of masquerade. Now tell us, what did you do with her?"

Betta, fully appreciating her moment of triumph, decided to enlighten the confounded Alec. "If you will look over at the group of boys around Bertie you will see Virginie's cousin Lucien. He's wearing a gray jacket and a specked cap."

"So what has that scruffy boy to do with anything?"

"My dear Alec," replied Betta, "Virginie has no cousin Lucien. That scruffy boy is our missing Lucy!"

"Lucy . . . it can't be. Why that's outrageous, Betta. What a joke on her father." Alec began to laugh. "If de Selles could see her now, he would give up in disgust.

"Please, Miss St. John, disclose to us your plan. It seems you have hidden talents . . . you become more fascinating by the moment." The earl's compliments were music to

Betta's ears, so much more satisfying to hear than simpering adulation about one's looks, or hair, or whatever.

The young woman quickly outlined all she and Virginie had planned against this moment. She told the Petries about elevating a kitchen maid who had a resemblance in coloring to Lucy to the parlor floor with Thompson's connivance. Thompson had been instructed to inform his master so that she could be shown to Wingate. It was hoped that Wingate, when faced with another girl who had dark hair and eyes and was about the same age, would give up the search for Lucy.

"We thought that Lucy's father might think that somewhere along the line he had been misled deliberately into thinking that Lucy was in this neighborhood and that he would return to London when he found she was not here." Betta elaborated: "Virginie and I thought at first Lucy would make a capital nursemaid for Virginie's children, but then when Virginie saw she was really so close to Bertie's size, she decided that it would be better if there were no female to trace. No one will notice a hobbledehoy youngster leaving with his family . . . so that's why we turned Lucy into Lucien."

"A capital idea, Betta." No one noticed Alexander's use of Betta's first name. "I think that should do the trick. Although if de Selles is with the man, he may smell a rat. His mind is very devious and never looks for the easy answer. What do you and Virginie propose to do with Lucy, once you turned her father to a different course?"

"Well, we had thought that she could go to Possingworth. In fact we thought that Philippe and Virginie should leave right away with Lucy. Do you think that's what should be done?" There was a worried tone in Betta's voice.

"If a carriage full of guests were to leave precipitously

126

this afternoon, before the ball, it would look very suspicious. And I'm sure that Wingate has a man keeping watch for just such a departure. Better, I think, if they stay until the morning and leave in the normal course of events. Lucy must not appear at the party tonight . . . she must behave just as though she were a lad. One of the youngsters visiting with parents. Except, of course, she will not join in their high jinks this evening. I think we had better find Virginie and advise her to lead Lucy back into the house as though she were really one of her children. It will be better if you and Robin don't have too much contact with Lucy where others can see you. After all, you don't have too much to do with the young boys of the other families visiting here today."

"Oh, she will be heartbroken to miss the dancing tonight. She has been talking of nothing else these past few days. Remember, Robin, how she spoke of her dress . . . and that she has never been to a party like this?" Betta turned to Robin with her question.

"We'll do something to keep up her spirits. I know, we'll have a midnight supper, just the few of us . . . that should keep her going." Robin enthusiastically made plans.

"I think we should let your parents in on the plan, Betta, and also give the news to Philippe and Virginie. They are probably expecting to leave any minute." The earl took the opportunity to take Betta's hand and tuck it into the crook of his elbow. She was so involved in making plans for Lucy that she absentmindedly permitted this intimacy. As the earl started walking toward the terrace she found herself attached to him, or so she felt, and was confused by her unwillingness to detach herself. There was a feeling of comfort and assurance that seemed to enfold her as well as a bubble of excitement that made her want to laugh out loud . . . at what, she hardly knew.

"I . . . I . . . do you think that we should, that is . . . I . . ." The assurance that came from Alexander was not the kind that helped control her tongue. "Oh, blast!" Finally anger at herself gave her control over her speech: "I don't think we should be walking like this, my lord."

"Why, whatever do you mean, Betta? Should you not accommodate a guest in your home? I . . . merely need some support in my infirmity. . . . You wouldn't want me to stumble and fall, would you?" Alec grinned shamelessly at her. "Now be a good girl and help me to the terrace."

Robin followed along, totally oblivious to the byplay between his brother and Betta. "Here comes your father, Betta. He looks to be in a good humor. Maybe he was successful in turning Wingate off."

"Hoy, you three." Mr. St. John huffed and puffed after his rapid walk down from the house. "I've been looking for you to let you know what that scoundrel had the effrontery to say. He's giving it out that Robin eloped with Lucy. Would hardly believe that you were here this past month with a broken leg. In fact, wanted to see for himself that you were incapacitated. I had a hard time not to throttle the man. Then I had a harder time not to laugh at his face when Thompson produced Betty for him. That was a clever move, daughter, to have arranged for her to be here. And she does look a bit like Lucy if you close one eye and wink the other!"

"Papa, you deserve a medal for your action. Above and beyond the call of duty, that was. What a nasty man he must be. It's a wonder that Lucy is so nice. Or maybe not such a wonder; she was lucky to have been with her nurse all these years."

As Mr. St. John listened to his daughter, he examined

Alec's and Betta's faces. The sight of them walking arm in arm surprised him. His Betta was rather shy with eligible young men. He found himself liking the thought of Petrie and his daughter making a pair of it. Petrie seemed a deep enough one to appreciate Betta and was certainly experienced enough to draw her out. The tales of his being a rake and a loosefish must be gossip engendered by the envious. Mr. St. John prided himself on his ability to judge human nature; based upon his knowledge of Robin and the few talks he'd had with the earl, he'd bet cash on the Petries, good breeding will show.

"Sir, you are a paragon among men." Robin's tone was admiring. "Pick-of-the-crop, that's what."

Betta's laugh rang out, accompanied by Alec's and her father's.

"Robin, go in and rest . . . all this is becoming too much for you. I can tell you're losing control. Pick-of-the-crop, indeed. You are speaking to my father, not to Albert. Where are your manners to assault his dignity like that?"

"My dear daughter, if my children have left me any dignity, I haven't noticed it, so why should Robin?" was her father's rejoinder. "Now, go along and tell your friends whatever the plans are. I'll back your decisions all the way because I don't like that man. . . . He'll be back tomorrow morning, so take that into consideration whatever you do."

Chapter 14

In the light of late twilight, the gardens of Watton Abbey had the look of a fairyland. Colored lanterns twinkled in the trees and bushes. The huge footed candelabras shone around a wooden dance floor that Mr. St. John had caused to be constructed just beyond the terrace. The striped peaked canvas roof that formed the pavilion above it was vaguely reminiscent of the tents of Araby. Musicians were tuning up in their enclosure at the far end of the pavilion as servants hurried about the terrace, setting up tables for the supper that would be served later. The pellucid air was fragrant with the scent of roses and honeysuckle, and the first star of the evening could be seen low in the sky to the west.

The members of the host's party were standing on the terrace awaiting Betta's appearance before forming the receiving line to greet the arriving guests. In a low voice Mr. St. John was commenting to his wife on his daughter's late arrival.

"I sent Parker to her with instructions to turn her out as though she were meeting the Prince of Wales tonight," Amelia told him. "This is one time when Betta is going to look her best. If I left it to her, she'd run a comb through her hair, throw on her clothes, and come down looking as though she were ready to go berrying. George, you know

I love her, but she rarely pays any attention to her appearance. Of course, she's so lovely to look at that one rarely sees what she wears, but tonight is important. More important than you realize, dear one. . . . I feel that tonight may have very interesting results, if my eyes haven't deceived me." She made a motion of her head toward the earl. "Alec has been showing a decided partiality for Betta's company, so . . ."

"But she seems not to care to be with him for the most part," Mr. St. John commented. "I rather thought Robin was more in her good books."

"Oh, George, you men are so blind. She practically flutters every time he gets near her. She's had some bee in her bonnet that he was involved with Lucy's father, but she seems to have realized finally that such an exercise is beneath his touch. He's a marvelous-looking man, and I think he's quite taken with our Betta, George. If he approaches you with an offer, will you be put off?"

"Of course not, Amelia, I like the man . . . he's got a head on his shoulders and would certainly be a feather in Betta's cap if he does come up to scratch. But it makes no difference to me. It's for Betta to accept or decline the honor." Mr. St. John was firm on that point. Turning to his son, he complimented him on his appearance and then, hearing the sound of carriages coming up the drive, began to shepherd his wife and Albert to the foyer, saying that it was time to form the receiving line. "Come along, come along. That includes you, and Robin, my lord, it's time to greet our guests."

Upstairs, Parker had just put the finishing touches to Betta's toilette. She stood back, bowing her head to acknowledge the applause from Lucy and Virginie, who had been watching the transformation. Betta gasped as she saw herself in the mirror. How could a new hairdo make such

131

a change? Well, the dress might have something to do with it, she thought. It's more than beautiful. The young woman saw herself robed in a gossamer dress of periwinkle-blue that floated about her figure, accenting her beautifully shaped breasts and narrow waist. The low-cut bodice was of a soft, lustrous velvet capped with draped sleeves that barely cupped her shoulders, leaving her arms bare. From just beneath the bustline, layers of chiffon de soie hung in soft folds to the floor, beaded here and there with seed pearls. The effect was that of moonlight on shadows.

Her new hairdo was a cascade of soft curls held back from her face by a wreath of violets, baby's breath, and seed pearls. Her tawny hair and translucent skin were accented by the color and textures of the gown and flowers. It was almost a stranger who stood there gazing back at her from the mirror.

"Oh, Betta . . . you look absolutely . . . absolutely . . . I can't think up a word that is fine enough!" was Lucy's rapturous response to her friend's questioning look.

"Ma chérie, tu es comme la lune, like the moon in that gown. Please," la comtesse asked laughingly, "please do not look at Philippe or he will be lost to me! And then I will have to have with you the duel, *n'est-ce pas?"*

"Oh, thank you, Parker, I don't know how you worked such magic, but I feel like a fairy princess whose godmother touched her with her wand." Betta gave Parker a hug and kiss, then turned to Lucy.

"Lucy, we'll all meet in the nursery at midnight, so you can get dressed up and enjoy your own private party. Thompson is arranging to have a table set and you will have everything except the dancing . . . it would be too noisy to have the musicians come upstairs. Parker, will you help her as you've helped me? Please." Lucy had quickly become a favorite with the household, and Parker willingly agreed to Betta's request. "Come, then, Virginie, we must make our appearance. . . . I vow, we shall be the most beautiful women at the party! Did I say that? Vanity, vanity thy name is woman!"

Softly laughing, Betta led Virginie from the room to join the family downstairs. The two could not have chosen their gowns for better effect had they planned in advance. Virginie's evening dress was of pale blush rose satin softened by an overdress of a paler tone of point-d'esprit lace. The straight line and tiny train gave height to her short, exquisite figure. Her black hair was drawn into a smooth chignon and capped with a diamond and ruby coronet that denoted her rank. Philippe and Alec, looking up at them from the foot of the stairs, were speechless at the sight of such extraordinary beauty.

"I don't know if I can walk down the stairs, my knees are shaking so," whispered Betta to her friend. "I can't imagine why I should have such a reaction. It must be that I was in the sun too long today without a sunshade."

"*Certainement,* if you think so," agreed Virginie. "I will hold you up and you will hold me up and we will make the elegant entrance in front of our two very handsome men, no?" Virginie took Betta's hand and began to walk down the steps.

"There," she said a moment later, "we have come safely down and now await the greeting from you, *mon cher* Philippe, and you, dear Alec."

Philippe drew Virginie toward the terrace, speaking rapidly to her in French, telling her exactly how he felt. Alec stood silently for a moment gazing at Betta, once again surprised at the feelings in his heart. He watched a blush turn the alabastered cream of her face to deep rose and then as quickly fade. He saw her violet eyes hidden by the sweep of her long lashes and then revealed in a

133

sidelong glance that melted his heart and brought a quick grin to his face. He extended his hand to the exquisite creature who stood before him and with a courtly bow asked permission to escort her to the reception area.

Betta stood for a moment, allowing the excited rhythm of her pulse beat to hold her. She felt heady with a power she had never before experienced. The admiration in Alec's eyes could not be denied, and it was intoxicating; she delighted in his presence and at the same time was frightened by the intensity of her emotions.

"Thank you, my lord. I feel quite flattered that you should undertake to be my escort." She dropped a deep curtsy, giving herself time to calm down as she responded with the courtesies in which she had been schooled. At the same time her thoughts were in a turmoil. It was true that she had accepted Virginie's estimate of Alec's character, but, but, but . . . he looked so rakish. The superb cut of his blue superfine jacket accenting the width of his shoulders, the sharp white of his shirt against his tanned face. The whole look of casual restrained elegance took her back to the London ballrooms. He always managed to send her pulses racing, and that simply couldn't be a good omen. Of course it could be her imagination . . . perhaps all this flattery and these intimate glances were just part of his usual behavior. Again but . . . but . . . but . . . it was very enjoyable and very exciting for once to have someone single her out for attention. Oh, well, perhaps she should just enjoy the sensation and expect to take up her rather quiet life on the morrow if she could. Tonight was an enchanted evening, she could tell just by the aura that seemed to surround everything.

After what seemed an interminable length of time, the last guest was greeted and the members of the receiving line were able to disband to enjoy the dancing. Before she had a chance to deny him the pleasure, Betta found herself circling the floor in a spirited waltz skillfully led by the earl. As she was whirled around, the effort of holding a conversation became too much, and she relaxed to the music, letting Alec's arm guide her. How fortunate that her stepmother had insisted that she take dancing lessons before she made her debut. Betta glanced up at the earl and her eyes were caught by his. Once again there was a long unspoken communication between them . . . and once again she felt confused and frightened by her response.

All too soon the music came to an end and the earl was walking with her to the edge of the floor. "May I count on another dance with you, Betta, before the evening ends?" Again he addressed her familiarly, with a caress in his voice.

Betta found it difficult to maintain her hard-won composure in the face of Alec's admiration. She found it better to retreat with the excuse that there were many neighbors and relatives who would be expecting her to partner them in the various country dances that were to predominate during the evening.

"In that event, I shall expect to escort you to supper and dance the waltz that will precede that intermission," was the earl's response. "Until then, I believe you have another partner awaiting your attention."

Philippe and Virginie had been observing the interplay between Betta and Alec with interest. "Virginie, can it be that my friend has finally found his heart's desire?" the handsome Frenchman asked.

"*Mon Dieu,* Philippe, if you cannot see what is on the front of your face, you are not as astute as I looked to see you." Virginie tapped him with her fan. "Not everyone can have his heart's desire fall into his arms like you, *mon coeur.* Some must work to find that delight! You found your adoring young nuisance still adoring you when you have become an old roué! Alec, I think, has the inkling that his future will be complete only with the lovely Betta. But Betta, oh . . . she is such a one . . . she thinks she is suffering from *une maladie* . . . she will not let herself believe that so fine a beau as Alexander could love her. *Pauvre petite,* she has had some bad times before, but I do not think ever she has given her heart."

"Do you think Robin will be offended that she prefers his brother to him?"

"Bravo, *stupide!* It must be that you are without the eyes to see. Robin sees only Lucy in that way . . . they are like two children playing, but Lucy will be his choice. She is young but has much sense. Me, Virginie, I shall arrange the whole. I shall be the putting-together person for the making of the match!" The comtesse clapped her hands. "So, now that I have settled that, you shall dance with me and we will forget about all the others and think only of ourselves, yes?"

"Yes, my dearest Virginie, let us dance and forget." Philippe held out his arms to her.

"I cannot imagine ever not loving you, my sweet one. All the times you followed me . . . so young, yet you knew . . . somehow you knew our souls were entwined." He drew her into his arms and began to move around the floor. "In my arrogance I passed you off as a nuisance, not realizing I needed your love. Never have I felt so much at home as with you, my love."

Virginie tilted her head back to look into her beloved's eyes. "*Mon amour,* always have I loved you. Everything that was good and strong and exciting was my Philippe. I never forgot—although I stopped hoping. But when Alec came . . . I followed you." She gave a delicate shrug of her shoulders. "But now—*you* shall follow me around and *I* shall hold *my* nose in the air!"

She gave a delighted tinkle of laughter as Philippe made a face. Quickly he whirled her to the side of the dance floor and into the shelter of a conveniently located tree.

"Now, my *gamine*," he said, "we shall see who will follow and who will lead." And he pulled her closer in an embrace that was a promise of their future.

On the sidelines, watching the activities, were Mr. and Mrs. St. John. The middle-aged robust man and his very attractive younger wife swayed to the sound of the music.

"How lucky we are not to be in London where it would be considered bad manners for us to dance together, George." Mrs. St. John tipped her head saucily. "You are planning on dancing with me, aren't you?"

"Of course, my love. There's no reason why we should not enjoy our son's party as much as all these other young people," was his laughing rejoinder. "Have you taken notice of our Betta? She is in radiant looks tonight. I don't think I've ever seen her looking so well."

"Dearest George, women in love always look radiant. Did I not tell you she had a partiality for the earl?" Mrs. St. John put her hand on her husband's arm. "After all, I have been in my best looks since I first met you. Haven't you noticed?"

"No one could ever compare with you, love, and I always notice . . . that you are the best as well as the most beautiful wife a man could have. Come, let's show these youngsters a thing or two about dancing. I was always thought to be a fair goer on the dance floor!" And with that he drew his wife into the nearest set and picked up the rhythm of the dance.

To Lucy, watching the party from Betta's window, it was apparent that everyone was having a good time.

Above the sound of the music floated the sounds of laughter and speech interwoven with the tinkle of glassware and china. Servants could be seen hurrying from the kitchen with trays of delicacies to be served to the guests and scurrying back for refills. A group of children of Albert's age were playing tag just outside the pavilion, stopping every now and then to watch a particularly complex dance figure being carried out. As the night sky deepened, the moon rose, shedding its cool light on the proceedings, bathing the scene with a lustrous glow.

Alec claimed Betta for the waltz before the supper break and had whirled her around until she was breathless. Once the dance was over he suggested that they walk in the garden a bit to cool down before partaking of the collation that was already being served.

Exhilarated by the dancing and the champagne she had imbibed, Betta felt more confident of her ability to cope with Alec. True, her blood sang with the excitement of his presence, and true, she felt a need to be close to him; but that was just a thing of the moment. No problem presented itself when he took her hand in his and then a little while later put his arm around her waist. It was just like in the waltz . . . well, maybe not quite the same, but not to be concerned about. When they reached the moon-bathed folly and he stood holding her in his arms, looking down at her uptilted face, it became a little more difficult to maintain her calm appearance. When he gently, sweetly touched her lips with his . . . well, anyone feeling a momentary dizziness would have to raise her arms and put them around the other person's neck just to maintain her balance. Which might have produced another kiss had Betta not heard her brother's voice calling her and awakened to her situation.

"Oh, I . . . What are you doing? I . . . really . . ."

"You tripped over a root, Miss St. John." Alec felt that the moment that had been one of informality now called for a more formal approach. "I merely put my arms around you to prevent you from falling."

"And . . ." Betta was not quite sure if she had dreamed a kiss or had really been kissed.

"And then your brother began to call you." Alec refused to acknowledge the delicious moment he had stolen. There would be time enough to teach her to accept his love. For now, he decided to be more circumspect in his actions. Don't rush your fences, man . . . you'll lose the fox if you do, he cautioned himself. Was ever a wooing harder, but was ever a goal more worthy of winning? "It's time to see what Albert wants."

The birthday celebrant had come looking for them with a message from Robin reminding them that it was time for Lucy's party.

"Come, love, we'll have time enough soon. You don't want Lucy to feel left out of the festivities." The earl led a bemused Betta back to the house.

Chapter 15

Betta ran lightly down the stairs, her heart filled with a persistent love for everything and everyone. As she passed Thompson in the foyer, she grasped his hands and whirled him around, caroling her good morning. Leaving him behind clutching at the newel post for stability, she moved quickly along the hall to the breakfast room. She was filled with an exuberance that bubbled in her veins. She would have some toast and coffee and then use some of this gorgeous morning to go for a ride. Hoping that there would be no one in the breakfast room—particularly not Alec . . . she couldn't face him yet—she pushed open the door to hear Letty's voice questioning about the propriety of little girls' watching the doings from the safety of the kitchen garden. To her dismay, the answering voice was the earl's, saying that although such action was to be condemned by most of the parents he knew, he himself had found such activities most enjoyable when he was a boy.

"Really, my lord, how can you encourage a child in such behavior? I should think . . ." Betta made the mistake of looking directly at Alec. His blue eyes were alight with a look that set her heart fluttering in her throat. Memories of the preceding evening, held tightly in check, skittered through her mind: the scent of roses, the touch of his hand on her waist, the moonlight and shadows in the garden, the softness of his lips lingering against hers. Her eyelids went down like shutters over a window lest he perceive the warmth of her response. She felt a threat in his regard, a threat to the tranquility of her existence.

Brought back to herself by Letty's persistent tug at her arm, she dismissed such thoughts as flights of fancy. Remnants of the magical effect of the music and the moonlight.

"Betta, I saw you dancing and I saw the squire pinch . . ."

"No, no Letty, don't tell me . . . you really are too much." Betta collapsed into a chair. "Why don't you bring me some toast instead of talking so much. I'm sure I'm as hungry as a bear in the springtime."

Pamela and Evianne jumped up. "Can we get you something, Betta?"

"Yes, you may bring me some berries, Pam, and you may bring me some ham, Evianne."

"Such a good sister," smiled the earl. "You could not have better service if you were a princess."

"Yes, well . . . they are very good to me." Betta didn't appreciate speaking about herself to Alec. "Did you sleep well, my lord?"

"Very well, Betta. But I thought we were friends and could stop being so formal with each other. Last night . . ."

"Oh, yes, last night. What a lovely party. Albert was really thrilled with his gifts, don't you think? Everyone looked so well. The cousins from Newscombe were in fine fettle and the food was just fine and the . . ." Betta began rattling on at a great pace, anything to stop his references to last night.

"Betta, did you have a beautiful time at the ball last

141

night? I tasted some champagne this morning. Ugh, it was horrible."

"Letty, what are talking about?" Betta asked. "Where did you get champagne?"

"There was a bottle with a little bit left in it behind the chair in the study, so I took a sip just to see what it tasted like."

"You took a sip out of the bottle?" Betta was horrified at her six-year-old sister.

"Well, how shall I know whether or not I will like it when I am grown up and going to parties and someone says would you like some champagne and I have to answer them and if I've never tasted it I can't tell the truth about whether I would like some or not, now, can I?" Letty finally ran out of breath.

Alec let out a bark of laughter at Letty's logic. "What you say has a certain validity, Letty, but ladies never, never drink from the bottle."

"Oh, Letty, that was a terrible thing to do . . . you must promise never to do it again." Betta cautioned the child in a stern voice. She could not completely control the giggles that threatened to overcome her at the thought of her littlest sister swigging from a bottle almost as big as herself. When she caught Alec's eye, she gave way and doubled over in laughter.

"It's really not all that funny, but, oh, dear, can't you just see it . . ."

"Letty, you are truly an original, although I remember Robin doing something similar. Don't tell anyone else about your adventure . . . with the bottle or in the garden. You might upset some of the other grown-ups. Not everyone is as understanding as your sister. Is that a promise?" the earl cautioned the little girls. Upon receiving Letty's undying word and the assistant promises of the twins, he suggested that they take themselves outdoors to see if they could find any favors left from last night's festivities.

Excited at the thought of such treasures, the three ran merrily from the room, leaving the earl sighing with relief and Betta sighing with trepidation.

"You are dressed for riding. Do you plan on going immediately following your breakfast?" Alec set about to restore Betta's equanimity. "I had planned on exercising your father's horse for him. Mr. St. John mentioned that he had had little opportunity to ride these last few days. Busy with the arrangements for the celebration and such."

"I had planned on riding for an hour or two. I must go soon or I shall not be able to go at all with all the company to be entertained. And if Philippe and Virginie are going to leave by twelve, I'll have to be back in time to help Lucy pack her things." Betta began to feel more at ease. As long as he didn't refer to last night, she felt that she would be able to cope with his presence.

"If you are finished then, shall we go? It's such a lovely morning, I'm really looking forward to the ride. The little I saw of the grounds as I came in seemed to indicate that your father has some unusual plantings. Robin mentioned that he is interested in botany."

Betta spent the time walking to the stables telling the earl about her father's experimentation with certain plants and his findings. The conversation moved naturally to an exchange of information of a more personal nature. Miss St. John felt a delicious sense of ease spiced with a current of excitement. She was able to speak without stammers and stutters about her outlook on life, her disapproval of the excesses of many members of the *ton* in their search for relief from boredom, and her love of country living. Together they agreed that Robin seemed to be cured of what might have become a madness for gambling and that he had shown a great good humor in his play with the younger St. Johns.

They found themselves agreeing on many things: the charm of the writings of Jane Austen, the need for friends, the beauty of the paintings of Constable, the joy of travel.

The Earl was enchanted by the young woman, and she responded to his subtly expressed approval. He realized she could easily be overwhelmed if he was too obviously the wooer. As long as she felt a modicum of safety from too deeply expressed emotions, she was able to behave with an engaging naturalness. Her personality opened like a flower, and soon she was laughing and talking with no self-consciousness. When he took her hand before throwing her up into the saddle, she relished the sweet languor that held her motionless. They gazèd deeply into each other's eyes, speaking wordless thoughts.

He studied her as she sat straight-backed on her horse, beautifully controlling the animal. The earl realized that he had at last found the one woman in the world for him. He decided to approach her father as soon as possible to ask permission to pay his addresses to Miss St. John. He also realized that he must do so in a way that would not expose his goal to the object of his desires . . . she was still too tentative in her feelings to take the chance and possibly face his disdain. No, this was to be a campaign that would win the prize—always providing the prize didn't take fright.

While Betta was being beguiled by the earl's persuasive ways, Watton Abbey was being visited by the two men who were the source of Lucy's problems. As he had promised when taking his leave the previous day, Jeremy Wingate had returned accompanied by his daughter's alleged fiancé, the Duc de Selles. Thompson, who had shown them to a small anteroom, notified Mr. St. John of their arrival and then, at his bidding, informed Lucy to remain in her room so that she would not risk the possibility of being discovered by the visitors.

"You see," Wingate addressed de Selles, "I told you we would not be denied the door. This St. John has nothing to hide, I'm convinced of it."

"You were ever a fool, my dear Jeremy, and ready to see that which was expedient." De Selles drew a handkerchief from his sleeve and waved it gracefully in front of his nose, inhaling the fragrance that came from its soft folds. "I have no doubt that we will find your daughter—you owe her to me for the sums I have already advanced to you—if not here, then wherever she has hidden herself. If you hadn't handled the matter with so little finesse, *mon cher,* she and I would already be on the high seas on route to Italy. You are a bumbler, Jeremy. . . . I don't know why I permitted you to conduct the affair."

Wingate turned pale at the implied threat in de Selles's voice when he mentioned the money owing him. "My dear de Selles, you exaggerate the problem . . . the girl was just shy and overcome with the honor you pay her. She shall probably turn up at her nurse's home all smiles and acceptance. She cannot realize the countenance being in your protection will give her. . . ."

"Even though I want the girl, Wingate, I cannot help feeling a disgust at your obsequious posturings. You haven't given one thought to the girl's well-being, so don't try to tell me anything otherwise. You have a mountain of debts that must be paid, or you will find yourself in the Fleet, so please be honest with me at least." The cold black eyes of the duc turned from Wingate's pale face. "You had better assume the pose of a grief-stricken parent once more. I think our host approaches."

Mr. Wingate took up a position in front of the fireplace

as the door opened to reveal a very congenial Mr. St. John. "Mr. Wingate, I had not expected to see you again. To what do I owe the pleasure of your visit?"

"I had mentioned that I would return this morning with my friend. May I make you known to the Duc de Selles, my daughter's affianced husband. He is practically prostrate with grief at her disappearance. Obviously the poor child was overcome at the magnificence of the life she faced as the Duchesse de Selles and in a moment of madness ran off . . . or was abducted by that scoundrel Petrie."

Mr. St. John's voice became frigid as he said, "Is it possible that I heard you make an accusation against me and a guest in my home?"

"No, no, not at all. I must persuade you to forgive a distraught father. . . ."

The Duc de Selles watched Mr. St. John with a calculating look in his eyes. "Is it possible that my friend, who is beside himself, can have made an error in his supposition that his daughter is here? We were told by one of your own villagers that she was seen to enter your carriage a few days ago. Naturally we would not question your word . . . in fact, we do not question . . . but you may have been deceived by the girl into thinking that she was other than she is."

Mr. St. John moved to the pull to summon a servant. "I shall have the young woman who was seen to enter the carriage brought here for your edification. Thompson." He addressed himself to the butler who had entered the room: "Please bring Betty here. These . . . gentlemen . . . wish to see her." He turned back to the two men, presenting a somewhat more affable face: "I can appreciate your concern, my lord. To have one's fiancée run off before the betrothal is even publicly announced is very . . . lowering to one's spirits, no?"

146

Mr. St. John's discourse was interrupted by the sudden arrival into the room of his daughter and the earl. Betta, still in her russet-colored riding habit, was rosy from the wind, her violet eyes aglow with enjoyment. The plumes of her dashing hat curved against her face, accenting the pure oval shape and enhancing the cream of her complexion. De Selles caught his breath in surprise. He had not expected to find a goddess in this out-of-the-way hamlet, and one he had never beheld on the scene in town. He turned his eyes to see who followed Betta into the room, and a curious look crossed his face at the sight of the Earl of Halwick. This proved more and more interesting and might be more worthwhile than tracking down that recalcitrant offspring of Wingate's.

Betta stopped abruptly upon realizing her father had guests. "Ok, I didn't know you had anyone with you, Papa. Forgive my storming in like this. . . ."

"My dear, you need not excuse yourself. This is Mr. Jeremy Wingate. He has come looking for his daughter, Lucy; and this is Lucy's betrothed, the Duc de Selles. Gentlemen, my daughter, Miss St. John. And our guest, Alexander Petrie, the Earl of Halwick."

"You needn't introduce us, sir." Alec's cold voice cut through the room. "The Duc de Selles and I have met before." He nodded briefly in acknowledgment of the older man's presence: "And Mr. Wingate and I have met over the gaming tables at White's several times in the past. Why are you looking for your daughter, Lucy, Wingate? Has she wandered away from you?" There was a mocking note in the earl's voice.

Wingate turned white at the derision he heard in the earl's tone. "Sir, you mock a grieving father. My daughter was snatched from me—yes, snatched from the bosom of her loving father by a scoundrel, sir, a scoundrel. We were given the information that the person who was involved with her disappearance was your own brother, Robin, but now find that he was discommoded by a broken leg, and . . . and . . ." Wingate's words slowed down as he faced the fury in Alec's face. ". . . but, but . . . of course we will accept Mr. St. John's word without any . . . um . . . um . . ." He stopped speaking, caught up in his own concoction of lies.

"Father, did you call for refreshments for the gentlemen?" Betta put in, hoping to lighten the tone of the meeting. "I am terribly thirsty from our ride and would love some coffee. . . . May I call for some for you also?" She turned questioning eyes on the visitors.

Relieved that someone was offering an escape from the difficult situation in which his thoughtless words had involved him, Wingate agreed that refreshments would be welcome, adding that he and the duc would have to leave shortly to make their return to London. He hoped to pick up Lucy's trail once again, but the correct one this time, not a blind-alley lead.

While they awaited the arrival of the refreshments, de Selles started up a conversation with Betta, ascertaining that she had not been on the London scene for several years owing to her duties at home, as she put it. For some reason she could not fathom, she was at ease with these strangers, even though she was repelled by something in the duc's manner. It was apparent to Alec that de Selles was attracted to the beautiful young woman, and from his own knowledge of the man, he was impatient to warn Betta to guard herself. He moved to seat himself in a position where he could hear the duc's sallies, but where he would not have to participate in the conversation. His concern was made note of by the duc, who had reason to take cognizance of the earl's actions. Indeed, the duc had

148

made a study of the earl in an attempt to find his weaknesses. If he was not wrong, today had given him that knowledge; now he had only to make use of it. Smoothly he began to talk with Betta about her interests, trying to draw her out. As she responded to his comments she felt a strong revulsion that she couldn't understand. He had made no overt motion that would give her a disgust for him, nor were his looks of the kind to put one off, and yet . . . Betta turned to draw the earl into the conversation, feeling a comfort in his presence that made discourse with the duc easier.

The door finally opened to Thompson, who was carrying the tray with coffee and cake, followed by Betty with a tray of wine and glasses. When they had set the trays down and served the company, the parlormaid asked Mr. St. John if there would be anything else that he required.

"Why, yes, Betty. Would you tell these two gentlemen when you started working here and how you arrived." Mr. St. John gestured toward an attentive Wingate and de Selles.

"Why I already told that gentleman yesterday"—Betty pointed to Wingate—"but if you bids me tell it again, sir . . ." And once again the servant told her story as she had the day before. Again her similarity to Lucy and the casual, open manner in which she told of coming to Watton Abbey convinced the two gamesters that there was some truth in her statements. De Selles focused his attention upon Betty—much like a snake focusing on its prey, came to Betta's mind. In a bored manner he asked one or two questions of the girl, inferring that the rewards for answering satisfactorily would bring her personal attention from the duc. Betta was so appalled by the blatant seduction in the manner of the duc that she excused herself to avoid having to express her disapprobation.

Mr. St. John's advice prior to this morning's visit enabled Betty to carry off her role of innocent parlormaid with ease. Her wide-eyed acceptance of de Selles's attention and her slightly gape-jawed awe of the nobleman convinced the Frenchman that she was as she professed to be. Once he had satisfied himself on this score, he and Wingate took their leave, assuring their host that they would be returning to town to further their search for Lucy, Mr. Wingate begging in impassioned tones to be notified if by any chance his missing daughter should arrive at Watton Abbey.

"I fear we have not heard the last from that pair" were Alec's words when he and Mr. St. John were alone. "You realize of course that it is de Selles who is the leader; Wingate is merely his tool. I have no doubt that he has done this sort of thing before . . . in fact, I know to my sorrow that he has. However, we have spent enough time on those two jobsters. We must get Lucy away from here instantly. Have Virginie and Philippe made their appearance yet?"

"Philippe has breakfasted and indicated that he and the comtesse would be ready to depart with Lucy as soon as you and Betta returned from your ride. But don't put me off, my dear Alec; what information about de Selles are you holding back? I really feel that the more I know about the man, the better I can protect Lucy and my family from his machinations." Mr. St. John was worried about the aftermath of the successful plot to foil the duc.

"If the situation were anywise other than it is, this story would remain untold, you understand that?" Alec studied the worried man as he spoke. "Naturally, I take it for granted that this will go no farther than this room . . . it concerns people very dear to me." Satisfied by the consent he saw in St. John's face, the earl began his story.

"Several years ago, I had a cousin, a delightful girl . . . very gentle, very beautiful, and very innocent. She was the daughter of Lady Westrich, my aunt, who is staying with us at Possingworth. The girl was in her first season, had just made her come-out, and was of such beauty and manner that she took the town by storm . . . despite the fact that she never sought such success. Part of the problem was that she had never been familiar with liars and cheats, had been protected and cosseted all her life, so when that . . . cur . . . began to pay her attention, she accepted him as a worthwhile man. I was not in town at the time, else I would have been able to warn my uncle and to protect Vanessa myself. To shorten the story, he made an assignation with her and talked her into eloping with him, promising the honorable thing. Needless to say, once he had used her to his satisfaction—and before she died she told me of some of his habits—he discarded her. . . . She was then with child and in precarious health. We finally found her . . . living in a hovel . . . merely existing. I took her home to her parents, but she lasted only a little more than a month. The deprivation to her spirit sapped her will to live, and she died. She was not quite nineteen years of age . . . much like Betta in looks and manner. The loss was such that we thought we would lose my Aunt Westrich as well, but it was my uncle who succumbed to his grief, although the doctors called it an affliction of the heart. Well, it was . . . but not in the way they meant. I had not meant to unburden myself of this tale to you, but it is just as well that you know the depths to which that man will sink."

"I understand fully, and I am grateful that you have shared this with me. I was aware that he was not quite up to the mark, but could not put my finger on it, not knowing anything about him other than hints you and Robin had dropped, and of course his action about Lucy." Mr. St. John put his hand on Alec's shoulder. "Well, I am fully warned now and feel better able to deal with him should he cross my path again. Now, what say you to some wine to wash the taste of this whole incident out of our mouths?"

"I would accept the wine, sir, but for another reason." Alec suddenly looked less at ease. His urbanity began to come apart at the seams as he continued to talk with Mr. St. John. "I am rather at a loss as to how to express myself. . . . I have recently discovered, that is, I realize how short a time . . . damn, I'm at a loss!"

"There, there, my boy, calm yourself. Here." Mr. St. John handed him a glass of wine. "Take this. Perhaps it will settle your mind and you will be better able to express yourself."

"Thank you, sir." Alec gulped his wine in a manner most unlike that of the usually composed, polished town beau that he was known to be. "I would guess the best way is the fast way . . . so here it is, sir. I love Betta. . . . I know that I have not known her for long and I have said nothing to her about my feelings, but I am a man of experience and have enough knowledge of myself to know that she is the woman with whom I wish to share the rest of my life. I hope that you will give me leave to address her, because it is my dearest wish to care for her, to win her, and to love her always."

"For a man of experience you surely approach a father all atwist, don't you?" Mr. St. John looked at Alec with a distinct twinkle. "But you did well all the same. If Betta should accept your suit, why Mrs. St. John and I will welcome you into our family. We already feel that you are one of us, and to have the right and privilege to call you son-in-law will suit us both. Just one word of advice, my boy, be easy with her. She's like an untrained colt . . . ready to shy at the least alarm."

"I thank you, sir. . . . I had seen how it is with Betta . . . so I planned on extra caution. I just wish we had more time together to give me time to pave the way, as it were, for a successful plea. I must take Robin back to Possingworth today or tomorrow. We've taken advantage of your more than kind hospitality for long enough. In addition to which I have Virginie and Philippe to think about, and my aunt, who is at the estate. But that may be the way. . . . Virginie and Betta have taken to each other very well. Perhaps she would accept an invitation to accompany Virginie and Lucy . . . to keep them company and help Lucy accustom herself to the new life she will hopefully be leading from now on. Do you think she will agree to something like that?"

Mr. St. John applauded the idea, cautioning, however, that Betta was no fool and might look askance at being the only member of the St. John family to join the traveling party. Alec agreed with him, remarking that he had had little time to study his beloved, being so surprised at finding himself in love. Mr. St. John suggested calling Mrs. St. John into the conference and was about to summon her when Alec began to smile broadly.

"But that's it exactly. I shall not invite Miss St. John; I shall invite the St. John family, to reciprocate the hospitality shown to the Petrie family! That should take care of the matter without any repining." Triumphantly the earl downed his wine with a salute to his future father-in-law.

The two men, in full agreement with each other, made their plans for the journey very carefully. Mr. St. John agreed not to mention Alec's proposal of marriage until such time as the earl had been successful in winning the woman he loved. It was settled that the Petries would leave with the departing guests that same day and that the St. John family, young and old—possibly even with Brindle—would set out for Possingworth in three days' time. The length of time of the visit was left open . . . both feeling that it might have to last as long as it would take for Betta to come to the realization that she returned the earl's love. In great amity with each other, the men parted, each to make his plans for the next few days.

Chapter 16

The waiter carried his tray into the pleasant wood-paneled parlor and set it down on the table. The tall autocratic man standing near the fireplace was engaged in examining his quizzing glass as he refuted the statement just finished by the shorter, less aristocratic gentleman who was sitting on the settle under the window.

"Wingate, you are not to be believed. It is no longer certain whether or not your daughter is with the St. Johns. Had you exerted a firmer control over the chit, this state of affairs would not exist and neither of us would have been so discommoded. That she has not left the St. John estate is the only thing we can be sure of."

Lucy's father shrugged pettishly. "If you hadn't been so forward with the wench, she wouldn't have taken fright and run like a scared rabbit. With all your *savoir-faire*, milord, you have bungled this as much as you claim I have." The little man was almost apprehensive of his defiance in the face of his wealthy patron's anger. "That is to say, I didn't consider her sensibilities and perhaps was a little blunt when informing her of your regard. How . . . un . . . how do you know that she hasn't departed the St. John estate . . . if indeed she is there?"

"My man, Achilles, has been keeping watch since we arrived. When it was necessary for him to attend me, my groom Corby took over the watch in his place. They have been particular in scrutinizing the departure of all the guests just in case she would try to leave in a disguise of some sort. Most likely if she were there, they would try to smuggle her out dressed as a nursemaid or abigail or some such. I think we can accept that she is elsewhere than Watton Abbey." A sardonic smile crossed the duc's face as he continued: "I am almost inclined to be glad about that . . . I have in mind to try to engage the beautiful Miss St. John. What a goddess . . . a fitting mate for one of the royal line of France."

"Engage Miss St. John . . . why, you must be all about in your head. Her father won't let you near her . . . you could see her reaction very plainly . . . took you in great dislike, she did. Haw . . . not quite so deedy when it comes to the gentler sex, milord. . . . Methinks you lost the touch of elegance that put you above the crowd these many years." Suddenly the purport of the Frenchman's words struck Wingate: "What do you mean, 'mate'? D'you mean to marry the chit? You're off your noodle, de Selles."

"Watch your tone, Wingate. . . . I have little liking for you and have countenanced you only because of what you owe me . . . but I can forget all that if you forget yourself. I find that you are rapidly becoming superfluous . . . especially since I am losing my desire for your daughter."

They continued to talk about their failure to find Lucy . . . Wingate castigating her in her absence for her disobedience and de Selles inclined to dismiss the affair now that he had become intrigued by Betta. The difference between the two men was very apparent as they sat at the table eating the lavish meal the innkeeper had prepared for them. De Selles, despite the decadence of his character, was the true aristocrat in his demeanor, his looks, his dress. His feelings of self-worth and consequence could almost have been a caricature had the impression of depraved power not accompanied his hauteur. Wingate, now that his dandified dress was in some disorder, had a more seedy look. An ineffectual whine and a face that was losing its weak good looks took away any pretention that he might have had to high estate.

"I must put myself in the way of meeting the beautiful Betta once more," the duc murmured. "What do you say to an evening of cards, Wingate, with a late supper thrown in?"

"What d'you mean? I'm not going to play cards with you; you've won everything I have except for the clothes on my back!" the slightly belligerent man answered.

The duc raised his quizzing glass and gave Wingate a long scrutiny. "I find it more and more difficult to restrain myself with you. . . . I have it on good authority that your father and mother were wellborn people. . . . What happened to you? My plan is to invite St. John and the younger Petrie to an evening of cards. It is more than likely that the young man will be bored with the lack of excitement and eager to try his hand at gaming again. You will be able to win some blunt against the inn bill and I will endeavor to make myself agreeable to the father of the goddess I have chosen for my mate. I *will* settle the Earl of Halwick once and for all. I owe him a debt that I can no longer allow to go unpaid."

"Don't see how you can settle a debt with Halwick by playing cards with his brother and St. John," Wingate said with a mixture of curiosity and caution in his voice.

"You will learn. In good time, you will learn, Jeremy. . . . First we must get in the good graces of the father, and then the daughter will fall like a ripe plum into our hands." For the first time, the duc smiled, a twisted sneer

157

that gave promise to the future he was planning for his gratification.

A note of invitation was quickly written and dispatched with the duc's groom. In anticipation of the arrival of his guests, the duc ordered the room cleared and the table prepared for cards. He spent some time with the host, discussing the proper dishes for a late supper, and finally approved the choices. His attention to detail was meticulous even though this was merely for a "friendly" card game. Once the arrangements were completed, the disparate pair sat back to await the arrival of their guests. Once or twice de Selles thought to caution Wingate about the amount of wine he was consuming, but was laughed at by his ally. Eventually the groom returned with a message from Mr. St. John thanking the duc for his hospitality but begging off from the engagement because the St. John family was leaving to visit other parts early in the morning.

"Damnation, this puts a crimp in my plan." He turned to Corby. "What did you learn about this trip?"

"The whole house was in a tizzy with excitement, milord," calmly answered the groom. "There is talk that the Earl of Halwick has offered for Miss St. John and they are to make a visit to his estate so the young lady can become better acquainted with the earl. One of the parlormaids overheard the earl make his offer to Mr. St. John and repeated it."

As he heard these words, the duc became still. So much so that he seemed to have stopped breathing. His face paled and then an angry flush covered his cheekbones, making apparent the virulent glitter in his eyes. In a voice almost too soft to be heard, he bade Wingate to entertain himself for the balance of the evening but to be prepared to leave on the morrow. Imperiously he waved Wingate out of the room, to the other man's great relief.

Lucy's father was not one to repine for long, so betook himself to the taproom looking for more congenial companionship. Just as he made his exit from the parlor he had been sharing with de Selles, he heard a woman's voice pleading with the landlord for help in her misfortune.

"Sir, I beg you, we must have lodging for the night. My carriage is in no condition to be used, the wheel is about to come off, and it is too late for the wheelwright to be summoned to make the repair. My maid and I can share . . ."

His curiosity aroused, Wingate walked to the door to see what the pother was about. When the woman, dressed in deep mourning, saw him, she turned to him and, holding out her hand in supplication, asked him in a voice bordering the tearful if he would help her make the landlord understand her great need.

The black of her clothing set off the translucent whiteness of the widow's skin and the rich auburn of her hair. She looked to be in her late twenties and, despite a trace of hardness in the set of her chin, could be considered a beauty. In the hope that her presence would enliven the evening, Wingate stepped forward to bring his authority to bear with the inn's owner.

"My dear madam, to what fortunate happenstance do we owe your presence in this drab corner of the world? Please, permit me to offer you the use of our private parlor. I am certain you do not wish to display yourself in the common room." Wingate was his most attentive self as he led the woman into the salon. Upon noticing her draw back when she saw de Selles, he quickly made the introduction, ending by asking the somberly dressed woman how she came to arrive at the inn at such a late hour.

The woman had seated herself with much fluttering and many murmurs of thanks and pleas that she not be allowed to discommode the two men. Her head held in a lowered attitude, she began finally to speak: "My name is Winifred Epping, late of Newcastle up on Tyne. I was the happiest of women until four months ago, when I received word that my dear husband, a captain in the Fourteenth Light Cavalry, was lost to me when he was thrown from his horse and killed." She stopped speaking, making heart-rending sobbing sounds behind her handkerchief. The men waited for her to regain control of herself, which she did in a few moments. "I am on my way to London now; I was supposed to be escorted by a brother officer of my husband's, but he was detained on company business." Mrs. Epping's voice had a waspishness to it. "He hired a chaise for me, but the idiot neglected to inspect the carriage and the wheel is hanging on by a thread." She looked up at her audience, halted in her narrative by a derisive sound from the duc. "Oh, I lose my manners in speaking about Major Church. . . . It is just that I am so tired . . . I feel rather faint . . ." And she dropped gracefully against the back of the high-backed chair in which she was sitting.

Wingate ran to her side and began chafing her wrists, begging her to calm herself, assuring her that they understood and had nothing but a wish to help her in their hearts. A quick glance at the duc from under her lashes told her that the nobleman was in no way seconding Wingate's statements. Maintaining her spurious swoon for a moment longer, Mrs. Epping tried to ascertain the most effective method of producing a modicum or better of financial gain from her hoped-for association with these

160

two men. She knew her story to be a farrago of lies and half-truths and suspected that the taller gentleman had reached that conclusion. She decided that her best chance to achieve at least a night's lodging and a decent meal (her pockets being almost totally to let) was to maintain a virtuous attitude and stick to her story. The evening would surely produce some information that she might put to good use.

"Dear lady, take a sip of this restorative. You needn't burden yourself with disclosing any more of your story . . . it obviously upsets you too much to do so. I will have the landlord bring you a tray, and once you have eaten you will feel more the thing." The duc marveled at Wingate's ability to involve himself with the woman so quickly. Part of his stock in trade was the wish always to appear charming; even as he stole a man's hearth and home he wanted only to be liked.

The duc examined the woman as she slowly sipped her wine. It was obvious that she had no money . . . or very little. Her dress was of a poor-quality material and her bonnet a copy of one of Madame Celestin's better designs. Her gloves had been mended in more than one place and her reticule had seen better days. Yet she had an air about her that they might put to use. De Selles let his mind play with certain ideas, searching for a stratagem that would defeat his enemy Alexander Petrie. Too many times in the past had the Earl of Halwick meddled in business that was no concern of his. . . . Perhaps through this woman the duc would achieve his revenge on Petrie. It would be enjoyable to see him defeated. Never before had he been so vulnerable as he was now that his interest was engaged by Miss St. John. The Frenchman continued to spin his spiderlike plans while the sounds of the voices of Wingate and Mrs. Epping washed over him. His attention was caught by the woman's speaking of her need to get to London to obtain a loan from a friend there. In flowery phrases Wingate was showing himself to be a well-wisher and champion, albeit one with empty pockets. The duc, on hearing his guesses about Mrs. Epping's financial status verified, realized that here was a potential partner in the scheme he had begun to conceive against his enemy.

"Have you had any acting practice, madam?" he asked, interrupting the conversation.

"Sir! What kind of woman do you take me for?" Mrs. Epping was indignant.

"I take you for whatever you wish, madam. I have need of one skilled in acting to take part in a . . . farce . . . I wish to present for the edification of an acquaintance of mine." The duc responded with a slight smile on his lips that left his eyes cold.

Wingate's face reflected his surprise as he began to bluster. "What about Petrie and Lucy and . . . and . . . our. . . . ? You sound all about in your head, duc. What can this lady do to help us?"

The duc ruthlessly told Wingate to shut his mouth and slowly outlined a plan to abduct Betta. The venom in his voice as he spoke of the earl's fascination for Miss St. John betrayed his hatred for the lord Halwick. He explained the need to have Petrie's home infiltrated by one who would be able to entice Betta away from the grounds of Possingworth without drawing attention to her action; this would be Mrs. Epping's role. His groom was to apply for a job as undergroom in order to be on hand to relay messages, with Mrs. Epping's maid as a second go-between. They would all remove themselves to the area of Possingworth the next morning, settling in at an inn convenient to the location. The specifics of the conspiracy needed more thought, but he would further instruct them after spending the night refining the scheme.

Mrs. Epping, grateful for the opportunity to earn the sum offered her by the duc, was not high-minded enough to consider her betrayal of the friendship she would soon profess for Betta to be an immoral act. She forgave herself any wrongdoing by allowing herself to believe that the young woman would have brought any such punishment upon her own head. Wingate, of course, found great enjoyment in the thought that Robin Petrie, although blameless of any acts against Lucy, would be brought low merely by his being a helpless bystander. So the three conspirators, each reveling in the mischief that the duc de Selles planned, took themselves off to bed, looking for a successful conclusion to their efforts to bring to life the stricture "How the mighty have fallen."

Chapter 17

The horses' hooves scattered the gravel of the broad curved driveway as they drew the traveling coach farther into the marches of the Earl of Halwick's great estate of Possingworth. The larger forward vehicle drew to a halt in front of the wide shallow stairway that fronted the palatial three-story building. Before the St. John postilions could dismount, the Halwick footmen had lowered the coach steps and opened the doors to allow the passengers to descend. On hand to greet his guests was the earl, accompanied by Virginie and Philippe and various children. The bustle of dismounting, greetings, and unloading gave Betta time to discipline her nervous start when she saw Alexander. He was as she had remembered: arrogantly handsome, but warm and friendly in his greeting of the family. Before she came face-to-face with him, she was taken by the hand by Virginie and pulled over to the side of the steps, where three young boys were standing.

"Before anything, dear Betta, I must make you acquainted with Philippe's nephew, Etienne, and my sons: Charlot . . . the littlest one . . . and my big boy, Pierre, who is always such a help to me." Virginie proudly presented her three charges to Betta, who responded by shaking each one's hand and then sweeping Charlot into her arms for a hug. To her great pleasure, the little one gave back squeeze for squeeze.

"I think the men in your family are truly first-rate." Betta put the little boy down and took his hand and beckoned the other two to follow her. "Now I would like to introduce the French group to an English troop." She conducted them to the St. John children and made the introductions. The formality of the French boys was apparent in the stiff little bows of acknowledgment they made to each of the St. John girls. Letty, as usual the leader of the three, immediately asserted her authority by announcing that she would be ready to explore in minutes . . . as soon as she took off her bonnet and left it with her governess. And she expected that the Possingworth boys would be more than happy to show them around. There was a slight contretemps as Étienne attempted to let the company know that he was the most worthy for the task of conducting the young visitors about and that Letty, as a girl and one younger than he and lower on the social ladder, must give way to his authority. Fortunately Albert knew to perfection how to control his little sister and was able to placate the already irate young French boy. After receiving permission from his rather harassed mother and a nod from the earl, he led the young contingent away to their own adventure.

Mrs. St. John laughingly expressed her opinion that Letty was the most managing female she had ever met . . . even though the child was her own daughter. "I can't imagine where she got that manner . . . it's not as though we encourage her pronouncements . . . for that's what they are. She never says 'perhaps,' she always speaks with such a positive way about her. . . ."

"At least she has arranged things so that we may have a quiet cup of tea together before you rest," Philippe offered. "Virginie, Alexander . . . are we going to stand out here with our guests for the rest of the afternoon? I'm sure Robin is waiting in anxious anticipation of the St. Johns' arrival. So, *en avant . . .*" The lively young man led the way into the mansion.

The visitors paused in the magnificence of the three-storied great hall, awed by the sheer size of the space. The walls were hung on either side with huge tapestries depicting the history of the Petrie family, the first scene being of a hunt for mythical creatures. The costumes of the hunters suggested that the tapestry dated from the fifteenth century, and the tower of Possingworth was shown in the background. Other panels showed a Petrie being honored by King Henry the Eighth, a family member being saluted by Queen Elizabeth. The most modern was of Charles the Second being handed his scepter at his coronation by the then Earl of Halwick.

The earl directed his majordomo to show his guests to their quarters so that they might freshen up before enjoying the promised cup of tea and their reunion with Robin. As they started to mount the remarkable curving staircase to their rooms, Lucy came flying into the hall from somewhere along the farther reaches of the area.

"Oh, to think I wasn't here for your arrival! I told Robin that I wished to be on the steps to greet you. Don't I look fine now that I'm a girl again. . . . Betta, how do you like the dress Virginie gave me? Her nurse, Mathilde, is a treasure . . . she sews so well . . . the dress was a trifle too large over here." In her enthusiasm Lucy forgot she was in mixed company and cupped her breasts to illustrate. Then, hearing Mr. St. John's soft chuckle, turned fiery red. "Oh, dear . . . I'm so sorry. What you must think of me. Robin keeps telling me I am such a noodle-head

. . . I'm beginning to think he's right. Oh, come upstairs where we can be private. Hurry!"

Virginie and Betta exchanged shrugs at the antics of their young friend, excusing her on the grounds of her mixed-up upbringing and youth. Then they forgot their more mature years and scampered up the stairs after her, giggling and chuckling like a pair of twelve-year-olds.

Mr. and Mrs. St. John followed at a more leisurely pace, accompanied by the urbane majordomo. The parents and younger children were installed in a suite of rooms clustered in the south wing of the manor that on one side overlooked the rose gardens (famous throughout the countryside for their unusual specimens) and on the other the broad lawn and topiary garden. In the distance, beyond the rose garden, the glint of water could be seen through the trees. Lucy commented that there was a large ornamental lake with a small island designed for the enjoyment of picnics. The rooms themselves were spacious and elegantly furnished. A large parlor equipped with comfortable settees and lounge chairs, a desk, and a small dining table and chairs was tastefully painted a rich cream color with molding and doors picked out in a soft blue. The drapes and cushion covers were a linen toile patterned in both colors. On a refectory table behind the larger of the two settees was a huge flower arrangement of cream-colored roses and blue irises. Several *sang de boeuf* porcelain vases and cachepots lent splashes of color to the room. On either side of the parlor were doors leading to the bedrooms.

Mr. and Mrs. St. John's room was of a luxury unknown to them. Velvet hangings bordered in gold braid were at the windows and around the bed. The rich burl of the wood furniture reflected a golden light that burnished the braid and was repeated in the gold leaf that outlined the dado and overhead moldings. The Aubusson rug under their feet was a priceless pile of thick, spongy wool, sculptured with green vines and pink roses.

"Oh . . . this is too beautiful . . . I swear I shan't sleep a wink in these surroundings. I shall spend my nights just enjoying the beauty!" was Mrs. St. John's comment.

"You'll soon spend your days sleeping, then," Mr. St. John answered with a wry grin, "and we will never see each other because I shall spend my nights sleeping . . . and then where will we be?"

"That's enough, George. Must you catch me every time I say something a little bit foolish? What's a woman to do with such a guard dog?"

"I don't know what you are going to do, Mama, but *I* wish to see the room Lucy and I shall share, and then I wish very much to have that tea that we were promised." Betta looked around for Virginie. "Let's go, Virginie . . . I'm truly famished. And I want to talk with you." She ended in a whisper private to the young comtesse.

Ascertaining that the St. Johns would be able to find their way to the lower hall if they were left to their own desires, Virginie first pointed out the bell pulls, should they need any service, and then took off with Betta and Lucy.

The three girls ran lightly down the corridor to the suite that had been prepared for them. Again there was a parlor, smaller than the St. Johns' and decorated in pale yellow and white; off the parlor were three bedrooms with small dressing rooms attached. Virginie and Lucy showed Betta to her chamber and pointed out the violet color that went so well with her eyes, the pristine white curtains and bed covers, and the deep blue and violet carpet that would comfort her feet. "See," said Lucy, "there's even a pretty footstool for when your feet are too tired from dancing!"

Betta rapidly straightened her hair and washed her face and hands, and then refreshed, settled down for a quick catching-up with her two friends. Unable to speak yet of the earl, she questioned Lucy about her plans for the future. Before Lucy could answer, Virginie responded with the news that she was sure that Lady Westrich was going to take Lucy under her wing.

"For she is all the crack, you know, and she claims friendship with Lucy's grandfather. She is sure that when he receives her letter and learns what Lucy's father tried to do to Lucy, he will take control and be responsible for her. As head of the family he has the authority to assume guardianship." Virginie gave a satisfied chuckle. "There, I said it all with great perfection, did I not? You see, my English is improving with great speed."

Lucy expressed her pleasure at the thought of going to London under Lady Westrich's aegis. "For she is so elegant, such a leader of the *ton,* and besides, Robin will be coming along to keep us company on the road."

This simple statement set the two older girls off into gales of laughter while Lucy looked at them uncomprehendingly. When she realized that their laughter was as much a release of excitement as aimed at her obvious preference for Robin's company, she joined in.

"Enough, enough. My sides are aching and my eyes are all teary," Betta complained. "Catch your breath, Virginie, and tell me of your plans. . . . Is there anything definite?"

"Oh . . . you mean with my so loving Philippe . . . but of course. We shall make the wedding while you are all here so that you will be my witnesses. Alexander is procuring the special license so that we will not have to wait until the banns are posted. Is this not of the most exciting?" Virginie's face was alight with pleasure. "We are to have

169

the betrothal ball (Alexander insists on calling it that) before you will return to Watton Abbey, and then the wedding will take place the following day."

"I am so pleased and excited for you . . . it's so romantic, to have traveled so far in time and distance to find your heart's love. . . . How I wish . . ." Betta fell silent as she looked into a dreamy, indistinct future.

"This is all very lovely . . . and I *do* want to talk about it at great length, but in the meantime everyone will be waiting tea for us, and I for one am *very* hungry." Lucy began to pull at Betta and Virginie in an effort to hurry them from their perches on the sofa. "We've made lots of plans for a wonderful visit and we can talk about it later, but let's go now . . . I'm starving." The plaintive cry moved the two to accompany Lucy.

As Virginie and Lucy continued chattering, Betta's thoughts turned to the earl. He had looked as though he had wanted to welcome her, but she had been pulled away so quickly, first by Virginie and then by Lucy, that she hadn't yet spoken a word to him. Fancy being in his home for an hour or more without having received a greeting from her host. What to do when he did finally approach her: Would she stammer and blush like the debutante she had been, or would she find that wondrous ease of communication they had shared the night of Albert's ball and the morning after when they had gone riding? A shiver of delight ran over her as she recalled the unusual agitation with which she seemed to respond to some of his glances . . . how peculiar to feel delight and agitation at the same time.

Betta's thoughts carried her down the grand stairway to the threshold of the summer parlor, where the guests had congregated with their host. She was recalled to the present by the voice of the subject of her thoughts speaking her name.

"Miss St. John . . . Betta? Are you all right?" Betta raised her eyes when she realized that she was being addressed. "For a moment you were so far away I thought I had lost you forever." The earl smiled at her with a quizzical look in his eyes. "You haven't allowed me to welcome you to Possingworth yet and already you have left me behind."

"Oh, no. I was just admiring the . . . the . . . wainscoting . . . so unusual." Betta excused her lack of attention, wondering as she did so why she felt the need to prevaricate at all.

"I had not known that you were a student of architecture." The earl's eyes danced. "You must let me show you the other marvels that abound here . . . it will give me great pleasure, you know."

"Oh, yes, architecture. Indeed, I have always . . . that is . . . Shall we have some tea? I haven't said hello to Robin . . . I'm sure he will feel slighted if I don't make my salaam to the Sultan of the Abbey!" Having made her initial stumble, Betta was more able to return to her easy style of speech. I shall just have to speak to him as though he is . . . Albert . . . that's it . . . Albert . . . she thought to herself. And then I shall have no problem . . . unless this foolish stomach of mine keeps doing flip-flops when he looks at me like that.

"I feel that I am losing you again, love. . . . Shall I take you to Robin and your family?" The earl allowed himself to grasp Betta's hand. "Through this door and here you are." He gestured expansively at the gathering. "Robin, here she is . . . your sister."

The room in which the company sat had a pleasant prospect of the rolling lawn and flower borders that were located beyond the expanse of terrace just outside the windows. To create a feeling of outdoors, the decorator had used touches of grass-green and daffodil-yellow in a predominantly off-white chamber. Pots of flowering plants from the greenhouses heightened the illusion of being in an outdoor arbor, and the paintings on the walls were for the most part watercolors of the surrounding landscape. The furniture was in the French style, covered with floral prints or solids in yellow or green. In the warmth of midsummer, the colors created a feeling of coolness and relief from the hot sun outdoors.

The graciousness of the pretty room and the smiling faces turned to her touched the edge of Betta's consciousness. Her attention was distracted by the word "love," with which the earl had addressed her. Perhaps the word was something other than she had heard; yes, that was it, he must have said something like "now" or "lady" or . . . perhaps it was just that he was being playful. He probably behaved so with all his female guests. The informality of being at his country estate would have produced such a lapse. Gradually Betta became aware that she was being spoken to by her father.

"My dear, you seem to be very distracted. Lady Westrich has been trying to attract your attention for these five minutes past." With a smile Mr. St. John recalled Betta to her social duty.

"Alexander, your description fell short of the real woman," Lady Westrich remarked to her nephew. "My dear, come sit beside me. Here's a table where you can place your cup and saucer while you eat some cake. I hate to have to balance a plate on my knee and a cup in my hand. I seem always to spill something and wind up feeling the most maladroit clunch in the room!" As she spoke to Betta she helped the young woman settle herself on the settee

172

next to her, handed her a cup of tea, and indicated that she should make a choice from the tray of cakes that the footman held for her.

"I know exactly what you mean, my lady." Betta turned to her stepmother. "Mama, do you remember the afternoon we visited Lady Gambidge-Stokes?" She turned back to Lady Westrich. "I don't know if you know the lady, but she is the most proper person I have ever met. We were bid to her house so that she could meet me before I made my formal bow, and it was a nightmare! I must have been a veritable comedy of errors just by myself. I tripped going into the drawing room, broke a Sèvres vase when I bumped into a table, and then could not juggle the tea and cakes and wound up dropping cream cakes on lady Gambidge-Stokes and tea all over myself. What a horrible experience! Thank goodness I seem to have outgrown such clumsiness." She started to laugh. "Now watch me make a liar of myself and do the same thing again!"

"I am sure you exaggerate, my dear. You look too graceful to have done anything like that. You must be funning me . . . just like Robin and Alexander. They think I am so guillible that they tell me the greatest whoppers just to see my reaction. But I *am* learning to recognize such moonshine. . . . I shall have my revenge!" Lady Westrich shook her finger at the Petries, warning them of the retribution she would seek.

Elizabeth was amazed to see the correct, fashionable lady behaving with such an ease and comfort of manner. She had never observed such behavior when she had been in London: there she had seen a formality that was almost a caricature of proper manners.

While Betta and Lady Westrich chatted, Philippe and Robin were making plans with Alec and Mr. St. John for the coming days. The earl, knowing of Mr. St. John's deep interest in the flora and fauna of England, was explaining a hunting party to the naturalist.

"Of course, sir, it is usual to hunt with guns, but I thought you might prefer to use a butterfly net and live-traps. There are some rare samples of plants in our woods bordering on the fens and some water plants in the fens that might interest you."

Betta, as she engaged in conversation with the females of the party, unobtrusively studied the earl and her father. They seemed to have a comfortable manner with each other. It puzzled her that they should get on so well, since, as far as she knew, they had not spent too much time together in the few days that Alec had been at Watton Abbey. Of course it could be that Robin was instrumental in bringing them together. He was such a romp that there could be no stiffness in his presence. Betta's gaze moved on to Lucy, who was participating in both conversations, making her comments somewhat incomprehensible to each party, since she would be facing the men as she answered something that Mrs. St. John put to her and alternately facing the women as she added a piece of information for Mr. St. John's enlightenment. At last, in order to alleviate the confusion she was creating, Mrs. St. John arose and asked Lady Westrich to walk with her on the terrace.

"I do think it a waste of this beautiful weather to be always indoors. From what I can see of the grounds, it will be a rewarding experience to view them." She included the younger women in her invitation.

The move from the room broke up the two groups into pairs and triads. Robin moved to Betta's side, using his crutches with great ease. He moved her away from the rest of the gathering, drawing her to one end of the terrace.

"Before Lucy comes over," he began, "I wanted to find

out if her father and that de Selles fellow had visited you again. Lucy was much more upset by the whole thing than she let on, although she played at being a boy with great verve. I think she is and has been crying inside all the time—that her father should be so uncaring."

As always in her dealings with Robin, Betta was surprised at the depth of sensitivity he displayed for the feelings of others. It was amazing to her in light of his brother's character . . . well, what she had been told of his character. Her eyes, more blue than violet this day, studied Robin's face, seeing an overlay of Alexander in the likeness of the younger brother. "Do you care for Lucy, Robin?"

"Well, of course I care for Lucy . . . but you mean in a different way, don't you?" Robin looked thoughtfully at Betta. "I think she's adorable and bright and a real delight . . . but I also think that she is too young to be tied down, and that a season with my Aunt Westrich will give her something pleasant to build her future on. I'm the first *young* man she has known, and she's very grateful to me, even though she doesn't call it that. . . . She should have a broader experience and go to dances and laugh with people and . . . well, then we'll see."

"Robin, how did you get to be so wise . . . and remain so foolish at the same time?" Betta's eyes had a mist of tears in them.

"Why, whatever can you mean . . . ? I'm *always* wise, never foolish . . . well, almost never!" Robin began to clown, unable to bear the tension that he had created. "Just because I gamble and wench and drink and display all the vices that my elders and betters do? 'Tis for the enjoyment and betterment of life, dear Betta. . . . And if such behavior lands me in the St. John household every time, don't look to see me stop!"

"You . . . you . . ." Betta began to laugh. "I must tell you that you are truly the best 'almost brother' I have ever had. . . . I do love you dearly, Robin, and hope you will be my friend forever."

Betta's back was turned to the terrace as she stood in front of Robin, speaking with him. She was unaware of the approach of the earl, but Robin, catching sight of the thundercloud on his face, was quick to explain Betta's declaration of love.

"Did you hear, Alec . . . she has declared her love . . . as a sister. The most beautiful woman I shall ever meet, and she loves me like a brother. I shall kill myself. No, no . . . I shall become a hermit and live in the woods. . . . Or shall I become a wastrel? And when I lie dying of unrequited love you shall find me and feel an abysmal guilt because you have spurned me!" Robin enlarged upon his act, carefully gauging Alec's temper. When he was satisfied that his brother had accepted his nonsense, he gracefully bowed himself away, leaving Betta still in the throes of laughter at his performance, and Alec, thundercloud now gone, contemplating his sudden jealousy.

Still chuckling at Robin's histrionics, Betta commented that the stage had lost as great a comedian in Robin as Edmond Kean was a tragedian.

"Can you not see Robin's gravedigger played to Kean's Hamlet? He would steal the scene from the great one!" Alec agreed. "And now, what would you like to do? May I show you around the estate?"

Before Betta could answer, the clamor of young voices could be heard. "I think any plans you may make will have to be set aside for the moment, my lord. More urgent business is at hand."

"Whatever it is, it sounds as if Letty is winning . . . at least her voice is loudest!" The earl moved swiftly toward the hubbub. "Here, here . . . what's all this? Why such an uproar? Is this the way young ladies and gentlemen behave?"

Rather shamefaced, but still carrying on, the three French boys and the three English girls came to a halt in front of the earl, who was now attended by his houseguests.

"Sir." Albert came running up. "I tried to stop them, but you know what Letty is like . . . and she thought Robin had been insulted by Étienne."

"Insulted, how?" was the astonished rejoinder to Albert's statement.

"We-ell, Étienne claims that you (he calls you Papa the earl all the time) were braver because of the trip to France and you saved their lives and had such adventures. And Letty says that Robin is, because he didn't even cry out when the doctor set his leg and has been so good and, and . . . that's about it." Albert looked somewhat embarrassed at being drawn into the affair.

"Really, Letty." Mrs. St. John looked at her youngster.

"Étienne, Étienne . . . is this how you show these English the courtesy of a true Frenchman?" Virginie looked at the straight-backed youngster with surprise and a strong hint of laughter in her eyes.

"Have I been insulted?" the earl asked with a twitch of his lips. "Robin, how shall we resolve this question?"

"I think this should be shelved for the moment . . . just until I can give it my full attention, of course, and the children should be shown the maze. We can have a game . . . the boys against the girls. Whoever gets out of the maze first shall have an extra cream cake for dessert tonight." Surrounded by clamoring children, Robin and Lucy led the parade to the maze. Robin explained that he and Lucy would show them to the center and they must find their way out. To make things fair, because Charlot was so little, Albert would be a member of the boys' team.

"What a genius that brother of mine is. And again, he surprises me with his quick understanding of children." The earl spoke to Betta as he casually guided her away from the maze and toward the rose garden. "I think his stay with your family did a great deal to bring him to maturity. He's no longer that harum-scarum lad that left London in a rage . . . how long ago was it? . . . two months?"

"Yes, I quite agree. My lord . . . are we not going through the maze with the children?" Betta looked up at the earl with a quick smile. "Or is there a back entrance to it?"

"No, my dear Betta. *We* are going to take advantage of everyone's preoccupation with the children and their trip through the maze and *we* shall view the roses. . . . They are said to be the finest blooms in the county, you know."

In great amity with each other, Betta and Alec strolled across the lawn toward the rose garden and arbors. Not quite holding hands (the earl decided it was too soon for that), they moved with slow steps, occasionally swaying toward one another, lightly touching at the shoulders or arms, enjoying the sounds of the countryside . . . the distant hum of bees, the liquid trill of a meadowlark, the rustle of leaves in the breeze. The sweet scent of newly cut grass mixed with the heavier perfume of flowers seemed to take part in separating them from the frame of their everyday selves. There was a gentle quality to the scene that was hypnotic in its effect. Betta felt as though she could walk like this with Alec forever. He wished for the moment to arrive when she would trust him always as she did now. Gradually, as they left the terrace and the rest of the party farther behind, they moved closer toward each other, and almost without volition their hands reached out and clasped.

Occasionally Betta would ask a question about the greenhouses or the woods or some piece of sculpture that caught her eye, and quietly Alec would murmur some words of information. For the most part they were content to let the mood of the afternoon wash over them without conversation.

On the terrace, Lady Westrich and Mrs. St. John stood talking together.

"Robin and Alec have told me so much about your family . . . especially about your daughters. The youngest ones, I mean." Lady Westrich moved to a marble bench that was placed next to the balustrade. "Do come and sit down with me for a while. Unless you'd rather retire to your rooms to rest . . ."

"Oh, no, I feel perfectly fine. The air is so lovely out here. . . . Just smell those pine trees. . . . One wouldn't think the scent would carry so far, but I suppose with the breeze coming in this direction . . . Such a placid view . . ." Mrs. St. John sat down with a sigh of contentment. "I must say that I love my home, but it's always so pleasant to visit . . . especially when one visits so fine an establishment as Possingworth."

"And the location is so convenient to Watton Abbey, should Alec and Elizabeth make a match of it. No, don't look so surprised. I've known that something happened to Alec while he was at your home. When Robin came back here all he could talk about was the wonderful Betta. For a while I thought it was Robin who was thinking of parson's mousetrap, but he quickly informed me that he has no desire to set up a nursery at such a young age." Lady Westrich patted Mrs. St. John's hand. "I wish you to know that I have begun to love your oldest daughter

179

already . . . not that my opinion matters one speck to Alec. He is a very opinionated man!"

"I don't know whether Betta has realized that she is falling in love with your nephew, but it's as plain as the nose on her face that she is. I trust Alec's good sense to know that he must not move too hastily . . . but then he already suggested that to my husband." Amelia looked at Lady Westrich with a smile on her fine features. "It certainly sets my mind at ease to know that you approve the match, my lady. From what Alec told us, you are very important to him, and I know your good opinion means a great deal."

Betta's mother and Alec's aunt continued their conversation, making plans to engage Betta's affections for Alec and to awaken her to her desire to become the Earl of Halwick's wife. They drew up schemes designed to give Betta a greater understanding of the earl and schemes to give the two time to be alone. They planned events for the coming days and parties for two or four or more for the coming evenings. In all, they had a most enjoyable time arranging for the future happiness of their loved ones.

Chapter 18

The quiet country sounds were lost in the eruption of cries of "we won, we won," "you cheated," and calls for Robin and Papa the earl. The tumble of children scolding and fighting brought several of the adults at a run. Faces flushed with anger and wet with tears of frustration turned toward the parents and relatives in appeal. The tall figure of the earl ran lightly to the angered children while his deep voice called out a single command. He stood surrounded by the six little ones with Albert trying to catch his attention from a few feet away. Betta, coming out of the bemused state she had been in while walking with him, compared him to a St. George surrounded by elves. The stern look on his face was belied by the twinkle in his eye as he listened to the complaints that the boys had won the maze race because of prior experience in running the labyrinth and because they were aided by Albert, who shouldn't be made to side against his sisters.

"Now, you can't have it both ways. Either one or the other. And it really isn't ladylike to call Robin a liar, which is what you are doing when you say that the boys have prior knowledge of the secret of getting through the maze." The earl then turned his attention to the little boys. "And I am surprised at you, to say such things about your guests . . . and lady guests at that. This is not the way of

181

a gentleman. I wish you all to apologize to each other first, then we shall all have a cooling drink and you will go to your rooms to rest for a while. No more arguing . . . I command it!" The earl beckoned to two footmen who had been hovering at the edge of the garden and bid them conduct the youngsters to the nursery area, where their various attendants could take charge of them. He omitted Albert from the group of children with a direct invitation to accompany the adults to the terrace, an act of kindness that served only to further the young man's high opinion of his idol.

Virginie and Philippe were already sitting with Mrs. St. John and Lady Westrich when Alec and Betta arrived accompanied by Robin, Lucy, and Albert. Virginie was explaining to Mrs. St. John that she and Philippe were to make their marriage vows on the following Sunday and that she wished the St. John family to be present, since they were her only friends other than the Petries.

"The dress I will wear for the wedding is one of Lady Westrich's . . . oh, so beautiful. It is of the color of gooseberries with the blond lace triming, with the bonnet of the same color of the lace, with the pale-green and blond plumes . . . very discreet, *très comme il faut.*" Virginie refused to allow the arrival of her friends to interrput her rhapsodizing on the coming ceremony. Her enthusiasm was contagious, and soon the women of the party were drawing up plans for the proposed ball preceding the event. Somehow, as Betta offered her ideas for the party, she began to visualize herself walking down the aisle to a shadowy figure whom she couldn't quite identify.

Her thoughts were interrupted by Albert's reminding Robin that he had promised to take them on a tour of the dungeons of the ancient fourteenth-century keep that was the original structure at Possingworth. It was not a part of the present building, but was kept in usable condition as a retreat for the occasional artist or writer who visited the estate. In fact, the earl told his listeners, it was here that Constable had sketched some of his tranquil country scenes.

Mr. St. John cautioned Albert not to bother himself about the sightseeing, then admitted that he would enjoy seeing the dungeon keep himself. "I must say that I haven't seen one that belonged to a private family; didn't think there were any still about."

It was agreed that the dinner hour was too close for this visit at present, but that the following afternoon would be a splendid time to go.

"I shall let Robin conduct the tour for those who wish to see the gloomy place while I take those who prefer the beauty of the outdoors on a picnic to Fortune's Island," the earl announced.

"Oh, that's not fair."

"What's Fortune's Island?"

"I never did like dank, dirty old dungeons anyway."

The protests and comments became too numerous to be discernible to the earl. Betta decided it was to his credit that he was not being arrogant in his plans, but just wanted to offer the most enjoyable pastime to his guests when he offered to save the dungeons for a rainy day. "We should take advantage of this weather to enjoy the outdoors. I'm sure it will rain soon enough," he remarked.

Robin seconded him by starting the story of the island with a description of the family fortunes during the time of the Roundheads. "As you have undoubtedly learned in your history books," he began, addressing the members of the group, "that was a period of great severity. Many noblemen were deprived of their homes, their lands, and even their lives. Our family was fortunate in that we were

183

left with our lives . . . or rather, the then earl was left with his life and the lives of his family. He remained true to the Crown and left for France to be with Charles the Second. In 1660, when Charles was invited back to England to resume the monarchy, Great-great-great-etc.-grandfather Halwick returned and was rewarded by the reestablishment of his grant of nobility and his properties. The grounds were enlarged by special decree, and as a personal gift the King ordered an ornamental lake to be created for the pleasure of the Earl of Halwick. The island was a part of the lake, and in honor of the change in his life, great, great, etc. named it Fortune's Island, and so it's been called ever since."

"Bravo . . . we have a storyteller in our midst." Virginie applauded.

"Robin, you did that very well." Betta seconded the applause. "Perhaps *you* should take up novel writing and I shall take up sewing."

"It's a possibility. . . . I still don't know what kind of a writer you are, sister. You never did let me read that vaunted novel!" Robin retorted with a grin. "I think, though, that I prefer historical writing. . . . Who knows? Perhaps someday I shall do something about it."

"Are we all agreed, then? A picnic on the island for tomorrow?" The earl looked questioningly at his guests.

The agreement was unanimous and hearty. Upon reaching the decision, the members of the group began to disperse to their rooms to rest and change for dinner. Before she had a chance to catch up with Virginie and Lucy, Betta was maneuvered away from the rest of the party by some swift intervention on the part of the earl.

"Before you make other plans for the morning," he said to her, "I wanted to ask you to join me in a ride. We have a new colt that you might like to see, and I would like you to see the other pond . . . your father might like to fish there." Alec couldn't seem to stop talking. Betta looked up at him with her head tilted to the side. Why, he might almost be chattering, she thought. It's almost as if he is less at ease with me than I with him. Strange . . . Her thought faded as her eyes once again became entangled with his. He reached to take her hand and brought it to his lips. The gentle pressure and warmth of the kiss that he placed in her palm started a tremor that swept through her whole body, leaving her weak and unable to move. Her eyes widened in surprise just as he let go of her hand and carefully turned her toward the door with a pressure on her waist. She felt a struggle within herself to stay where she was that stopped almost as it started. What kind of behavior was this for a proper young woman? She moved along the terrace, guided by his hand at her back, almost as though they were doing an open step in the waltz, she wishing that they would never reach the doorway, praying that they would get there before she fainted from an excess of emotion. What kind of a ninny am I . . . to feel like this . . . ? And yet . . . and yet . . .

The morning ride that Alec proposed was the first of many. In the ensuing days of informal association Betta was able to relax in his presence. With a growth of poise, her ready wit and lively manner were uncovered to her new friends.

When a few days later Betta ran down the stairs calling a morning greeting to Alec, he looked up at her, wondering at the delightful change from hesitant, fearfully shy girl to a more confident, adorable woman. She had come to enjoy the game of courtship with a gusto that might have been unbecoming had it not been so innocent. Her former fear of engaging in social activities had completely disappeared as she became assured of Alec's attention and regard. The zest with which she lived gave each day a flavor that brought new satisfaction to Alec's life. He felt that the time was rapidly approaching when he could speak to Betta of his love; even though he had not yet spoken in words, he knew that she was aware of his regard.

"Shall we have a good breakfast, my lord, or just break the fast with the thought of those delicious foods to bring us back from our ride more swiftly?" Betta's hand on the newel post steadied her balance as she swung around the stairway, giving Alec a provocative look from her violet eyes. She was able to chuckle with satisfaction at the approving response on his face.

"Oh, at least rolls and coffee before we escape the crowd," Alec answered her. "As much as I'd like to, I cannot live on love alone."

Betta was less nervous at Alec's mention of love than she had been, although it still sent a frisson of . . . something . . . up her spine to know that he was speaking of his love for her. With pleasure and anticipation, she allowed herself to look forward to hearing his declaration. More and more she would permit herself to think of the glory of being Halwick's wife. Their minds seemed to find such a meeting ground . . . so close were their thoughts that at times they would speak the same words in unison. She had dreamed of such a closeness, but had never hoped to find it. Spinsterhood had been the preferable choice in lieu of that focus of two minds, one for the other.

"Come along, then. I shall pour your coffee and you shall butter my toast. Only let's hurry before that gaggle of scamps catches us." Betta's eyes sparkled as she walked into the breakfast room ahead of Alec. The earl followed closely, keeping a tight rein on his desire to sweep her into his arms and cover her face with kisses. He gave himself leave to touch her cheek lightly before moving to the sideboard to help himself to an assortment of breads.

They ate quickly, wanting only to be uninterrupted in their blossoming love. The mood was broken by the hullabaloo of children's voices coming from the upper landing. Putting his finger to his lips, Alec quickly led Betta away from the table and through the butler's pantry to the back hall.

"We'll do much better to escape through here," he told her, "than if we try to run past them and out the great hall. They've been tracking us these past four days, and today I wish to be free of them. You shall concentrate on me, my dear, no one else!"

Betta found herself walking through the kitchen garden to the side terrace. She smiled at his adept escape from the tyranny of the seven youngsters.

Ahead of them stood a groom holding the earl's stallion and the young filly that had been Betta's choice to ride. Alec threw Betta up into the saddle and moved to mount his horse. He looked at the groom, about to direct him to release the animals. To his surprise, the man was unknown to him, an unusual happening at Possingworth. It was Alec's habit to interview all employees personally.

"What's your name?" he asked abruptly. Upon being answered with a gruff "Corby, milord," accompanied by a pull at his cap, Alec continued questioning the groom about his term of work on the estate, not quite liking the manner of the man. He found nothing in the answers he heard to make him ill at ease, so decided to leave the matter for the moment.

"Let go the horses, Corby; we're ready to go. We'll leave them in the home paddock when we return. You'll hear the whistle when you're needed to tend them." Then, with a challenge to Betta for a race, Alec wheeled his horse around and took off.

The horses seemed to fly down the path, so rapid was their gallop. A silvery laugh trailed back to the watching groom. The riders soon slowed to a walk, exhilarated by the short gallop, the winelike morning air, and their enjoyment of being with each other. There were moments of contented silence between them, followed by discussion that included personal histories, politics, travel, the arts . . . any and all of the subjects that occupy the minds of bright, alert people.

They reached a sunlit glade in the wooded landscape and dismounted to rest in the enchanted setting for a while. Betta sat down on a large boulder, removing her dashing white peaked hat, remarking that the plumes that wound round her chin were excessively warm.

"I wonder why women are required to cover their heads even in the informality of their own gardens. . . . I suppose it's really to protect one's skin from the sun. Whiteness is considered so ladylike," she mused aloud. "And yet I have always thought I looked rather more attractive slightly browned from the sun. Fashion is so difficult to deal with."

Alexander started to chuckle at this ingenuous statement. "But so important to live with. It's like the manners that we are taught to live by: some of them necessary to ease the perplexities of our daily lives, and some to . . . one doesn't even know the why or wherefore of the rule."

Betta agreed with the earl. "It makes friendships so difficult sometimes. . . . If you consider it, our being here without a groom or chaperone is out of all prescriptions for proper behavior, and yet"—she cast her lovely eyes at the handsome man standing before her—"I must confess to feeling comfortable with you. Which in itself is odd considering how I didn't care for you a bit when we first met."

A burst of laughter left the earl's lips as he remembered the furious young goddess he had tangled with on his arrival at Watton Abbey. "I am relieved to hear you say that you feel 'comfortable' with me. . . ." He sat himself down on the grass at her feet. "I would like to hope that you feel more than comfortable, Betta." He took her hand and began to play with her fingers, examining them as though they were the first fingers he had ever seen. "I confess that my feelings, while they include 'comfortable,' are rather more warm than that." He glanced at her face, trying to find an indication of her response to his less than subtle hint as to the true state of his emotions. Her head was turned slightly away from him, giving him a view of her delicately molded cheek and the line of her eyebrow. Her eyes were resolutely hidden by the pale cover of her eyelids. He was encouraged by the fact that she had not withdrawn her fingers from his, nor had she jumped up and run away from him as he had been afraid she might.

"If you would rather not hear me talk about this any further, love, just say so . . . I will understand. And I promise not to harbor a grudge against you." He waited for her answer.

Pure joy flooded through Betta's being at Alec's words. Her response to the idea that he loved her came with a surge of excitement so strong that she herself was astonished. Never had she thought herself capable of the degree of ardor his words had kindled, and she was intoxicated by it and at the same time somewhat disconcerted that the proper young woman that she supposed herself to be should be capable of such transports. Her cheeks turned fiery rose and then blanched; her fingers tingled where his hand touched hers. All the symptoms that she had previously felt—the loss of breath, the weakness of her limbs, the pounding of her heart—were once more upon her to the point that she felt she would swoon. Then her wry sense of humor saved her. She turned to Alec, the flush once again staining her cheeks: "You are most unfair, my lord, to provoke me without warning like this. Even to save my soul, how could I possibly put down such a generous attitude? You will not hold a grudge against me, indeed. And what if I hold a grudge against you for taking up the subject in such an informal setting? I should have expected you on bended knee, at least, in the best parlor!" She looked at his startled face and let out a tiny giggle. "I would love to hear you. . . . I should be ashamed to be so forward, but I like to hear you call me 'love.' "

Alec had risen to his feet in response to her first few words, sure that she was about to give him a thorough set-down, but when he heard the last words he swept her to her feet and drew her into his arms. "You are the most adorable, outrageous, winsome witch in the world . . . and I love you, my Betta." His lips met hers for a long moment, until he felt her arms steal about his neck. He raised his head, his brilliant sapphire eyes holding hers. "You are my delight . . . but I think you will lead me a merry dance before you have shaped me to suit your pleasure."

Her arms tightly clasped around his neck, Betta studied Alec's face. "I can't imagine that I once thought you cold and uncaring. You'll never know . . ."

"Tell me all," Alec cried. "I know I loved you from the moment I saw you stop your horse, in a flaming rage at this upstart who had almost run you down!" He nuzzled her neck, setting small kisses along the lines of her jaw.

Breathless from the delicate tremors his lips caused, she

began to tell him about seeing him in London years ago. She told him how she had decided to use him as a villain in her projected novel.

"Novel? My dearest—you are a writer?"

"No, not really. I think I wrote for company. It was so much easier to create a world on paper than to go out into the real world." Betta let her hand wander over Alec's face, outlining his eyebrows and lips, tracing his nose and jaw. Carried away, she turned her face up for his kisses, reveling in the sensuous pleasure of his touch. She wanted only to stay in his arms, feeling the touch of his hands, the warmth of his ardor.

After a long kiss that left them both flushed with passion, Alec said with a rueful smile, "If we keep this up, love, we are liable to bed before we wed . . . and I will not have that. I want everything perfect for you—so move away from me, my dear delight, while I am still in control!"

Blushing a little at herself, Betta allowed Alec to seat her once more, keeping his arms around her and pulling her head to his shoulder. They sought respite from the violence of their emotions. Quietly they continued to explore their new status, discussing the reactions of their families and friends.

"You know that Robin decided this was to be our destiny before ever I came to Watton Abbey," the earl told his love. "I arrived thinking that you had trapped him by playing the helpful, tender nurse to his ailing patient. Then I was afraid that he did have strong feelings for you . . . more so, because I began to realize that *my* love was engaged. Why do you smile?"

"I think *my* love was engaged when I saw you at Almack's five years ago . . . and ever after there was no one who could come up to the perfection I had been exposed to. You could even say that I waited for you." Betta bent slightly to place a kiss on Alec's head. "But I fought my partiality for your person and assigned you a place in my novel as a villain." Betta wasn't quite ready to confess her belief that the earl was a part of Jeremy Wingate's infamy and the subsequent unjust accusations she had made about him.

The quiet of the woods was broken by the sound of a horse galloping toward them. They stood up to see who was in such a hurry to intrude upon this enchanted hour. To their surprise it was Corby, the new groom.

"My lord, my lord," he called to them while still a distance away, "there's been an accident at the entrance." He jumped down from his horse and proceeded to enlighten them as to his sudden appearance. "I was driving the supply wagon and was just turning out of the gate when this coach came traveling down the high road as though the devil himself were after it. I couldn't pull up the horses in time, and there was a real mix-up."

"Why were you driving the supply wagon?" the earl asked in a hard voice. "Houseman is usually the driver when the housekeeper goes to pick up supplies."

"Houseman was taking care of one of the horses, my lord, so I took it upon myself to drive . . . to ease the burden for him, sir."

The sly implication that the groom cared more for Houseman's well-being than did the earl did little to lessen Alec's dislike for the man. He bade the man continue his story.

"Well, my lord, the passenger from the coach, a Mrs. Epping, was a-fainting and a-carrying on something fierce, so I sent her coachman . . . he wasn't hurt at all . . . to fetch Mr. Sedgely and somebody else to help decide what to do. One of the women took the lady up to the house while me and the coachman looked over the coach to see if it could be righted without too much trouble. We got it up, but the axle on the front end snapped when it turned over . . . must have been a weakness in the wood . . . and now she can't go no place without it gets fixed first. So Sedgely sent me to ask you to come back to the house first thing."

"What a muddle. . . . I sincerely hope that this Mrs. Epping has suffered nothing more than a shaking up. You take yourself back to Sedgely, Corby, and tell him I will be right behind you with Miss St. John." Alec waved the groom on and turned to help Betta mount her horse. "My love, I am so sorry to have our time together disrupted. The thought of a stranger becoming a member of our party at this time doesn't please me too much either. But we shall weather it . . . we have much time ahead for interludes like this, and even more pleasant ones."

Betta accepted a last touch of the earl's lips on hers, not wanting to return to pressures of caring for the unexpected guest and the explanations of her newly found standing with her beloved Alec. Putting a cheerful face on the matter, she gave him a dazzling smile and a toss of her head. "Still the forward one . . . I am not so sure that I should accept your advances, sir. I have my reputation to think about, you know."

"You need not worry about your reputation, my girl, but just you wait . . . I shall give you other things . . . not to worry about precisely, but to participate in . . . and even to love!" Alec tossed Betta up onto her sidesaddle, then mounted his horse. "Come, now, a race to see who gets to take care of the problem of the mysterious Mrs. Epping first."

193

Chapter 19

The beautiful auburn-haired widow gasped as the vinaigrette bottle was passed under her nose by a solicitous Virginie. Anxiously Lady Westrich and Mrs. St. John chafed the stranger's hands, trying to bring her back to consciousness. Her swoon had seemed to be so deep that they feared that she had suffered severe physical harm in the unfortunate accident that had brought her into the environs of Possingworth.

"Ohhh, where am I? What has happened to me?" the swooning woman moaned. Her eyelids fluttered, then slowly lifted to reveal eyes that seemed to have a measuring quality to them. Virginie reached out, exchanging the vinaigrette for a small glass of brandy, which she held to the woman's lips. "Here, drink a bit of this, it will make you feel better."

The widow drank the brandy, which revived her enough so that she was able to push herself up into a sitting position on the green figured settee where she had been placed by the footmen. Gracefully she raised a hand to her forehead, pushing back the somewhat tumbled weight of her hair. She looked around at the circle of concerned faces surrounding her, letting her eyes linger on Philippe and Robin before regarding the women in the group.

"I . . . was there an accident? How did I get here

. . . and where am I?" she asked in a weak, fluting voice. "My head, and my back . . . Ohh, I am in pain."

"You were hurt, madam, when your coach and the estate supply wagon collided. I don't know how it came to happen . . . a new groom . . . carelessness . . . but we will try to make you comfortable. There is no question but that you will stay here until you feel sufficiently recovered to continue your journey." Lady Westrich spoke as the earl's hostess. "As soon as you feel stronger, you must tell us who you are so that we may inform your family as to your whereabouts."

"You are too kind . . . but please tell me, where am I?" The woman lay back against the cushions of the sofa, looking expectantly at Lady Westrich.

Before her ladyship could answer, Alec entered the conversation. He and Betta had been standing in the doorway watching the proceedings.

"You are in my home, madam. I am the Earl of Halwick, Alexander Petrie. Around you are members of my family and my guests. When you are more recovered they will be properly presented to you. I wish to express my deep regret at the carelessness of my groom, which led to this unfortunate incident, and to tell you that any expense incurred in the repair of your vehicle will be taken care of."

"Too kind . . . I do not wish to make a burden of myself, but if I could just rest here for a day or so until I feel more the thing. I don't think I could travel any further with my back in such pain." The lady's voice became fainter as she finished her sentence. "My name is Winifred Epping. If you will just have a little patience with me, I will tell you my story. . . . But could I first beg a cup of tea . . . I think it will help to revive me more quickly. . . ."

"Oh, you poor thing. Of course you shall have tea

. . . and anything else you feel up to having." Virginie sent Sedgely, who had been hovering on the edge of the circle, to order the tea and some other refreshments. "We will have it for you in a moment. You must rest quietly for a while . . . so you will be better able to sit up to enjoy your tea." Virginie turned to the others. "Move away, now," she commanded. "This lady must rest *tranquillement*, and having *tout le monde* to stare at her does not make for this."

As everyone moved away from her, murmuring softly to each other, Mrs. Epping examined the various faces. They had accepted her as the victim of an accident, not knowing that the whole event had been planned carefully by the Duc de Selles and arranged with Corby's assistance. That was why he had been driving the wagon. . . . There had been no actual accident; the duc's men had overturned the coach and then broken the axle. She had arranged herself artfully half in and half out of the coach so that it would look as though she had been seriously injured. And now she had broached the stronghold and would soon be in a position of intimacy to do her damage. Even had she had qualms about upsetting the lives of the people involved, she was too afraid of the duc to change any of his instructions. His subtle intimation of the results of treachery bound her to her appointed task. She relaxed against the cushions. Her first step was to engage the attention of the earl. With this in mind, she watched his movements until he turned toward her and she was able to catch his eye. With a slight gesture of her head, she beckoned him to her side.

"I feel as though in some way this occurence is my fault," she started. "No, no. Do not contradict me . . . I know a man does not like to let a woman accept responsibility." She gazed up at him from beneath sweeping eyelashes. "Won't you sit here"—she gestured to the foot of the sofa—"then I won't have to hurt my neck trying to look up at you."

Alec was somewhat taken aback at her informality . . . but being accustomed to having women try to attach him, did not place too much significance on her action. He was not interested in any case. . . . He had his Betta, and she was and would be his life. He thanked Mrs. Epping but refused the sofa, saying that his weight on the seat might cause her back discomfort. He drew a small straight-backed chair to the side of the couch and sat down to listen to her.

"I fear I've interrupted a family party," she said. "Will you tell me who everyone is. So much easier than being introduced all at one time. Especially, who is the beautiful young woman who came in with you? She has a certain glow about her that makes her most attractive, and a sweet look that makes one wish for her acquaintance."

Again the earl felt that he was listening to an actress reading lines, then decided that the visitor's way of speaking was a result of the weakness she felt owing to the fracas with the wagon. With a pleasant smile he began to enumerate the names and some of the qualities of the people in the room. Just as particularly as Mrs. Epping had asked about Betta, so was the earl as particular in not singling her out for special attention. To the onlookers, the manner in which Mrs. Epping and Alec spoke seemed to suggest an intimacy between them. Still aglow from the hour she had spent with Alec, Betta was surprised that he had not bid any of the members of the party to come and be properly introduced to Mrs. Epping. One could almost suppose that he was keeping her to himself . . . especially if one noticed the way they were smiling and nodding at one another . . . and speaking in such a cordial way for two who had only just met.

Gradually the lovely light that had been in Betta's eyes began to fade. She was still too insecure to be able to cope with the green-eyed monster, jealousy. As she thought back to the rendezvous in the wood, she felt perhaps that she had been a bit too free with her favors in allowing the earl to kiss her. But then her good sense caught up with her and she began to recall the sound of Alec's voice as he told her of his love, which recalled to mind the unusual (for her) questions that were hers as she responded to his kisses. Surely he was just being a thoughtful host in speaking quietly with Mrs. Epping. The thing to do was to gather up Lucy and Virginie and to present themselves to the lady. Then she could suggest that Virginie see that a chamber be prepared for the uninvited guest. That course of action would surely be more appropriate than standing here worrying about . . . things.

Before she acted upon her resolution, Mrs. St. John, who had been watching and interpreting the play of changes on Betta's face, moved to the side of the reclining woman.

"My dear Mrs. Epping, I am Amelia St. John, a guest of Lord Halwick's. May I lend you the service of my maid. . . . I am sure you would like to lie down for a while after such a disastrous happening. Men don't usually appreciate the fact that we are the weaker sex and do have to consider our sensibilities in the light of the urgencies of our lives." Mrs. St. John smiled kindly at the stricken woman while she spun a farrago of nonsense designed to removed Mrs. Epping from the room without being too obvious about it.

"Thank you so much for your kindness, dear Mrs. St. John," was the sweetly voiced response, "but I do have my maid with me. She is probably still at the coach . . . waiting to be told what to do. If someone could fetch her for me, I should like to retire for a while. The earl . . . so thoughtful . . . has bade me welcome until I feel more myself." There was a gleam of triumph in the lady's eyes that Mrs. St. John remarked upon to herself. Something smoky was taking place, and she would be sure to ferret out the whys and wherefores of the game. Especially since Betta seemed in some way to be concerned.

Alec called to two of the footmen standing at attention in the great hall to come and carry Mrs. Epping to the chamber assigned for her comfort. He assured her that her maid would be sent to her immediately upon her arrival at the house, but until that moment one of the parlormaids would help her.

"Too kind . . . always the most . . . Really, my lord . . . thank you." The flurry of words were spoken in a soft, almost whispery voice, with much fluttering of lashes and telling glances. Mrs. Epping, once the footmen had lifted her, held out her hand to the earl with a look of promise. "I shall see you . . . later, my lord?" The slightly questioning sentence was almost an invitation to a late-hour tryst.

"Yes, of course, Mrs. Epping, we will meet again at the dinner table," was the crisp answer. "If you should decide it will be too much for you to make the descent to the dining room, the chef will prepare a tray for you and we will see you in the morning." Alec refused the widow's implied invitation, being too downy to get caught in such an obvious trap. He gestured to the footmen to carry his guest to her room, and with a sigh of relief turned back to his favorite people.

When Nettie, Mrs. Epping's maid, arrived at her mistress's chamber, she found her to be as hearty as when she had left the inn earlier that day. She was pacing the floor, impatient to get on with her plan. She greeted Nettie

199

crossly, upbraiding her for taking so long to arrive at the mansion.

"Why, how can you call me to task for that, when it was yourself that told me to wait at the coach until I was sent for? And a proper job of it I did; cried and carried on as though I thought you was dying. And when I spoke to the butler I told him I was glad that this turned out to be the Earl of Halwick's home, even though we hadn't known it to be. Sort of pretended that we had met him before without saying so outright . . . just as you told me.

"Do you think he believed? Well, it doesn't matter if he didn't. He's sure to spread the tale to some of the other servants. That will do for a beginning. Petrie and that girl Betta came in smelling of June and roses. . . . He's probably about to pop the question, if he hasn't already. Well, we'll see what we can do to change her opinion of him . . . the duc's plan seems to be well able to run true. It had better come off or I shall be in deep trouble . . . I'm truly afraid of him. We must be successful. We *must!*" The suddenly fearful woman looked at Nettie as though asking her for help. She had done many things in her life that would not hold up under close scrutiny, and she had been involved with many a scoundrel, but never had she had to partner one so evil as the Duc de Selles. His satisfaction came from the hurt he did to others . . . and he had no qualms about the innocence of those who came to his attention. Better for her to ignore any personal feelings she might have and do exactly as he had told her.

"You will have to make yourself a friend of Miss St. John's maid," she directed Nettie, "and you shall have to find out something about the habits of the earl from his man. I need the information so that I can speak of him as though from intimate knowledge. When you can, hint that we have known each other for several years and perhaps that there is even a child in the background. Yes . . . that should be a very potent factor in changing Miss St. John's regard. Now you will have to press my dress for the evening. It's too bad I am supposed to be a widow. At least I don't have to appear in black. I can wear half-mourning. The gray and white with the double ruching around the hem . . . it has an almost naive look . . . should give me a purity that I will carry out with my sighing away and swooning manner." Mrs. Epping, satisfied with her choice of gown for the evening, sent the woman about her business.

The next few hours saw the laying of the groundwork for the promoting of the duc's nefarious plans. Nettie ingratiated herself with the household servants, and in particular with Polly, the young abigail assigned to wait on Betta. She offered her services in the guise of an older, more experienced person giving help to one newly on the job. Since she did it in a manner so casual and without any undue attention, she had no trouble winning the girl over. She was able to offer advice on the best way to press a ruffle, the best way to affix a feather to a headband, and the best way to remove a stain from silk. When put into practice, the advice won Betta's praise and made the abigail grateful to Nettie.

After dinner that evening, Mrs. Epping began to insinuate herself into Betta's good graces. She spun a fine tale about her widowhood and the care she had given her elderly husband in his final illness. Her manner was so confiding and so sorrowful that her listener was in full sympathy with her. The actress then began delicately to probe Betta's relationship with the master of Possingworth. She observed the rosy tint that stained Betta's cheeks as the young woman gently but determinedly changed the subject to less personal matters. Carefully the older woman began to insert general observations on the character of rakes and runabouts into the conversation.

"Of course there are those who will profess to being reformed from their outré behavior," she commented, "but are actually doing so only to gain their dishonorable objective. Oh, my dear"—she leaned confidingly toward her listener—"if I could but tell you . . . The earl . . ." She let her voice die away, not having said a thing, but having suggested everything.

Betta's face paled as she heard the woman's words. Was it possible that Alec's courtship was merely a game to him? It didn't seem real . . . that he would so deceive her. . . .

"Mrs. Epping, I believe you do not only the earl, but yourself, a great injustice by hinting and suggesting such vile behavior. He has shown me and my family nothing but the most gracious kindness. . . . Why, look at what he did for Virginie. . . ." Betta's confidence in the earl's fidelity grew stronger as she spoke.

"But, my dear girl, of course you would think that . . . it is to your credit that you are so loyal." The treacherous guest looked at Betta with great pity. "I believe he was alone with the comtesse for some weeks. . . ."

"Oh, no, I will not accept that . . . not Virginie. Mrs. Epping, please excuse me, I have the migraine. I . . . I shall see you in the morning. Pray forgive me. . . ." Somewhat distraught, Betta arose from her seat to leave the room.

From across the salon Alexander and Robin had been discussing the arrival of the beautiful widow. They spoke softly together, not wanting their guests to overhear their words.

"She's a tough 'un," was Robin's comment. "Very beautiful, but she looks as though this might be her second or third time round."

"There's something smoky about her and I can't quite tell what it is," the earl answered. His eyes took on a steely look as he noted Betta's growing agitation. "She's up to something, but I don't know what or why. I don't think I've ever seen her before, or heard of her, for that matter." He clapped his brother on the shoulder. "Keep close to her if you can. Perhaps your youthful charm will appeal to her!"

Robin stared at his brother with a startled look on his face. "Get away with you. What kind of fustian are you talking? Youthful charms!" Robin was distracted by Betta's abrupt departure from the salon. "Where did Betta go off to? Alec, something's going on . . . she looked ready to faint."

"You go over to the widow and be charming, I'll send Virginie after Elizabeth. Perhaps she'll be able to find out just what the lady is up to. Take Lucy with you . . . our *inconnue* may fall victim more easily if you disguise your intention by hiding behind an innocent young thing. I think I'll turn Aunt Beatrice loose as soon as you two are finished with her. Lady Westrich is a very impressive person once she gets on her high horse. She has a way with her, half autocratic and half sympathetic. That should get through the widow's guard." The earl's face hardened. "If that woman has caused Betta a moment's concern, she'll answer to me for it!"

By the time Virginie had followed Betta to their suite, the light was out in Betta's room. Virginie knocked gently at the door, but was answered with silence. Inside the bedchamber Betta lay curled up on her bed trying to put the visitor's wounding words away from her. It seemed impossible to her that Alec would deceive her so outrageously. Yet when they had spoken together today in the woods, he had been everything that she could have wished for in a man. He had been tender, gentle, and loving. Not for one moment had he made her feel as though he were playing a role; no, he had been truly speaking his love, his words were sincere. But he hadn't then seen Mrs. Epping; it was only when he returned to the house that he realized it was she. It was possible that the earl merely pretended not to know the widow; he may not have wished to acknowledge his relationship with the beautiful woman.

Oh, Betta cried to herself, it was just too much to have to contend with. She would much rather have believed that Alec was all that she wished him to be, but her lack of experience tempted her to believe Mrs. Epping.

Confused and unhappy, Betta was unable to sleep until late into the night. She heard Lucy and Virginie chatting softly when they came up to bed, but chose not to answer when their voices quickly called her name. Every now and then Lucy's voice would raise with a vehement sound, as though she were arguing with Virginie, then the tone would soften and Betta would hear no more. While she wondered what the two girls could be arguing about she fell asleep, a few tears still wet on her cheeks.

Chapter 20

The next morning, for the first time since the St. Johns had arrived at Possingworth, Betta did not come down to ride with Alec. She had been unable to bring herself to face him without having resolved her feelings about Mrs. Epping. She found herself wavering back and forth, first believing the widow, then believing in her love. The shock of facing the possibility that the man she loved was not the decent human being she had come to trust in destroyed her equanimity. Any self-confidence she might have been feeling in the light of Alec's love deserted her, and once more she felt like the stammering, inept miss that had faced the London *ton*.

Betta was sitting on the window seat of her bedroom glumly watching the earl ride down the drive when Lucy danced into the room.

"Guess what, Betta? Lady Westrich is going to take me to London right after Philippe and Virginie are married. She says that it would be harmful to my reputation to stay here with Robin and Alec without a proper chaperon . . . and she wants to get back to town to order her wardrobe for the fall season." The young girl whirled around the room in excitement. "Whoever thought that *I* would be going back to London in such style!" She looked at Betta, noticing the older girl's lack of enthusiasm. "Betta . . . whatever is wrong with you? You look ill. Aren't you feeling well? I'd better call your mother . . . you look so pale."

"No, no, Lucy, don't call Mama. I'm just suffering from the . . . oh, I don't know . . . I think I just want to get back home to my own room and my own place." The unhappy girl's eyes blurred with tears. "Isn't it silly of me? Here is all the luxury one could want, and all I want is my tatty old stables and my own room. I knew I shouldn't have come . . . it's just too much to bear."

"What *are* you talking about? You were having a grand time until yesterday. What happened to change your mind? Did you quarrel with Alec?" Lucy stopped for a moment in recollection. "Oh, no. Oh, Betta, don't tell me that you've let that awful Mrs. Epping upset you? Why, I'll warrant she's been saying nasty things about Alec and you've believed her. Well, if that's all you can think about him, then you deserve to be unhappy. You know that he's the best there is . . . except for Robin . . . and that he'd never stoop so low as to have an affair with her! Why, she's not even top of the heap, she's just a common . . . I don't know what to call her, but she is common."

"Lucy, stop talking like that . . . you know nothing of the matter. Yes, I know all about the things you saw when your father was taking you about, but *I* saw the high-flyers that men like the earl were paying tribute to when I was in London. Mrs. Epping is just as beautiful as any dancer or opera singer or . . . or . . . any of those kinds of women. And I can quite easily see how he would be attracted to her. She's very beautiful . . . and very—knowing—about men.

"I think the earl was just amusing himself with me to pass the time so he wouldn't be bored. He probably felt that he owed the St. John family the courtesy of a visit because we took care of Robin. . . . That's why he invited us all to Possingworth . . . but that's all he meant, I'm sure. I just let myself get caught up in a daydream, but now I *am* back to earth and no more silliness. He doesn't have to pretend anymore. As soon as I can convince Mama and Papa that I really want to go home, we shall leave."

"Aren't you going to stay for Virginie's wedding?" Anxiously Lucy tried to divert Betta. "I think she would be hurt if you were to leave without being a witness. You know she especially asked you to be here."

"I suppose we shall have to stay till then, but I think I shall be too busy to go riding anymore . . . or walking in the garden." A tear slid down Betta's cheek. The past few days had been the most wonderful of her life. All the things she had dreamed about had seemed to be coming true. To be loved by someone like Alexander Petrie, to be cared for by his family . . . had been a lovely dream; but like most dreams, it had turned to a reality that didn't quite match the dream.

Alexander became aware of Betta's withdrawal from him; he was puzzled by her sudden coldness. They had been so close, so in touch with each other, that he was, for the moment, unable to react quickly. He knew that in some way Mrs. Epping was responsible for the situation, but never having met the woman before, could not attribute a motive to her. She was, he realized, a rather low person with whom he might have, in the distant past, set up a flirt. She was not polished enough or intelligent enough to have attracted him into a more serious affair. And yet it was obvious to him that Betta believed that he had foisted his *inamorata* upon his guests; why Mrs. Epping had allowed or even encouraged that belief was the problem.

Lady Westrich, who had seen her nephew gaze at Betta

with such a look of hopelessness that she could have wept, was of the school that believed action was better than idleness. Casually she asked her dresser, who had been with her for years, if there had been any talk among the servants.

"My lady, you must have the ears of a magician to have guessed something was about in the servants' hall. Why, just this morning that Nettie was telling Miss St. John's abigail some fol-de-rol about when the earl visited Mrs. Epping. She kind of hinted that there is a child—supposedly the earl's. It's all a hum, if you ask me. The look on that Nettie's face . . . I could tell she was up to mischief."

"A child—impossible. I would never believe Alec so far gone as to have an affair with that woman. I guessed something on that order might be the story going around. The shamelessness of that woman . . . What is she up to? Lady Westrich impatiently threw down the fan she had been playing with. "You and I, my girl, will have to put a block in her path, or else she will ruin my nephew's life and hurt that lovely young woman beyond saving. Now here is what I want you to do, Perkins: give out that you and I have come to a parting of the ways. You are looking to leave my service. Sound out this Nettie, cozy up to her and be sympathetic to her mistress. You could tell her that you would like to get even with me for being so . . . stingy . . . with you."

Perkins pulled back in alarm. "Oh, my lady, I couldn't say anything like that; why, no one would believe me."

"Nonsense . . . just act nasty enough and everyone will believe you. And even if the other servants don't, it only needs the one to believe. The others would never say nay to any story you put about if you tip them the wink first." Lady Westrich continued to outline her plan to foil Mrs.

Epping's actions. Her trust in Alec's integrity was such that she had no need to confront him with the nebulous insinuations that were being circulated. She trusted his good taste and good sense.

Mistress and maid continued to refine their plan to learn Mrs. Epping's scheme.

Betta meanwhile avoided the company of the earl by staying close to her stepmother and the children. She had lost some of her ebullience, but managed to invent new games or spin new stories for the amusement of the youngsters. Virginie was too involved with the final plans for her wedding to Philippe to be aware of Betta's misery. Even though Lucy sought her advice, she pooh-poohed the young woman's anxiety by claiming a lovers' quarrel as the cause of the sad look of Betta's face and the unusual reserve on the part of the earl.

Dinner that evening was rather solemn compared to the effervescent occasions of the last several evenings. Mr. St. John and Robin carried on a rather subdued conversation, trying to include a reticent Alec; while Mrs. St. John and Lady Westrich tried to lure Betta into a talk about things that she usually found of interest. Even Lucy, usually so gay, was abnormally restrained. The only one who behaved with what might be referred to as her customary manner was the uninvited guest, Mrs. Epping. She entered the drawing room once again dressed in half-mourning, her beautiful hair arranged in the Grecian mode. Her eyes sparkled with a hint of malice that was apparent to the knowing look of Lady Westrich, but her manner was as gentle as a June breeze.

"You are all so quiet this evening. . . . Is there something wrong?" she asked in a singularly "cooing" tone of voice. "I am feeling so much better after being cosseted with so much attention this afternoon. I think I will be able to be about my business by the day following tomorrow. Will that be all right with you, my lord?" She addressed her question to Alec before continuing on about her proposed departure.

Alec could barely conceal his distaste for this woman who had so unexpectedly come between Betta and himself. It had taken such effort to win Betta's confidence; the patience and planning that had gone into breaching her stiff reserve was now for nothing, lost by forfeit to some mysterious design on the part of this unprincipled woman. After exchanging a few pleasantries with her as they strolled about the salon, he left her with Mr. and Mrs. St. John. Once out of her hearing, he beckoned Philippe to his side.

"Dear friend, I can hardly speak in a civil tone to this woman. Would you try to entertain her for a while? Virginie knows you to be safe from the widow's wiles, so please, have a go at divining her plan. I confess I'm at a loss to know what she is doing or why she's playing her game. Enough to know she's made Betta unhappy." The brilliant blue eyes had a puzzled look in them as they rested on the vivacious face of Mrs. Epping. "I can't get close enough to Betta to find out what the widow has said to her. . . . I leave it to you, my friend. You must rescue me and the one I wish to make my bride."

Philippe studied Alec's face, seeing for the first time a haggardness that he had never observed there—not even when the earl had thought Robin desperately ill. Halwick had always been in control of the situations in which he found himself . . . always trusted in his own ability to find his way. Now, for the first time in his life, he seemed to be floundering in a morass of molasses . . . unable to move quickly enough to effect a safe plan of action.

Philippe nodded his head in understanding. "I shall

save the day for you, my friend. No woman is able to resist the charm of a Frenchman . . . especially one so fascinating as myself! I have but one favor to ask. Please inform my sweet Virginie that what I am about to do is for you; never would I undergo so dangerous a trial for anyone else! So, *en avant,* into battle . . ." With a brisk little nod, at variance with his relaxed, easy saunter, Philippe moved to Mr. St. John's side and entered the conversation with a compliment to the widow. Few women can resist a handsome man's admiration; Mrs. Epping wasn't one of the few. She preened herself and fluttered her eyelashes under the warm glances from Philippe's flashing eyes. In her enthusiastic response to Philippe's lavish praise, Mrs. Epping missed the cynical expression that crossed his face. Despite his efforts, however, he was able to ascertain little more about the woman than she had already disclosed to the earl.

With the exception of the uninvited guest, it was a sadly disconcerted group of people that dispersed to their bedchambers that night. All were aware of Betta's pain and the earl's frustration, but none felt adequate to help. None, that is, except Lady Westrich. The indomitable woman spent the next hour in conference with Perkins, assessing the modicum of information that her dresser was able to give her.

Her ladyship leaned back against the huge white ruffled pillows of her bed, giving a twitch to the pretty green nightcap that matched her nightrobe. Her forehead was wrinkled in thought as she drummed her fingers against the bedcover.

"It's too bad we can't listen to those two . . . I'm sure they have a deal to say to each other when they're private, Perkins. She's up to no good, we all know that . . . but for what purpose? What plan?" The earl's aunt sat up in her bed and slapped at the mattress. "Well, we're not dished yet. . . . You must try to overhear them tomorrow morning. . . . She mentioned something about leaving the following day . . . so if she's going to do anything, it will be sure to be tomorrow. I just have a feeling . . ."

"Don't you worrit your head, milady. . . . Remember when you thought you wouldn't be able to get Lord Westrich to speak for you? We managed then, and we'll manage now," Perkins reassured her mistress. "There's no one set for the room next t'the lady's . . . the earl had her put in the other wing. . . ."

"You could hide in the dressing closet there . . . it shares a wall with the widow's bedroom. . . . That's it, Perkins . . . you shall be the spy. Best you go to bed now and be up at the crack of dawn. Come to me as soon as you learn anything of import." Lady Westrich instructed her maid: "That woman will never believe that we're on to her . . . she doesn't realize that I can be as underhanded as she when it comes to protecting my own. I feel much better now, Perkins. I know I shall sleep well."

Pleased with her scheme to outwit the visitor, her ladyship was able to sink into restful slumber almost immediately upon touching head to pillow.

A few hours later, Perkins quietly entered the empty chamber next to Mrs. Epping's room. Even as she opened the closet door she heard the murmur of voices. "They're up early to do their tricks," she muttered to herself, "but not too early to outwit my lady." Gently she placed the water glass she carried with her against the wall and put her ear to the open end. The sound of voices was immediately magnified, the words becoming clear enough for her to understand.

"Now, you listen here, Winnie," the flat voice of Mrs. Epping's maid was heard to say, "we're in a heap of trou-

212

ble, and if you don't pull this off, we're apt to be . . . well, maybe not dead, but as good as, if that Duc de Selles's to be believed."

"Oh, Nettie, I'm not sure I can go through with it . . . I thought it would be easy . . . but the earl has eyes that go through one like a knife for all he's so loverlike with the St. John chit. If we don't succeed in getting her to de Selles, he'll have his revenge on us; and if we do succeed, the earl is likely to be after us." Mrs. Epping's voice had a note of hysteria in it.

"You just keep your head together, Winnie. I'll do all the arranging. You've got to ask the St. John girl to join you in a drive around the park this afternoon; Corby will make sure he's the driver. As soon as I let him know the time, he's going to ride to the inn to tell the duc so he and Wingate'll be ready to stop the carriage and capture Miss St. John. You just have to return to the house in a state of shock and no one will even guess that you were involved in the abduction." Nettie's matter-of-fact voice was almost as shocking as the words she was speaking. Perkins's mouth was muttering imprecations against the two women, but soundlessly, she mustn't be heard . . . this was too important.

"Did you hear him when he said that he knew just the house to take her to in France?" There was a rising note of fear in the words spoken by Mrs. Epping. "He sounded insane . . . he hates Petrie so much that he'll ruin the wench for his revenge. She's like to lose her mind with the treatment she'll find there . . . and no escape for her except death. Oh, God, I don't know whether I can go through with this, Nettie."

The sound of a sharp slap came through the wall, then: "Enough of your caterwauling. Get yourself together. You may be my sister, but if you don't stop this acting,

I'll take the strap to you . . . and don't think I can't do it. If only I had the looks instead of you. . . . I'm tired of pushing you, Winnie . . . I'll leave you flat and get a job as dresser with Madame Delauney. She has plenty of men eager to give out handsome tips to the one who puts them in good with the madame. Now let's get you dressed . . . you've got to see Betta first thing to make the arrangements with her so I can tell Corby."

Perkins kept her ear glued to the glass for a few moments longer, but heard nothing other than directions from one sister to the other about the clothing to be worn and the style of hairdo for the day. Deeply affected by the words she had overheard, Perkins hurried to her mistress. It was imperative that they counter the duc's base intent before he had a chance to bring harm to Miss Betta.

"My lady, my lady, wake up . . . wake up." Perkins shook Lady Westrich's shoulder. "It's time to get up, my lady."

"Yes, Perkins, I'm awake, no need to shake my bones so." Lady Westrich sat up, putting her hand out to stop Perkins. "You must have heard something important . . . you're all out of breath."

Perkins quickly repeated the conversation between Nettie and Mrs. Epping. That the maid and Mrs. Epping were sisters was not as shocking to Lady Westrich as it had been to Perkins. "I knew she was ordinary; she and her sister were probably both in service until she was taken up by one of her masters. So the whole thing is a plot devised by the Duc de Selles. That is a surprise . . . but not, I suppose, unexpected. The Petrie family has much to forgive the Duc de Selles . . . and now to add to it this infamous plan for Betta. I must tell Alexander. . . . Quickly, Perkins, help me dress. I'll wear my blue walking dress with the deep-blue shawl and the white shoes. I'll not take my parasol

214

down with me. If I need it, I'll call you. I must find Alexander."

Giving Perkins the shortest time possible to dress her, Lady Westrich was soon on her way to the breakfast room. She walked in hoping to find the earl, but saw his already cleared place. Sure that she would have been early enough to meet with him, she questioned the waiting footman as to the earl's whereabouts.

"He breakfasted very early, my lady, along with Mr. St. John and Monsooer Beaumont. They had an appointment over to Lord Harringford's to look at his matched grays. M'lord said something about needing new carriage horses or some such."

"When did he expect to return, James?" the agitated woman asked.

"I dunno for sure, ma'am, but I don't think he expects to get back before the dinner hour. He and Mr. St. John said something about letting the ladies be for the day, my lady." The young servitor blushed slightly at his temerity in offering a personal opinion as he said: "I do believe he's right upset about that new lady, Mrs. Epping. She do be following him around something awful, my lady, and the talk in the . . . oh, beg pardon, my lady, I shouldn't have . . ."

"No, no, James. I know you have Lord Halwick's best interest at heart. What is being said backstairs? This will be just between you and me." The graciousness of Lady Westrich's manner invited the confidence of the servant.

"Well, it do be the thought of us that my lord was about to offer for Miss Betta, and a real right one she is—oh, sorry, my lady." The young man stopped in confusion, then seeing no censure on Lady Westrich's face, continued: "Seems as though that Nettie has been talking to Miss Betta's abigail and telling her without telling her, if

215

you take my meaning, ma'am, that the earl and Mrs. Epping have some sort of an understanding. She kind of pretended that she felt sorry for Miss Betta, about to engage herself to a . . . a . . . beg pardon, m'lady, a rake. She kind of hinted that maybe Polly should tell Miss Betta, so as not to let her get into troubled waters over the earl. She's a real bad'un, she is. Pardon if I've been too forward, my lady." James stopped, relieved to be through with his story.

"Good God, what am I going to do? . . ." Lady Westrich thought for a moment, then began to give the footman orders. "Have Jackson sent to me at once, then have someone find Miss Betta (if she's with me, that witch can't get her off alone) and have her join me in the summer parlor. Umm . . . tell her I need help with the invitations. Then send my maid to me." James left to follow her directions as she poured herself a steaming cup of coffee and considered what she must do. "I will have to go with them for the carriage ride . . . the best way to foil de Selles's plan is to catch him at his evil work. Unfortunately, the best way is going to be the most dangerous way. I'm so hungry . . . all this intrigue must be good for the appetite." While she laid her plans, the noblewoman helped herself generously to slices of the pink ham that was on the buffet. As though she hadn't a care in the world, she sat at the table, buttered herself some toast, and began to eat her breakfast. Before she had finished, Jackson arrived to receive her directions.

"Jackson, do you know where the earl has gone off to?" Lady Westrich asked as soon as the earl's retainer entered the breakfast parlor. "Now, no excuses. It's of the utmost importance . . . Miss Betta's safety is at stake."

"Aye, mum, I know where to find him. . . . What's about that is so needful of his presence?" Jackson held a special position by virtue of his having acted as riding teacher and counselor to both Petries as they grew up.

Lady Westrich wasted no time as she directed Jackson to prepare to ride for the earl. She gave him a sketchy outline of the plot against Betta, urging him to hurry himself in getting a horse ready while she wrote a note of warning to the earl. Before he would consent to go, she had to convince the man of the importance of catching the Duc de Selles in the act, so to speak. "Lord Halwick allowed him his life once before," she said bitterly, "and now he's up to his despicable mischief again."

As soon as Jackson had left the room to get himself ready for the ride to Lord Harringford's estate, she called for writing materials. In the note to the earl she outlined de Selles's plot to abduct Betta and take her to France. She stressed the urgency of his return and assured him that she would do all in her power to delay the proceedings. Before sealing the missive, she once more bade him make all haste.

When Jackson returned to the parlor, Lady Westrich handed him the note. "Ride as fast as you can, Jackson; much depends on your speed. How long do you think it will take you to get to Harringford Park?"

"I reckon on it taking me some two hours, my lady. I shall have to take time for the horse to rest, else he'll collapse under me. Howsoever, it's still early, so if you can delay the drive until after the midday meal, we should come about all right and tight."

"Four hours or more until you get back. . . . What's the time now?" Lady Westrich had not realized that the earl had gone so far to find peace from the invader now in his home.

"It's early, my lady, just half after ten. . . . We should be back by three o' the clock. If you know what inn they'll

217

be at, we should be able to cut some time off from that by not coming back to Possingworth, but going directly there. I took the liberty of taking weapons with me for the earl and the other gentlemen. I'll pack them on another pony so as not to load my horse down. And I also brought this along for you, ma'am." Jackson pulled a small pearl-handled pistol out of his belt and handed it to Lady Westrich. "It's just the right size to fit into that little carryall you take with you when you go about. I'd just be a little more at ease about giving it to you if I knew you could shoot it."

Lady Westrich started to smile at Jackson's thoughtful-ness. "Don't worry, Jackson. Years ago, when I was just newly married, my husband felt it was necessary for me to learn to shoot straight. I can hit my target right on; as long as the gun is loaded, I'll shoot straight!"

"Well, that relieves my mind a bit . . . the gun will fire two shots. If you have to fire it, make sure they count," Jackson advised the earl's aunt. "Now, can you tell me the name of the inn where the duc do be staying?"

Lady Westrich gestured impatiently. "No. Perkins didn't find that out, but I shall do my best to get that information. Someone will meet you at the crossroads this side of Wroxham . . . if all goes as I plan."

"Mayhap you should set someone to follow the carriage also, ma'am . . . like making a little extra luck," Jackson suggested.

"That's a good idea, Jackson. I hadn't thought to do anything like that. Who do you think would be good for that?"

"I would suggest Houseman, my lady. He knows how to handle himself and he's a crafty one. You won't notice him on your trail, but you can be sure he'll know where you are."

Relieved to find that she could make arrangements to ensure that the plot, whatever it was, would be made known to the earl, Lady Westrich gave permission to Jackson to bring Houseman into the plan.

"Now," her ladyship said to herself when Jackson had left, "now to see to it that Mrs. Epping doesn't get to speak to Betta alone. If her arrangements have been made, she won't be able to change them; and if I play the giddy old lady, she won't be able to object to my accompanying them on their exploration."

Her counterplot drawn up and instituted, Lady Westrich betook herself to the conservatory, where she had been advised she would find Betta. The windows of the almost-all-glass room had been opened to the summer breezes. Tropical flowers of brilliant hues were in full bloom, scenting the air with their fragrance. Carefully swept brick-lined paths wound through the spacious area, creating a sense of the outdoors that was enhanced by the sounds of exotic birds caged among the leaves of the taller plants.

The walk followed by the lady led to a central terrace-like alcove lined with comfortable seats and small tables. Betta was seated on a high-backed India chair, gazing abstractedly into the distance. Her face had a look of sadness and melancholy that tore at Lady Westrich's heart. All the more angered because of the falseness of the accusations that had produced that look, the older woman would have liked to let go a diatribe against the false witness. However, she realized that to do so would be to lose track of the ultimate quarry, who might then act against Betta without the safeguards she was endeavoring to provide.

"Dear child, you look quite blue-deviled. Is something troubling you? Would you like to talk about it?" the lady

219

gently asked. "Sometimes it helps to talk . . . things that seem hopeless turn out to be quite promising when examined with another person."

Betta's violet eyes blurred with tears for a moment. Then she gave a little smile and shook her head. "Thank you for your concern, my lady, but I shall come about in a bit. I just allowed myself to get mopish over a foolish fancy. . . ." She stopped for a moment and then gave herself a slight shake. "It's a schoolgirl whim, and I forgot I'm beyond such things. There, I'm feeling better already." The discipline of her background took control and forced Betta to put aside her sorrow while she was in another's company . . . especially the company of the earl's aunt. There was no reason to make such a very nice person suffer for the misdeeds of a relative; telling Lady Westrich in no way would change the fact that the earl was, indeed, the kind of person she had at first thought him to be. That was before he had beguiled her with his gentle manner and kind way.

"Oh, my dear, I wish . . ." Lady Westrich stopped herself before she said anymore, fighting to overcome her wish to assure Betta of the earl's worthiness. Before she was able to say anything else, a voice was heard calling Betta's name. Mrs. Epping had arrived on the scene. Betta responded to the "Where are you"s by directing the newcomer to the central area of the conservatory. Bubbling with virtuous "good mornings," Mrs. Epping began an encomium of the service and of the kindness of the household. She inquired about the health of the various members of the party and made sure to compliment Lady Westrich on her good health and handsome looks. When she had finished her paean of approbation, she turned to Betta, commenting that she looked just a tiniest bit haggish.

"Can it be that your migraine is still bothering you, Miss St. John?" she asked with great solicitude. "I have the perfect remedy for the headache . . . and would be more than happy to give you an amount for one or two doses." She finished with a questioning look, as if to say that she really knew the reason for Betta's downcast disposition.

"You are very thoughtful, Mrs. Epping, thank you. I don't require any medication, just a little quiet." Betta tried to indicate she would rather be alone than in company. "I find that to be the best remedy for the headache . . . don't you?"

"Well, yes, that's true sometimes. But if I don't take my medicine, the other prescription I use is to take a drive. The movement of the carriage and the smell of the fresh air and country sounds seem to be very efficacious. . . . Have you ever tried that?"

"I have rarely found a remedy necessary, Mrs. Epping," Betta answered, "because I rarely suffer from the migraine. . . . It's just that I think there has been too much socializing for me . . . I'm accustomed to leading a very quiet life, you see."

"Well, do let me take you for a drive, then, Miss St. John. I'm sure you would feel ever so much better for it. We could go immediately . . . the sooner you start the cure, the faster you will feel the thing."

"Oh, no, that's impossible," Lady Westrich announced. "Betta is engaged to help me with the invitations to the ball celebrating the wedding of Virginie and Philippe."

Betta's eyes widened in surprise at Lady Westrich's remark. To the best of her recollection the invitations had been sent out the day before yesterday. Perhaps there was something else to be done that she had forgotten . . . she'd wait for Lady Westrich to explain.

"Oh . . . oh, I didn't realize . . . I thought that Betta—I beg your pardon, Miss St. John—would be free this morning." Mrs. Epping paled at the thought that the arrangements with the duc might have to be called off. She had already sent word to him that the plan was in motion, but had not yet mentioned a time. Before she had a chance to offer a countersuggestion, she was relieved to hear Lady Westrich suggest postponing the drive until the afternoon.

"I should think we would be finished with the work we have to do in an hour or so, and then we can have some nuncheon before we leave. Betta, what do you say to half after two for our drive?"

Mrs. Epping began to disagree, expressing a wish to be alone with Betta "to get to know her better." Lady Westrich, while arguing that it was so important to become familiar with newly met friends, ignored the widow's preference and included herself as desiring to become more knowledgeable about Mrs. Epping. "Well—on your own head be it," muttered the erstwhile betrayer under her breath as she smilingly agreed.

Swept up by Lady Westrich's plans, Betta nodded her head in agreement. She would rather have been alone, but couldn't deny what she felt was the kindness intended by the solicitude of the two ladies.

"Very well, that's settled, then." Lady Westrich almost crowed with triumph that her circumvention of the duc's plot was beginning to work. "We'll go for a drive at that time, then. It should prove the best time of day!"

Chapter 21

A few minutes before the appointed time for the carriage ride, Lady Westrich could be found in consultation with one of Lord Halwick's workers, the man Houseman. It looked as though she were giving him instructions about something, because he could be seen to nod in response to certain of her statements. Once she had finished and had turned away from him, he might have been seen moving toward the stable. Had there been a watcher keeping an eye out, he would further have seen Houseman saddle a horse, equip himself with a gun, and then lead his horse down the riding path to a clump of pines and laurels, in which he hid himself and his horse.

Shortly after finishing with Houseman, Lady Westrich made her way to the side portico, where Corby was waiting with the landeau hitched up to two elegant, matched bays. Neither Betta nor Mrs. Epping had yet arrived, which lack elicited a comment from Lady Westrich to the effect that younger women seemed so often to be unpunctual. Idly, the lady tried to engage the groom in conversation suitable between employer and employee. As she asked certain innocuous questions about his family and antecedents, Lady Westrich examined the countenance of the earl's newest hostler. "He's a shifty-eyed one," she remarked to herself, "a real ruffian if ever I saw one." It's unlike Alexander to hire anyone like that . . . her thoughts continued . . . I wonder if he is connected to this whole havey-cavey scheme. We'll find out soon enough. . . . "Betta, my dear, and Mrs. Epping. Why, I had quite thought you must have decided not to come for the drive, you were so late," she said in greeting when the two women arrived at the carriage.

"Oh, my dear Lady Westrich, you couldn't think that we would be so thoughtless as to change our plans without informing you?" trilled Mrs. Epping. "I was just this minute saying to Miss St. John that I really look forward to this delightful ride. I'm sure the estate must be one of the great estates of England, and to see it in your company will make it an even more enjoyable experience."

The quizzing glass that hung around Lady Westrich's neck on a long gold chain was brought into play with a damping effect on Mrs. Epping's gush of words. The lady then focused on Betta, noting that the young woman looked drawn and unhappy. "My dear Betta, are you feeling up to this ride?" The older woman's voice was sympathetic. "If it is too much for you, we can postpone it until another time."

Before Betta could express her preference, Mrs. Epping answered for her with a hasty denial that it would cause any discomfort. "Why it would be the best thing for her to take in the air . . . nothing better, I assure you."

"It's perfectly all right, Lady Westrich. I really do feel that the drive would help me." Betta's usually lively tone was low and spiritless. "I'd just as soon go as stay behind . . . and I don't want to spoil anyone else's pleasure."

"There, you see. I told you it would be the best thing for her." Mrs. Epping's voice was triumphant. Inwardly she was thanking her good fortune that she wouldn't have to face a disgruntled de Selles.

224

Lady Westrich's intelligent eyes took note of the look of relief that crossed Mrs. Epping's face at Betta's acquiescence. She also intercepted the look that passed between Mrs. Epping and the driver, and his little nod. At Mrs. Epping's gesture, the groom jumped down from his seat to hand the ladies into the carriage before shutting the doors and resuming his place.

Mrs. Epping kept up a flow of conversation, alternately asking questions about the various sights they passed and passing on the latest on-dits she had culled from the most recent gossip columns. Lady Westrich responded occasionally with an appropriate comment, but Betta remained silent, contemplating the passing scene, detesting the sound of Mrs. Epping's voice. With a start she realized that the carriage had turned and was taking a side road that led to the highway.

"Where are we supposed to be going?" she asked Mrs. Epping. "I think Corby has taken a wrong turning. This road leads away from the park, and we'll be on the main highroad in a few minutes."

Mrs. Epping pretended a lack of concern. "I asked Corby to show me the direction my coach would have to take tomorrow. . . . I shall be going on to London then, you see."

Lady Westrich, knowing that this was a part of the plan to abduct Betta, kept quiet while the discussion went on between Betta and the widow.

"You must stop the carriage this instant, Corby," Betta called out to the groom. "There is no need to continue on this road. If you turn about we can go back by way of the lake."

"Be quiet, miss," commanded Mrs. Epping. "You have nothing to say about our destination . . . that's already been arranged."

225

Betta looked at Mrs. Epping in surprise. The widow's heretofore pleasant expression had become unyielding. Her vulgar background now manifested itself in her almost immediate loss of the cultivated veneer of manners she had assumed as Mrs. Epping. "You've lost, Miss St. John—almost Lady Halwick—that life's no longer for you, ducks; you're destined for a different ending. A great lord has chosen you for a somewhat less quiet life!"

"A great lord?" Betta whispered in shock.

"The Duc de Selles. . . . He's paying me a great deal of money to deliver you to his hand. Although what he's going to do with this old girl, I don't know. She'll probably be taken along as your maid!" The thought of the elegant Lady Westrich becoming maid to the woman who might have been her nephew's bride sent the iniquitous woman into gales of laughter.

Lady Westrich, meanwhile, in order to appear less resolute than she was, moaned and sobbed, calling for her vinaigrette as she rolled her eyes and announced that she was fainting. Had Betta been less confounded by the turn of events, she would have realized that Lady Westrich was enacting a role that was in direct opposition to her natural character.

"Corby, Corby . . . please, you must turn the horses . . . please . . ." Betta cried. When the groom responded by cracking his whip over the horses' backs to urge them on to greater speed, she stood up in the swaying vehicle, trying to climb up on the seat that backed the driver's perch. From under her half-closed eyelids Lady Westrich saw Betta's attempt and screamed her name in an effort to stop her. At the same moment Mrs. Epping jumped up and grabbed Betta around the knees. Unable to balance herself on the cushion of the seat, doubly hampered by the rapidly seesawing motion of the landeau, Betta fell backward against the side of the carriage. Her head hit the edge of the door with a sharp crack and her body collapsed limply, half on the seat and half on the floor.

"Oh, my God, I've killed her," the suddenly shattered Mrs. Epping moaned. "He'll murder me. . . . Oh, God . . ."

Lady Westrich quickly put her hand on Betta's chest to feel for a heartbeat. Greatly relieved when she felt the strong, even pulsing, she snapped an order to Mrs. Epping to help her lift Betta to a more comfortable position on the seat. Once Betta had been settled securely in place, Lady Westrich resumed her swooning, assured by Mrs. Epping's panic-stricken behavior that the wretched woman would not recall her lapse. Hoping that Houseman was staying out of sight as he followed them, the lady sent up a prayer that Jackson's horse would suffer no fall in racing to the earl. Betta's only hope lay in the earl's timely arrival. The evil Duc de Selles might still be successful in the abduction, in which case Lady Westrich knew that she would be *de trop* and would soon be gotten rid of by the amoral man.

She allowed herself to relax against the cushions, knowing from the motion of the carriage that Corby was slowing the horses. Above the sounds of the horses and wheels, she heard men's voices hailing him as he drew the horses to a halt. Keeping her eyes shut, Lady Westrich listened to the hysterical voice of their erstwhile companion urging the newly arrived plotters to hurry with the transfer of the object of their nefarious scheme. In a moment footsteps were heard approaching the side of the carriage, then the door was pulled open. Lady Westrich allowed her eyes to open the merest fraction; through her lashes she beheld the long saturnine face of the Duc de Selles, livid with anger at beholding her unwanted presence. Delicately she

227

moaned . . . a tiny sound that produced an explosive reaction.

"I made no bid for this person," the duc hissed. "What is she doing here . . . and in this condition . . . ? You fool, how do you expect to return to the manor to tell your story with her to bear witness against you?"

"I couldn't help it. She glued herself to us . . . wouldn't let us leave without her. I'm sure she didn't suspect anything . . . she's just a busybody . . . probably bored with the run of the guests and wished for an outing with us. But I can't take her back," Mrs. Epping protested in a whining voice. "She'd inform the earl that I was involved. You'll have to take her with you." The widow's voice became vindictive. "Your little ladybird will need a maid . . . use the old harridan for that."

Old harridan, indeed, was the thought in Lady Westrich's mind. You can't be more than ten years younger than I am. Just wait until this is over, my girl . . . you'll feel my wrath. Softly she again let out a moan.

"Quickly, quickly, get them into our coach. . . . If she wakes up, she's liable to start screaming, and there's no telling who might be in the area." Lady Westrich recognized Jeremy Wingate's voice, high-pitched and frantic though it was. "De Selles, we can decide as soon as we get them to the Broken Crown. Corby's got to get Winnie back to Possingworth before they decide to send out a search party."

"Silence! Your caterwauling and her screeching will give notice to the neighborhood before this woman will. Mrs. Epping . . . you will be certain to advise the earl and his friends that the coach turned towards the London road." The Duc de Selles once more was in command: "You will give out the story that you were stopped by common highwaymen; three plus a leader should be enough. You could suggest that the leader had a soldierly air about him and that he let fall the destination as being the Inn of the Three Maidens in Cheatham. If he asks why the name should have been mentioned in your presence, you can tell him that you were thought to be in a deep swoon. I'm sure you will be able to beguile him enough so that he will accept your story."

The duc beckoned Corby to climb into the carriage and lift Betta's shoulders while he took her feet. Together they handed her to the duc's valet, who tossed her over his shoulder and carried her to the coach. Lady Westrich was soon given the same treatment, to her dismay! It being difficult to maintain the illusion of being in a faint while jouncing inelegantly over the shoulder of a ruffian who had no thought for one's comfort.

Before the doors of the coach were closed on the two women and their captors, Lady Westrich could hear the sound of the carriage driving away. Now she began to worry that Houseman might be seen by Corby as he drove back to the mansion. If that were to happen, they would be really in a pickle; there was no way that the earl would know for sure where they had been taken.

Once the coachman had whipped the horses into starting on their way, the duc began to curse in soft, sibilant phrases, failing to omit his thoughts about hirelings who couldn't follow directions, the inefficacy of using women to do a man's job, and the pea-brained activities of certain women of the upper classes, Lady Westrich in particular. On this note Lady Westrich decided to regain consciousness. If she could have been certain that all would end well, she would have thoroughly enjoyed herself; it had always been a secret desire of hers to be an actress, and now she was fulfilling that ambition to its fullest. The inconsistency was that their lives, hers and Betta's, might now depend on her ability to enact the proverbial Cheltenham tragedy for the benefit of their abductor.

"Oh, where are we? What's happened . . . ? Mrs. Epping struck Betta. . . . I feel I am going to faint again . . . oh, help." She lifted her head and fluttered her eyelashes as if the weight of her eyelids was too much for the actual act of opening her eyes. She allowed herself to droop disarmingly before becoming aware of the two men sitting opposite her.

"Is that you, my lord de Selles? Have you rescued us from that wicked woman?" She clasped her hands in the time-honored gesture of pleading. "Take us to a safe place, my lord, before she can attack us again. Thank goodness we have such a brave man with us." She permitted herself to swoon again. Let them make what they can of my gratitude, she thought, if we can pretend that we think them our saviors, our treatment may be somewhat better for the moment.

At her outrageous remarks the two men exchanged glances. Was it possible that this woman was so totty-headed as to believe that they had come to her rescue? All to the good if that were so . . . she and the St. John chit would be that much easier to handle during the few hours that they would have to await the arrival of the boat that would take them to France. While they spoke softly to each other about Lady Westrich's supposition, Betta began to regain consciousness. She lifted her hand to her head, wincing as she tried to move herself into a more upright position.

"What happened? My head . . . it hurts so. . . ." She noticed Lady Westrich's partly recumbent figure next to her on the wide seat. "My lady, what's wrong with you . . . ? Please, my lady . . ." She was answered by a groan and then a spate of requests for Perkins, vinaigrette, pillows; and supplications to heaven, my lord, the world in general, and Betta in particular. So involved for the moment in trying to make Lady Westrich more comfortable, Betta paid no attention to the figures seated on the other side of the coach. As she bent over the earl's aunt, the older woman whispered in her ear the command that she go along with whatever the lady would say . . . their lives depended upon her. Unfortunately Betta thought that Lady Westrich was suffering a lapse of sanity brought about by the rough handling in the carriage. She soothed the older woman as best she could, not realizing she was utterly mistaken in her assessment of the situation. She chafed Lady Westrich's hands, attempting to bring her to full consciousness, unaware that her ladyship was keenly awake, and turned to seek help from the two figures she perceived seated across from her.

"Sir," she started, then stopped when she recognized the satanic features of the Duc de Selles. "What are you doing here? How did you get . . . How did we get into this coach? Where's Corby and Mrs. Epping?" she demanded.

"I shall give you your answers and then give you your options," the duc announced in answer to Betta's questions. "Mrs. Epping has returned to Possingworth with Corby. Her story is that you were abducted by some highwaymen and taken towards London. In reality, I have taken a fancy to you . . . you are much too captivating a piece to be left to Alexander Petrie. If you are obliging, I shall set you up in a pretty apartment in Paris, on the Faubourg Saint-Honoré. You will undoubtedly become a leading light of the demimonde. If you are not so obliging, you shall immediately be sent to the House of the Golden Foxes . . . called so because all the women are blonde like yourself. You will not be treated so gently, and coming

231

from the background that you do, will probably not last too long before you become too docile for their needs. In addition, your companion may remain your companion only as long as I find you entertaining and agreeable. Should you create any problems, she is *phhfftt!*" The duc made a gesture across his throat with the side of his hand.

Betta looked at the duc with uncomprehending eyes. "How can you do something like this? What did I ever do to you to exact such treatment from you? And Lady Westrich . . . why did you not let her go with Mrs. Epping? I don't understand this . . . it must be a nightmare . . . you can't be serious."

Lady Westrich took Betta's hand. As soon as she heard the duc's plan, she realized that it would no longer help their situation for her to pretend. It would not do to fully expose her strength, but she must help Betta to cope with this terrible future that he had offered her.

"I fear he is serious, my dear. He is known to be without a conscience and has done things like this before . . . as I know to my sorrow." The knowledge that she still had her reticule reassured Lady Westrich. If the worst should occur, and Alec not be able to save them, she had the gun . . . and two shots. That would be enough as long as she could keep her hand steady. But not yet. . . . Houseman must be successful in tracking them and then getting the information to Alexander. Just a few short hours and they would be safe . . . please God, she added in a prayer.

"Listen, de Selles." Jeremy Wingate made himself heard in a somewhat frightened whine. "I will not go to France. . . . I want my money as soon as we get to the inn, and then I'm off for the north of England. I've a ladyfriend who's been badgering me to spend some time with her, so I shall be safe enough until this blows over."

"Yes, Jeremy," the soft voice of the duc spoke, "you

shall be safe. . . . Have patience; there is no need for you to journey with us to France. You shall be safe."

Almost mesmerized by the duc's monotone and dark eyes, Betta sank back into her seat. Her mind was working in bursts of thought . . . examining and discarding first one plan and then another. Her primary concern was the safety of Lady Westrich. If she could persuade the duc to leave her ladyship in England when they embarked to France, she would have solved half her problems. Once aboard the ship she would pretend to be enamoured of the Frenchman, and given the chance would cast herself overboard. Better to die in the clean waters of the Channel than to exist in the kind of life he had outlined for her. As long as she could hold him off, she would be able to pretend. If he should do more than hand her down from the coach, the touch of his flesh against hers would undoubtedly cause her to cringe from him. Then she would be finished, and Lady Westrich would be . . . no good to think about that.

While her thoughts skittered around in her head, the coach arrived at the Broken Crown. It was located at the landward edge of a small coastal village that had the smell and look of a not too successful fishing center. As Betta descended from the vehicle she took a quick glance around, hoping to see a face that had a friendly look. Other than the hostler, who stood at hand to help with the horses, there was no one about. The day seemed to have turned cold and gray, and the sharp smell of sea and of fish hung over the yard. Betta shivered, then put her arm around Lady Westrich, who had tottered to her side.

Again Lady Westrich tried to warn Betta. "Don't make a fuss," she whispered as the girl helped her into the building, "go along with whatever he says. . . . If necessary, faint!" Before she had a chance to say anything else about their predicament, the duc motioned them into the low thatch-roofed building. Inside, they were led into a small room, warmed by a fire burning in the fireplace. The room, intended to be used as a parlor, was supplied with the minimum of furniture. The duc walked to the fireplace and stood resting his shoulders against the mantel. He watched Betta seat herself on the high-backed wooden settle next to Lady Westrich. Nowhere in the room could one find a hint of grace or beauty to ease the square, hard surfaces and corners. Despite the warmth of the fire, there was an impression of cold and unwelcome. Again Betta shivered. She felt that not even a fur wrap could do away with the intense cold that came from within her.

Lady Westrich sat pinched and silent, huddled against Betta in an attitude of extreme dejection. She was doing her best to give the impression that she was a weak and useless old lady. The duc had said that they would be resting in this godforsaken place for some time . . . the best thing for her and Betta would be to have a cup of tea and something to eat. She knew that Betta had barely touched her morning meal. Something hot always heartened one, so since she obviously was the general of her two-member army, she took action. In a pathetic, dying-away voice, she asked to be allowed to have something for her thirst; she would be most grateful for something hot.

"Go find someone, Wingate," commanded the duc. "Order a tray for the ladies."

Wingate started to object, blustering that it was not his place to serve as a lackey, but a glance at the glacial eye of the duc quickly changed his tune. He slipped out of the room in an almost stealthy manner. His fear of the duc was apparent, although he tried to act as though he shared command with the Frenchman.

"Well, Miss St. John, have you given any thought to

234

your predicament?" asked the Frenchman in a conversational tone of voice. "Have you decided to accept your role as my *petite amie*? You will be the envy of all Paris. Or shall I have to express my displeasure by installing you in what is rudely called a brothel?"

Betta lifted her head proudly, about to give de Selles a setdown, when she felt an elbow poking her in the ribs. She allowed herself to give the duc a look of intense dislike and then bent her head slightly. Discretion was the better part of valor; in this case it would be discreet to agree. "I will do as you ask, but in return I would that you might grant me my request. There is really no need for Lady Westrich to accompany us . . . she is too frail to retain her health on so arduous a journey." Betta put her arm around the lady. "You can see she is not well, and already in difficulty. Her heart could give out at any moment."

Brilliant thinking, Betta. Lady Westrich silently congratulated Betta. . . . But don't count on his swallowing this whopper . . . he wasn't born yesterday. She let out a delicate moan followed by a small cough, as though to punctuate Betta's description of her frailty.

De Selles let out a dry laugh. "I had not thought, madam, that you would have the temerity to bargain with me. It is not up to you to demand concessions in this situation. We have time to decide the course of action to be followed. For now it will suffice that you guarantee your strict obedience to my rules."

"Your rules, sir? And what may they be?" Betta put the question with dread.

"If any strangers should arrive, which I very much doubt, you will make no move to ask for assistance. Lady Westrich will be the one to suffer should you attempt any communication with other than our party. Secondly, you will promise to do nothing to harm yourself. . . . Again

Lady Westrich will be the sufferer. And thirdly, you will write the letter that I am going to dictate to you . . . . Your former host must be apprised of your plans for the future." The duc was gloating at his victory over his hated enemy. "This will pay him well for the troubles he has caused me . . . he will think twice before he cuts across my path again."

At this point the intrepid Lady Westrich decided that she and Betta needed to confer together. She must let Betta know that Alec would be arriving at any moment. The girl might do something foolish to thwart de Selles without the assurance that they would not be leaving for France. Once again she thrust an elbow into Betta's side, whispering, "Privacy!" in the hope that the young woman would understand. Betta gave a tiny nod of understanding, whereupon Lady Westrich gave out a bloodcurdling scream and fell in a heap at Betta's feet.

"Oh, my lady . . . it's . . . it's . . . her heart! She's had a convulsion of the heart. She must have privacy . . . I have to loosen her clothes. Please, my lord." Betta appealed to the duc: "Please allow us to retire to a chamber where I may restore Lady Westrich to consciousness."

Grudgingly the duc agreed to Betta's plea. He called a servant and had Lady Westrich carried up the stairs to a small room just under the eaves. Before Betta followed, he cautioned her against trying to escape, again threatening bodily harm to Lady Westrich. Without hesitation Betta gave her pledge and hurried to the lady's side.

In short order she was leaning over Lady Westrich, loosening the fastenings of her gown. "We're alone, my lady. Are you all right?" she whispered to the supposedly stricken woman.

"You're a clever and a good girl, child. . . . I'm fine . . . but I had to talk to you. You must pretend that you agree with the duc's demands. We must distract him until Alec arrives."

"Alec . . . How will he arrive? He knows not of this fix we are in."

"I've known that this was going to happen since early this morning. It seems so long ago . . . I think I'm getting too old for this kind of activity. Mrs. Epping is a protégée of the duc's. It was through her connivance that we arrived at this situation. My Perkins overheard Epping and her maid (who happens to be her sister) discussing the plan for your abduction. That's why I wouldn't let you go off alone with her this afternoon. Of all times for that nephew of mine to have gone off . . . and to take your father and Philippe with him!" Lady Westrich stopped to contemplate her nephew's untimely action. "As soon as I heard the plot, I sent Jackson after them with an outline of the proposed abduction. Then I arranged for Houseman to follow us so that he will be able to meet and guide the men to this hovel. Now, I have taken us this far. Do you have any suggestions?"

"Well—we could demand some dinner . . . and we need warmer clothes if we are going out on the Channel. And, and . . . oh, I really can't think of anything else," the astonished girl answered. "But I don't want to be left alone with *HIM*, so please, my lady, you will have to recover from your 'faint' and join me in the parlor."

"Don't worry, my dear, I have no intention of leaving you alone with that lascivious *roué!* He's had a career of evil-doing for over twenty-five years that I know of, and I sincerely hope it will be brought to an end today!" The elegantly *soignée* lady was as fierce as any savage protecting her charge.

Despite the danger of their predicament—for they were still not safe and would not be until the earl arrived—

Betta had to smile at the indomitable will of Lady Westrich. She would have made a good soldier had she been born a boy, she had such will and such courage. From the look on her face she was actually enjoying the hazard—incredible!

"Well, come along, my dear," the earl's unconquerable aunt commanded. "Let us go forth and defeat the enemy!"

Chapter 22

The scene in the parlor was almost one of congeniality. The four protagonists were seated around a table that had been placed in front of the fireplace. The duc was lounging back in his chair, having just replaced his wineglass on the table. Wingate was about to dip some snuff in a manner aped from Beau Brummel, but sadly lacking the flair shown by that great "setter of fashion." Betta and Lady Westrich were sitting in a relaxed attitude listening to the duc animadverting on the deficiencies of their host to provide a decent meal.

"You shall see, Miss St. John, the distinction of the Parisian scene," he announced in a dry tone. "There is nothing in England to compare with that noble city. And once I have taken you to the great couturieres of France, the best of whom are in Paris, you will never again think that London offers anything of fashion."

"Why, my lord," Betta returned as she rose from the table, "I could almost look forward to my visit to your country if the circumstances were any different." She arranged a shawl on one of the chairs, then addressed Lady Westrich: "My lady, you might be more comfortable over here. It's getting a bit warm by the fire." Returning her attention to the duc, she asked why he had left France if he loved it so much. As he answered her question, she moved a chair next to Lady Westrich. The two women had decided to remain in proximity to each other against the time when the earl should arrive. They would be better able to protect each other and be out of way of being used by Wingate or de Selles.

The duc, so positive of having gained his victory over Alexander Petrie, was relaxed in his triumph. He could not help, as cold a man as he was, feeling a degree of satisfaction at Betta's interest in him. He knew that he had inordinate success with women . . . even under these circumstances; here was evidence that the chit could not resist him . . . she was absolutely flirting her eyes at him. Usually a man in total control of himself and fortune, he made the mistake of allowing himself to bask in the warmth of his proposed liaison with Betta. . . . From his point of view it should be most enjoyable. Even though her resistance was crumbling, she was still apprehensive enough to offer a challenge to his mastery over the art of seduction. Yes, he thought, once we are rid of the old woman, it should be a very satisfying experience.

"Y'know, I've been thinking, de Selles." Wingate, who was somewhat the worse for drinking and had been silent throughout most of the meal, suddenly started to speak. "You're going to get what you want, but I still won't have my Lucy. . . . She's supposed to be my insurance against a rainy day."

"You horrible man . . ." Betta began, glad to be able to let loose her anger at last. "What . . ." Her tirade was interrupted by the crash of the door being thrown back on its hinges. Then a soft, very welcome voice was heard: "Give you greetings, de Selles. It looks as though you are having a dinner party. How could you not have invited me?"

The duc froze at the unexpected sight of Alexander

240

Petrie leaning against the doorpost, one hand fiddling with his quizzing glass, the other hanging loosely at his side. In the midst of the squalid little room, his broad shoulders, clad in a many-caped riding coat, and his bright sapphire-blue eyes were the most welcome sights that Betta had ever seen.

As welcome as his presence was to Betta, just so fearful was it to Jeremy Wingate, still somewhat bleary eyed from overindulging in the landlord's wine. He jumped up from his chair, knocking it over in the process, and backed up to the mantel. He reached out to the mantelpiece as though to steady himself, but made a grab for the gun that was lying there. As he grasped the handle, Lady Westrich reached into her reticule for the tiny pistol that Jackson had given her so many hours ago. The small pearl handle exactly fitted into her hand. Jeremy Wingate had taken hold of the gun on the mantel and was raising it, aiming at the earl. A shot sounded, accompanied by a gasp from one of the women. The blast reverberated in the small, stone-walled room, deafening the occupants for a moment. Betta watched the earl, expecting to see him fall, wounded by Wingate's bullet; instead, it was Lucy's father who slowly, slowly clutched at his stomach and folded up on himself, to fall in a heap on the hearth.

Lady Westrich looked at the little weapon in her hand with satisfaction. "I told Jackson I could hit my target!"

"Aunt, you've done very well. . . . Now permit me to take over." Alec said with a laugh. He smiled at Betta. "Are you all right, my love?" Before she could answer, her father pushed past the earl to come to her side.

"Father . . . I'm so glad to see you . . . I thought you would never get here." At last the tears began to trickle from her eyes. "It's been horrible. The man must be mad."

She looked at Alexander. "You know you will never be safe from him . . . his hatred has made him mad, I think."

"I know," answered the earl, "this is the last time this dog will ever put any of my loved ones in danger again. Aunt, I wish you and Betta to leave the room. Jackson is outside with Philippe . . . they have Corby and the landlord prisoner. Please, the two of you, go and get into the carriage. I won't be long."

Lady Westrich voiced a strong objection to such a desertion on her part. "I wish to see this villain get his comeuppance, and I will not permit you to fight a duel in this room."

The duc finally stood up, straightening his cuffs and lapels as he did so. "I take it that this will be a fair fight, Petrie?"

Alec made a deep bow. "My lord, I would never treat you with the duplicity that is your trademark. Of course it will be fair. My future father-in-law shall examine the guns. . . ."

"Guns? Why not the sword?"

"My lord, the duel with swords has always been thought to be too honorable for such as you. It will be guns or a horsewhip. You prefer . . . ?" Alec raised an eyebrow questioningly.

"I am forced to agree . . . but what of a doctor? There is none present."

"Neither you nor I will need a doctor when this is over, de Selles." Alec shrugged his shoulders. "This is to be the end for one of us. . . . I may say, with hope that you understand, that I prefer that it be you."

Betta, horrified by the thought that Alexander might die before she had a chance to enjoy a life with him, moved away from the door, held to the room by the drama that was taking place.

Mr. St. John opened the box of dueling pistols he had been holding. He lifted them out of the box. They were a matched pair, designed and made by the famous Manton; the polished wood and inlaid silver beautifying their deadly purpose. The earl picked them up to examine them, then handed them to Betta's father to load.

Mr. St. John carefully loaded the first gun while de Selles and Alec watched. He handed it to Alec and then loaded the second. As he was so occupied, the duc turned away from the scene for a moment as though to make peace with himself.

Betta watched him curiously . . . his move did not seem natural to the moment. She saw his shoulders twitch, as though he were setting his coat in place, then with the speed of a striking snake he whirled, lifting his arm as he did so. Betta screamed when she saw the glint of metal in his hand and the satanic look on his face. With unbelievable swiftness Alec raised his pistol and fired, just as the knife left the hand of the duc. Before it entered Alec's shoulder, the Frenchman was dead, fallen across his henchman and tool, Jeremy Wingate. Betta, her father, and Lady Westrich were held motionless by the duc's lightninglike attempt on the earl's life. Their immobility was disturbed by the sound of a gasp and then the earl's voice.

"Mr. St. John, would you help me? I . . . I seem to have a knife stuck in my shoulder!" With that soft remark, the earl fell in a faint.

"Oh, no . . . oh, Alec . . . help him, someone. . . ." Betta dropped to her knees beside the unconscious man. She reached a trembling hand for the knife, then pulled back, afraid to touch the silver handle that extended from the smooth fabric of the caped coat. She kneeled there for what seemed an eternity, watching the blood begin to seep from the wound, until she felt her father's hand on her shoulder.

"Come, child, let us take care of him. I don't think the wound a fatal one . . . your warning prevented that tragedy. Betta, move yourself . . . go to Lady Westrich . . . she seems quite overcome by all of this." Mr. St. John helped the trembling girl to rise, then seated her next to Lady Westrich.

Before he was able to do more, a wild-eyed Philippe Beaumont ran into the room, almost tripping over the Earl of Halwick's still body.

"Alexander, my friend, what has happened to you? Where is that *canaille?* I will kill him myself!" his anguished voice cried out.

"Nonsense, you can't. I finished him off." A weak voice issued from the earl's lips. "Isn't anyone going to remove this blasted stiletto from me?"

Four pairs of eyes looked at the stricken earl with astonishment that almost immediately turned to joy. The resultant babble forced Mr. St. John finally to raise a calming hand, calling for silence from the other three. "Philippe, call Jackson . . . he is the one best able to remove the knife from the wound. My lord," he addressed the earl, whose hand was now being held by a thankful Betta, "until the weapon has been removed from your shoulder, I think it better that you remain where you are. Then you will be placed in the duc's coach with the ladies and returned to Possingworth, where you can receive proper medical attention. Betta, you may put a pillow under his head, if such a thing is to be found in this benighted place." He turned his attention to Lady Westrich: "Lady Beatrice, are you all right? Let me pour a glass of wine for you. . . ."

"No, thank you, dear sir; knowing that that dog is

finally dead is restorative enough. Thank God you arrived when you did . . . I don't think we could have kept up the pretense for much longer . . . although your daughter, sir, is a wonder . . . a perfect addition to the Petrie family. I shall be happy to call her niece."

By now Betta had relinquished her place to Jackson, who asked that she find hot water and towels. "The servants do all be locked in the shed outside, miss, and I would not trust a one of them to do my bidding. So if you would be so kind, we'll have the earl fixed up all right and tight instanter."

In a short time, a time filled with torment for those who loved the earl, the knife was removed and the wound pronounced to be clean and well bound. The earl was removed to the coach, accompanied by a tremulous Betta and a relieved Lady Westrich.

As Mr. St. John handed them into the conveyance, he assured them that the events that had just taken place would in no way be made known to the world at large. "It will look as though the two scoundrels fell out and killed each other. Other than the family and those of us who are Alexander's guests, no one will know of your presence and that of Betta in this place. Do not concern yourself with the rest of it. Now, be on your way. . . . Philippe and Houseman will be your coachmen . . . Jackson and I will attend to everything necessary here."

He climbed into the coach to give his daughter a reassuring hug and a kiss, then removed himself, shouting to Philippe to get on with it . . . time was awasting.

Alexander was stretched out on the well-upholstered bench seat, his head on Betta's lap. He felt a trifle weak, but otherwise in good spirits. He gazed up into Betta's violet eyes, enjoying the love that flooded his being. The quality of his glance brought a rosy color to Betta's

245

cheeks. Despite herself, her hand began to smooth the tousled hair away from Alec's brow with a gentleness and love that she at last gave into. Without saying anything, the wounded man reached for his beloved's hand, bringing it to his lips for a kiss, then holding it against his cheek.

"I had wished to make my declaration in a much more beautiful setting," he began, "but can wait no longer to ask you. With my aunt as witness, I wish you to know that I love you, Betta. Love you above and beyond my life . . . and I want you to be my cherished and precious wife."

"I . . . I . . . Oh, yes . . . I would, I will . . . I mean I do. . . ." Betta started to giggle. "I can't even answer a proposal properly, my tongue gets so twisted about." Then she bent her head and gently kissed Alexander on the lips. "There, I've sealed our betrothal with a kiss . . . you cannot renege now. Isn't that right, Lady Westrich?"

Her ladyship beamed at her nephew and Betta. "I had hoped for this. I saw Alec was head over heels as soon as he returned from Watton Abbey . . . and then when I saw you, my dearest Betta, I knew you would make a perfect pair." A tear coursed down Lady Westrich's cheek. "I insist now that you both be quiet, we all need the rest. . . . I feel as though it's been weeks since we left Possingworth. Just let me close my eyes for a few moments. . . ."

"Oh, Alec—I feel such a fool for having allowed that Epping woman to fill my head with such libelous thoughts." Betta's eyes filled with tears. "I must have been so afraid of my love for you that I was ready to believe her lies."

"She was very clever, sweetheart." Alec brought Betta's hand to his lips to place a kiss in her palm. "I confess I didn't understand what was happening, although I knew she was the source of our trouble."

"If ever I behave so . . . so . . . stupidly"—Betta smoothed Alec's hair from his brow—"you have my permission to punish me severely."

"Then let the punishment begin now with this." Alex reached up with his good arm and drew Betta's head down to kiss her soundly. When he finally let her go she was rosy with color.

"I may 'argol-bargol,' as Jackson would say, for the rest of our lives, my dearest, but I shall never trust another before you. I love you too much to ever hurt you like that again. You have sealed your fate, sirrah," she said, "and now must suffer the consequences. Now rest, my love, my dearest."

It seemed just a short drive to the two lovers before the coach turned in at the gates to Possingworth. The two weary women and their wounded champion were greeted by the rousing cheers from the family, friends, and servants. Astonished by this welcome, Lady Westrich and Betta descended from the coach into the arms of their loved ones. Alec, his arm in a sling, was able to climb down with a little support from his butler.

"*Vite, vite,* take up Lord Halwick . . . don't let him walk . . . carry him into the summer parlor." Virginie strove to direct the proceedings as she threw her arms around Betta and whispered how glad she was that her friend was all right.

"Don't be foolish, Virginie, my dear, I can walk . . . . It's but a small wound," Alec told the worried comtesse.

Questions flew from adults and children alike. How had he gotten the wound, what was the outcome of the rescue aside, of course, from Betta and Lady Westrich being here? Where were Philippe and Mr. St. John? What was it all about, anyway?

"We'll tell you the whole story around the tea table," Lady Westrich assured the concerned people. "Just let us get settled. While we await the arrival of the doctor, Alec and I will tell you what happened . . . won't we, Alec?" She looked to her nephew for affirmation.

At his nod, they were allowed to continue to the green and white summer parlor, there to have something to restore their energy and to tell their story.

"First, what happened to Mrs. Epping?" asked the earl.

"Oh, she and her maid—Perkins says she was a sister, not a maid—couldn't get away from here fast enough. She came flying in screaming that you two ladies had been taken by highwaymen." Mrs. St. John recounted the story. "Then she called for her carriage to be readied and she and that person, Nettie, left. Why, their clothes were hanging out of their satchels, they packed so fast!"

"She's lucky she left before I returned," announced Alec. "She wouldn't have had the chance elsewise." He then went on to explain Mrs. Epping's arrival and involvement with the abduction and the whole nefarious plan of the duc. He was not so blunt as to describe Betta's alternative to accepting the duc's offer of "protection," but the adult listeners understood the unspoken words.

"What I cannot understand, *mon vieux,* is why the duc had such hatred for you? What was it that you have done to him?" Virginie's face expressed her puzzlement.

"That was because of me, my dear." Lady Westrich interrupted. "I once had a beautiful daughter, Vanessa. She looked much as you do, Lucy . . . and she was about your age when she first met the duc at Almack's. He was ten years younger then and accepted everywhere by the *ton.* Vanessa was very special. . . . She was not a great

248

beauty, but she had a vivacity and intelligence that placed her on a par with beauties of the first water . . . and attracted him to her. It was about the time of my husband's last illness. He was too weakened to go about in society, but insisted that Vanessa should make her come-out and have her season. . . ." Her ladyship's voice dropped. "He said that there would be enough time for mourning after his death, and no reason for her to mourn before."

"A dear friend of mine undertook to chaperone her when I couldn't be in town, and it was at just this time that the duc began to reel in his fish. He had a way with him, no one can deny that, and she was too innocent to understand what he was doing . . . and so, in the end, she ran away with him. When she became pregnant, he dropped her . . . left her with little money, no friends, and no wish to live. She was too ashamed to contact us. When Alexander found her she was living in a hovel, ill and despairing. He brought her home, where she died shortly after. Then he went after the duc."

Alec took up the story. "I found him and was able, with the help of the young man who had been in love with Vanessa, to overcome him. I then horsewhipped him like the animal he was, and loaded him into a fishing boat that was to drop him on the coast of France. I expect that he's been waiting for an opportunity to repay me since that night. Thank God it's all over now and my dear reward is sitting here with me. . . ." He looked at Betta, who was sitting across the room from him.

"Why are you blushing, Betta?" the outspoken young Letty asked, causing her sister to redden even more.

"Really, Letty," exclaimed Lucy, "can't you tell yet . . . Oh, no, I forgot for the moment how young you really are!"

"Tell what, Lucy . . . tell what?" Letty refused to be silenced.

"I will tell you what, Letty. Your oldest sister has agreed to marry me. How do you like that?" Lord Halwick said, to the delight of his brother and the rest of the company.

"I suppose it's all right, as long as it doesn't interfere with my getting to marry Robin when I'm old enough." The precocious young miss turned to a laughing Robin. "You will wait for me, won't you? I shall try to hurry as fast as possible!"

The earl stood up, walked over to Betta, and drew her up from the chair. "You and Robin will have to take that up with your parents, Letty. . . . For now, Betta and I wish to say a few things to each other . . . so do, please, excuse us?" He led the smiling young woman out of the room, putting his arm around her as he did so. They moved to the rose arbor at the end of the terrace. There, surrounded by the soft pink blossoms and the rich perfume of the flowers, Alec turned Betta to him. Putting his good arm around her, he pulled her against his lean body, so close that she could feel his warmth through the thin dress she was wearing.

"You agree you are mine," he said as his eyes, brilliantly blue, gazed into hers, "and that we are as one?"

Throwing off the shyness that had always been her bane, Betta slowly brought her arms up around Alec's neck. She placed a hand on the back of his head, pressing her body against his. "We shall ever be one, forever," she said before she lifted her lips to his, drinking deeply of his kiss. Behind them, standing in the shadow of a tree, Virginie and Philippe watched the two.

"*Enfin*," Virginie said, "I have told you they were for

each other, and so it proves. And now they will live happily ever after. *N'est-ce pas?* Just as we shall."

Joyous laughter exploded in the air, a precursor of the happiness to come.

Love—the way you want it!

Candlelight Romances

		TITLE NO.	
☐ A MAN OF HER CHOOSING by Nina Pykare	$1.50	#554	(15133-3)
☐ PASSING FANCY by Mary Linn Roby	$1.50	#555	(16770-1)
☐ THE DEMON COUNT by Anne Stuart	$1.25	#557	(11906-5)
☐ WHERE SHADOWS LINGER by Janis Susan May	$1.25	#556	(19777-5)
☐ OMEN FOR LOVE by Esther Boyd	$1.25	#552	(16108-8)
☐ MAYBE TOMORROW by Marie Pershing	$1.25	#553	(14909-6)
☐ LOVE IN DISGUISE by Nina Pykare	$1.50	#548	(15229-1)
☐ THE RUNAWAY HEIRESS by Lillian Cheatham	$1.50	#549	(18083-X)
☐ HOME TO THE HIGHLANDS by Jessica Eliot	$1.25	#550	(13104-9)
☐ DARK LEGACY by Candace Connell	$1.25	#551	(11771-2)
☐ LEGACY OF THE HEART by Lorena McCourtney	$1.25	#546	(15645-9)
☐ THE SLEEPING HEIRESS by Phyllis Taylor Pianka	$1.50	#543	(17551-8)
☐ DAISY by Jennie Tremaine	$1.50	#542	(11683-X)
☐ RING THE BELL SOFTLY by Margaret James	$1.25	#545	(17626-3)
☐ GUARDIAN OF INNOCENCE by Judy Boynton	$1.25	#544	(11862-X)
☐ THE LONG ENCHANTMENT by Helen Nuelle	$1.25	#540	(15407-3)
☐ SECRET LONGINGS by Nancy Kennedy	$1.25	#541	(17609-3)

At your local bookstore or use this handy coupon for ordering:

 DELL BOOKS
P.O. BOX 1000, PINEBROOK, N.J. 07058

Please send me the books I have checked above. I am enclosing $_____
(please add 75¢ per copy to cover postage and handling). Send check or money order—no cash or C.O.D.'s. Please allow up to 8 weeks for shipment.

Mr/Mrs/Miss _____

Address _____

City _____ State/Zip _____

From the bestselling author of
Loving, The Promise, and Palomino

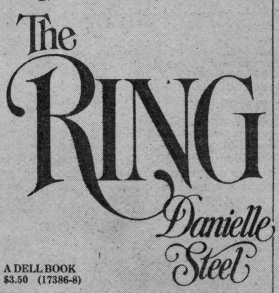

The
RING

Danielle
Steel

A DELL BOOK
$3.50   (17386-8)

A magnificent novel that spans this century's most
dramatic years, *The Ring* is the unforgettable story
of families driven apart by passion—and brought
together by enduring compassion and love.

At your local bookstore or use this handy coupon for ordering:

Dell	**DELL BOOKS** **P.O. BOX 1000, PINEBROOK, N.J. 07058**	THE RING $3.50 (17386-8)

Please send me the above title. I am enclosing $ _____
(please add 75¢ per copy to cover postage and handling). Send check or money
order—no cash or C.O.D.'s. Please allow up to 8 weeks for shipment.

Mr/Mrs/Miss _____

Address _____

City _____ State/Zip _____

Candlelight Ecstasy Romances

At your local bookstore or use this handy coupon for ordering:

Dell **DELL BOOKS**
P.O. BOX 1000, PINE BROOK, N.J. 07058

Please send me the books I have checked above. I am enclosing $_____
including 75¢ for the first book, 25¢ for each additional book up to $1.50 maximum
postage and handling charge.
Please send check or money order—no cash or C.O.D.s. *Please allow up to 8 weeks for
delivery.*

Mr./Mrs._____

Address_____

City_____State/Zip_____

*Breathtaking sagas
of adventure
and
romance*

VALERIE VAYLE

☐ **LADY OF FIRE** $2.50   (15444-8)
Garlanda was a passionate pirate of the heart that no man
could resist or forget. But Roque, the daring buccaneer,
was the only man who could conquer her fiery spirit.

☐ **SEAFLAME** $2.75   (17693-X)
The sensational saga that began with *Lady of Fire* contin-
ues as Evonne and Genevieve search for their mother, Sa-
belle—the most infamous lady pirate of them all.

☐ **ORIANA** $2.95   (16779-5)
After inheriting a vast shipping empire, Oriana sailed the
raging seas—and found Gaerith, a bold adventurer with
whom she would learn the heat of passion, the pain of sepa-
ration, and the burning sweetness of love.

At your local bookstore or use this handy coupon for ordering:

| Dell | **DELL BOOKS**
P.O. BOX 1000, PINEBROOK, N.J. 07058 |

Please send me the above title. I am enclosing $ _____
(please add 75¢ per copy to cover postage and handling). Send check or money
order—no cash or C.O.D.'s. Please allow up to 8 weeks for shipment.

Mr/Mrs/Miss _____

Address _____

City _____ State/Zip _____

Bestsellers

☐ **THE RING** by Danielle Steel $3.50 (17386-8)
☐ **INGRID BERGMAN: MY STORY**
  by Ingrid Bergman and Alan Burgess $3.95 (14085-4)
☐ **SOLO** by Jack Higgins $2.95 (18165-8)
☐ **THY NEIGHBOR'S WIFE** by Gay Talese....$3.95 (18689-7)
☐ **THE CRADLE WILL FALL** by Mary H. Clark $3.50 (11476-4)
☐ **RANDOM WINDS** by Belva Plain $3.50 (17158-X)
☐ **WHEN THE WIND BLOWS** by John Saul $3.50 (19857-7)
☐ **LITTLE GLORIA . . . HAPPY AT LAST**
  by Barbara Goldsmith $3.50 (15109-0)
☐ **CHANGE OF HEART** by Sally Mandel $2.95 (11355-5)
☐ **THE PROMISE** by Danielle Steel $3.50 (17079-6)
☐ **FLOWERS OF THE FIELD**
  by Sarah Harrison $3.95 (12584-7)
☐ **LOVING** by Danielle Steel $3.50 (14657-7)
☐ **CORNISH HEIRESS** by Roberta Gellis $3.50 (11515-9)
☐ **BLOOD RED WINE** by Laurence Delaney....$2.95 (10714-8)
☐ **COURT OF THE FLOWERING PEACH**
  by Janette Radcliffe $3.50 (11497-7)
☐ **FAIR WARNING**
  by George Simpson and Neal Burger $3.50 (12478-6)

At your local bookstore or use this handy coupon for ordering:

DELL BOOKS
P.O. BOX 1000, PINEBROOK, N.J. 07058

Please send me the books I have checked above. I am enclosing $ _____
(please add 75¢ per copy to cover postage and handling). Send check or money
order—no cash or C.O.D.'s. Please allow up to 8 weeks for shipment.

Mr/Mrs/Miss _____

Address _____

City _____ State/Zip _____